How long would i[illegible] Daniela to win C[illegible] trust and accom[illegible]

Would she win hi[illegible]

As if he'd picke[illegible] Professor Thorne [illegible] the papers on his podium, his [illegible] weeping the crowded room before coming t[illegible] on hers. Daniela's breath hitched, her skin tingling as if he'd physically reached out and touched her.

But a second later, his gaze shifted away, leaving Daniela to wonder if he'd noticed her at all.

Her classmate April seemed to think so, seizing Daniela's arm in excitement. "Did you see that? He looked right at you!"

"We're seated in his direct line of vision," Daniela said drolly.

"And yet, you're the only one he looked at."

Daniela felt a tiny thrill of pleasure. Maybe there was hope after all.

MAUREEN SMITH

has enjoyed writing for as long as she can remember, and secretly suspects she was born with a pen in her hand. She received a B.A. in English from the University of Maryland and worked as a freelance writer while she penned her first novel. To her delight, *Ghosts of Fire* was nominated for a *Romantic Times BOOKreviews* Reviewers' Choice Award and an Emma Award for Favorite New Author, and won the Romance in Color Reviewers' Choice Awards for New Author of the Year and Romantic Suspense of the Year. Her subsequent novel also garnered praise from critics and readers.

Maureen lives in San Antonio, Texas, with her husband, two children, a cat and a miniature schnauzer. She loves to hear from readers and can be reached at author@maureen-smith.com.

MAUREEN SMITH

A LEGAL *Affair*

To my sister, Juliet Morah, who was going through her own trials and tribulations while I was working on this novel. Thank you for overcoming, and for teaching me the true meaning of "survivor."

ISBN-13: 978-1-58314-792-4
ISBN-10: 1-58314-792-6

A LEGAL AFFAIR

www.kimanipress.com

Printed in U.S.A.

Dear Reader,

I have enjoyed reading Harlequin romances ever since I was thirteen years old, when I used to sneak books from my mother's endless supply and devour them in one day. Those romantic, heartwarming stories made me realize that there was something quite extraordinary about two people meeting and overcoming all odds to be together. I never dreamed that someday *I* would be given the opportunity to join the wonderful family of Harlequin authors!

A Legal Affair was my first foray into writing contemporary romance without a suspense subplot, and it was an incredible experience. I learned so much about myself as a writer, and as a romance reader. For me, the hardest part about writing this story was having Daniela enter Caleb's life under false pretenses. Just as she struggled with her duplicity, so did I—and *I* had the advantage of knowing everything would turn out well in the end!

Anyway, I truly hope you enjoyed following Caleb and Daniela on their roller-coaster journey to falling in love, and I hope you'll come back for Noah Roarke's story.

I love to hear from readers! Please e-mail me at author@maureen-smith.com, and visit my Web site at www.maureen-smith.com for news and updates on my upcoming releases.

Enjoy the love!

Maureen Smith

Acknowledgments

To family, of course, without whom none of this would be possible.

With warm gratitude to Nathasha Brooks, Angie Daniels, Katherine D. Jones, and Yahrah St. John—beautiful, talented authors whose friendship and support have meant the world to me.

Thanks to the following friends who welcomed me to San Antonio with open arms and have enthusiastically supported my writing—Frederick Williams, Patricia Garza, Beverly Evans, Shawn Harward, Alyssia Woolard, Paul Vallejo, Lisa McDaniel, Lynda Cruz, Renata Serafin, Jeannette Jones, and Sanjuanita "Janie" Scott who humorously allowed me to "borrow" her likeness.

A special thanks to the following folks at St. Mary's University—Professor Jeffrey F. Addicott, who graciously allowed me to sit in on his civil procedure class; Director of Recruitment Carolyn Meegan, who kindly made the arrangements; and diva extraordinaire Noemi Garcia, who patiently answered all of my questions about being a law student.

Chapter 1

Daniela Roarke knew she was in trouble the minute she stepped through the double glass doors of Roarke Investigations and saw her older brother's smiling face.

Kenneth Roarke never smiled before noon.

Not on a Monday morning, and definitely not on the first of the month, when the rent was due and utility bills had to be paid.

So the smile softening his features that morning was disconcerting, to say the least.

Daniela eyed him warily as she entered the single-story brick building that housed the private detective agency she owned with Kenneth and their brother, Noah. A pair of ancient ceiling fans whirred noisily overhead, circulating humid air that promised to become unbearable as the temperature outside soared, climbing toward another record-breaking June day in

San Antonio, Texas. Even the potted ferns arranged around the sparsely furnished reception area had wilted in anticipation of the coming heat wave.

"'Mornin', sis," Kenneth greeted her cheerfully. "How was traffic? Not too bad, I hope?"

"No, not at—" Daniela's gaze narrowed on her brother's face, scanning the strong, rugged features cast in rich chestnut tones. "Wait a minute. What's going on here?"

Before Kenneth could respond, the door behind him opened. Daniela's eyes widened in surprise as a tall, gray-haired gentleman dressed in an expensively tailored navy suit emerged from Kenneth's office, followed by Noah Roarke.

"I really must be going," the visitor said to Kenneth in a deep bass that rang with authority. "I'm expected at a charity auction this morning, and if I'm even thirty seconds late, Tessa will have my head on a spit."

Kenneth chuckled humorously. "I understand. My wife is the same way. Before you go, I'd like to introduce you to our sister, Daniela. El, this is—"

"I know who he is," Daniela said, palm outstretched as she stepped forward. "It's a pleasure to meet you, Mayor Philbin."

"The pleasure's all mine, Miss Roarke." Former mayor Hoyt Philbin clasped Daniela's hand and offered the relaxed, congenial smile that had served him well during twenty-five years in public office. "I regret that I can't stay longer to visit with you. Your brothers have been singing your praises all morning."

"Oh, is that right?" Daniela divided a suspicious look between her two older siblings. Both smiled gamely at her.

Something was *definitely* up.

"Indeed, they have," said Philbin. Shrewd blue eyes roamed across Daniela's face, lingering on full lips slicked with cinnamon-spice gloss, long-lashed dark eyes and riotous black curls that tumbled to slender shoulders draped in silk. Hoyt Philbin gave an imperceptible nod, leaving Daniela with the distinct impression that her appearance had passed muster.

Carefully she withdrew her hand from his firm grasp. "What brings you to our neck of the woods, Mr. Philbin?"

Again he flashed that trademark smile. "I'll let your brothers fill you in on the reason for my visit." A silent look passed between the three men as Philbin moved toward the double glass doors. "Thanks for your time, gentlemen. I'll be in touch."

Daniela rounded on her brothers as soon as they were alone. "Will someone please tell me what's going on?"

Kenneth gestured toward his office. "We can talk in there." Over his shoulder he said to his brother, "Noah, why don't you bring Daniela a cup of coffee—with cream and three sugars?"

Daniela stared at her oldest brother as if he'd suddenly grown two heads. Since when did Kenneth Roarke remember the way she took her coffee? He had a hard enough time remembering her birthday, let alone her hot-beverage preferences.

He ushered her into his large office and pulled out one of the two visitor chairs opposite his desk. Daniela sat, still eyeing him as if she'd never seen him before.

Kenneth perched his hip on a corner of the cluttered desk and folded his arms across his broad chest. "How's Mom doing? How'd her appointment go this morning?"

"It went okay. Her blood pressure's still a little too high. Dr. Molina asked me to keep an eye on her, make sure she sticks to the low-carb diet he prescribed. He may as well have asked me to build a flying saucer equipped with Internet access," she grumbled, thinking of her mother's stubborn refusal to give up the high-cholesterol, albeit scrumptious, foods she'd always prepared for her family with great pride.

Daniela pushed out a deep breath that stirred a lock of hair above her right eye. "Other than that, he says she's doing pretty well for someone who suffered a stroke eight months ago."

"Mom's a survivor," Kenneth said, and the two siblings shared a moment of quiet reflection that was interrupted by Noah Roarke's return.

"Thanks, Noah," Daniela murmured, accepting a steaming cup of coffee and taking a careful sip. The brew was a little weak, and nowhere near as good as hers. But then, she'd had plenty of practice. Three years of making coffee for their clients had rendered her something of an expert.

She leaned back in her seat as Noah claimed the chair beside her, stretching out long legs covered in khaki trousers. His features were the mirror image of his brother's, the resemblance between them so striking that strangers often mistook them for twins. But the similarities ended there, for though they'd both chosen careers in law enforcement, Kenneth had opted for a desk job in Internal Affairs, while Noah had worked as a beat cop before being promoted to homicide detective.

"What did Mayor Philbin want?" Daniela asked.

"Our services," Kenneth answered. "He wants to hire us for a big assignment."

Daniela felt a surge of excitement, but kept her expression neutral. She knew, from past experience, that big cases were usually handled by her brothers, with little or no involvement from her. "I'm listening."

"Have you ever heard of Crandall Thorne?"

She frowned. "Is that a trick question? Who in this town *hasn't* heard of Crandall Thorne? He's a hotshot defense attorney who specializes in helping white-collar criminals beat the rap—like that scumbag CEO three years ago who defrauded his employees of their retirement savings, but got off because the government couldn't make the charges stick. Or the labor union boss who was charged with racketeering and money laundering, but walked away scot-free thanks to his fork-tongued attorney." Her mouth twisted cynically. "Again I ask, Who *hasn't* heard of Crandall Thorne?"

Kenneth and Noah exchanged amused glances. "Gee, El, don't be afraid to tell us what you *really* think," Noah teased.

Daniela took aim at his shin with the pointy toe of her alligator-skin sling-back pumps. He laughed, wisely moving his leg out of harm's way.

She returned her attention to Kenneth. "What does Hoyt Philbin have to do with Crandall Thorne?"

"While in office, Philbin spent a great deal of time and resources investigating Thorne's law firm. He believes that Thorne has ties to the Mexican mafia and is guilty of everything from bribery and witness tampering to economic espionage and public corruption. Unfortunately—or perhaps fortunately for us—he hasn't been able to prove any of it. His failure to take down Crandall Thorne has been, if you'll pardon the pun, a thorn in his side. Now that he's out of office and retired from politics, he's free to use his wealth any way he sees fit." A slow grin crawled across Kenneth's face. "And he's chosen to share some of that wealth with us. All we have to do is establish a link between Thorne and the Mexican mafia, or provide some incontrovertible proof of the firm's criminal negligence. Then Philbin and his buddies at the U.S. Attorney's Office will take care of the rest."

Daniela frowned, taking a sip of coffee. "With all due respect, how are we supposed to get the dirt on Thorne when all the king's men have failed? I mean, don't get me wrong, fellas—we're good. But if the mayor and his arsenal of investigators couldn't get the job done, what chance do we have?"

Kenneth smiled as if at some private amusement. "What we have over 'all the king's men' is a secret weapon."

"Which is?"

"You."

Daniela blinked, nonplussed. "I don't understand."

Kenneth stood and rounded the desk to claim the leather executive throne behind it. He not only had the largest office in the building, but the best furniture. "Crandall Thorne is very ill. He's suffering from acute renal failure, according to Philbin's sources, and there's talk that his only son, Caleb, will soon step in to run the law firm. That's where you come in, Daniela."

Daniela had a sneaking suspicion she wasn't going to like what her brother said next. So she said it for him. "You want me to befriend Caleb Thorne in order to get the goods on his father."

"That's the general idea." Kenneth traded a speaking look with his brother before adding, "Of course, making him fall in love with you would almost guarantee we get the kind of dirt we really want."

Daniela gaped first at Kenneth, then Noah. She set her cup down on the desk, sloshing hot coffee onto the mahogany surface, and lunged to her feet. "I don't believe this! You're asking me to *sleep* with a complete stranger?"

Noah looked stricken. "Of course not! We wouldn't—"

"*You* might not, but I wouldn't put anything past *him,*" she fumed, jabbing an accusing finger toward Kenneth's face. "For the right price, Kenneth Roarke would sell his own mother to the devil!"

"Hey, that's not fair!" he protested, indignation propelling him forward in his chair. "For your information, the main reason I accepted this assignment *was* Mom! Philbin's paying us enough money to make sure she never even thinks about working another day in her life. If you don't believe me, take a look at the retainer he left behind."

Daniela hesitated, then grudgingly reached for the check he'd thrust at her. She thought her eyes were deceiving her when she saw the amount made payable to Roarke Investigations.

She lifted incredulous eyes to Kenneth's face. "This c-can't be right."

"Oh, it is, believe me. Hoyt Philbin is very serious about securing our services." In the gentle, conciliatory tone he used to calm hysterical wives hell-bent on catching their husbands in the act of cheating, Kenneth said, "Sit down, Daniela. Hear us out before you make any hasty decisions. Please?"

She sat, but only because he'd asked nicely. She passed the check back to him, half-afraid it would turn to fairy dust if she clutched it a moment longer. That kind of money would not only ensure their widowed mother's permanent retirement from nursing, but would give Pamela Roarke the down payment necessary for the Hill Country ranch she'd secretly dreamed of owning for years. Daniela would have to be a fool, or the worst kind of daughter, to turn down such a golden opportunity.

Still, it rankled that her brothers had accepted an assignment—in which she would play a crucial role—without her knowledge or consent.

"No one's asking you to sleep with Caleb Thorne," Noah began, with a pointed look at his brother. "What Kenny was *going* to say earlier is that there are other ways to make a man fall for you, ways that don't necessarily lead to the bedroom." He flushed, as if he couldn't believe he was actually attempting to school his baby sister on the art of seduction.

Smothering a grin at his obvious discomfiture, Daniela reached over and squeezed his well-muscled shoulder. "It's all right, Noah," she said with sham gravity. "I'm twenty-seven years old. I think I've been around long enough to figure out how to make a boy like me without compromising my virtue."

Kenneth roared with laughter, and Noah scowled. "All I was trying to say is—"

"You're a very beautiful woman, Daniela," Kenneth interjected dryly. "You've never had any trouble attracting members of the opposite sex—at least, not since you were a gawky preteen with a mouthful of braces and Buckwheat-wild hair."

"Gee, thanks for the reminder," Daniela grumbled, unable to rally a comeback because Kenneth Roarke had always been good-looking and popular with the girls. So had Noah, for that matter.

"The point is," Kenneth continued, "you should have no problem turning Caleb Thorne's head and lulling him into sharing confidences with you. It may take some time, though. From what I know about the man, he doesn't trust very easily—with a father like Crandall Thorne, who can blame him?"

"What if he doesn't know anything about his father's business dealings?" Daniela countered, her conscience pricked with guilt at the thought of deceiving an innocent man. "Or what if he has no plans to run the law firm?"

Kenneth shook his head, dismissing both possibilities. "After graduating from law school, Caleb went to work for the old man. He was good in the courtroom—damn good. His style was completely different from his father's, but just as effective. He was sharp, cunning and methodical, almost predatory. He kept prosecutors on their heels, many of whom were downright terrified of him.

"But after five years at the firm, he suddenly walked away. Seems he and the old man had a falling-out. Over what, God only knows. Maybe the kid developed principles and his father didn't want to hear it. Anyway, Caleb wound up as a law professor at St. Mary's University, and from what I've heard, he's as much a natural in the classroom as in the courtroom. But I don't doubt for one second that he misses litigating and would go back to it in a heartbeat if the right opportunity presented itself. Especially since he and his father have recently reconciled. Sounds to me like it's only a matter of time before Junior steps in to take over the family business."

"So," Daniela said with a deep, resigned sigh, "just how am I supposed to meet Caleb Thorne?"

"As one of his students." At her dumbfounded look, Kenneth chuckled. "For three years you've been hounding us to give you a 'real' assignment—something other than running background checks on new corporate employees and chasing down unfaithful spouses. Well, you've gotten your wish. This fall, you're going undercover as a first-year law student at St. Mary's University. Hoyt Philbin just happens to serve on the Board of Regents, so he'll have no problem pulling strings to get you admitted on such short notice. We'll take care of obtaining fake transcripts and LSAT scores, and Philbin will take care of the rest.

"If all goes well, you'll get him the information he needs to bring down Crandall Thorne, and in the process Mom will be set for life, and Roarke Investigations will never again have to accept assignments we don't want. I think our first order of business," added Kenneth, basking in his role as senior partner and chief decision-maker, "should be to hire a full-time secretary and buy some nice furniture for the reception area."

"Hallelujah," muttered Daniela. "And while we're at it, Big Spender, could we also get the air-conditioning fixed?"

Chapter 2

Two months later

"I'm late. I can't believe I'm late."

Daniela uttered the words to herself as she hurried across the manicured grounds of St. Mary's University toward the Law Classroom Building located in the center of campus. It was the first day of classes, and she was late for her eight o'clock civil procedure course.

Despite weeks of planning and preparing for the undercover assignment, Daniela couldn't have foreseen that her mother would come down with the flu the day before the fall semester began, and that she would spend the entire night nursing Pamela Roarke back to health. She couldn't possibly have known that after dragging her tired body from bed and going through the motions of showering and getting dressed, she'd be faced with her next obstacle: finding her car keys. She'd searched for close to an hour before locating the keys where she'd left them the night before—still buried in the front-door lock, where she'd forgotten them in her haste to investigate the source of the violent retching she'd been greeted with upon arriving home.

When Daniela finally left the house that morning, her mother had been sleeping soundly, and Kenneth's wife, Janie, was on her way over to take the second shift. Not for the first time, Daniela thanked God for blessing her with a sister-in-law who was a stay-at-home mom.

Daniela slipped inside the air-conditioned coolness of the Law Classroom Building and strode down the tiled corridor in search of her classroom.

Even before she rounded the corner and saw him, she heard The Voice. Deep, husky, with pure masculine tones that rippled along her nerve endings. Like sinuous curls of smoke from a sorcerer's flame, it reached out to her, wrapping around her, drawing her closer.

Daniela stepped from the hallway and into the dark, piercing gaze of Caleb Thorne. Her pulse hammered at the base of her throat, and for one awkward moment she hovered in the doorway.

Firm, sculpted lips curved upward in a mocking half smile. "So nice of you to join us, Miss—?"

"Moreau," she said, the alias wobbling off a tongue that seemed stuck to the roof of her mouth. Funny, she hadn't counted on being blindsided by an attraction to her intended victim. "Sorry I'm late."

"I'm sure your clients will appreciate knowing that every time you show up late for trial," Caleb Thorne said dryly.

Daniela's face burned with embarrassment as her classmates laughed. Bravely squaring her shoulders, she looked around quickly before sliding into a vacant chair in the fourth row. An attractive young Asian woman seated next to her offered a sympathetic "Better you than me" look that only made Daniela feel worse about her ill-fated entrance.

So much for making a good first impression.

After taking a minute to compose herself, Daniela allowed her gaze to drift back toward Caleb Thorne, then found that she couldn't look away.

To say that the man was sublime would be an understatement. The hard, masculine line of his square jaw accentuated cheekbones that could have been carved from granite, and his strong chin hinted at a dimple that was incredibly sexy. His skin was the deep brown of toasted walnut, and his jaw held the beginnings of a shadow that only heightened his utter maleness. He was tall, easily six-three, a towering specimen of male authority as he prowled back and forth in front of the lecture hall with relaxed, powerful strides Daniela would not soon forget. Wearing a short-sleeved black shirt that stretched taut across broad shoulders and blue jeans that rode low on lean hips, Caleb Thorne's appearance was a marked departure from the bookish law professor of Daniela's imagination. No wonder practically every seat in the first row was occupied by a wide-eyed female eagerly hanging on to his every word.

The vibrations of his deep voice quivered like a caress across Daniela's skin. She was captivated, shamelessly so, and when those deep-set onyx eyes came to rest on hers once again, she actually shivered in response.

"What about you, Miss Moreau?" Caleb asked, arms folded across his wide chest. "What are your expectations for this course?"

It took Daniela several seconds to realize that he'd actually addressed her, so preoccupied was she with watching that sensuous mouth and wondering what it would feel like against her own.

She was pulled from her trance by a discreet cough to her right—her "Better you than me" friend again.

Nervously Daniela passed her tongue over dry lips. "I, um, have no expectations for this course," she mumbled.

One thick black brow sketched upward. "Is that right?"

Daniela resisted the urge to squirm under that incisive gaze. "One thing I've come to understand about myself is that if I approach anything with too many expectations, I don't learn or grow as much as I should, because my perceptions are shaped by my expectations. So I came here today with an open mind, which I think is good practice for anyone aspiring to enter the legal profession."

Complete silence descended, as if the sixty-four other occupants of the room were holding a collective breath, awaiting Caleb Thorne's verdict on her response.

He nodded once, a trace of amusement and something akin to curiosity glinting in his dark eyes. He studied her a moment longer before turning away.

"Memorize Miss Moreau's answer," he told the class in a voice laced with humor. "It might show up on the final exam."

The announcement was met with laughter and a few

muffled guffaws. The young woman seated beside Daniela gave her a thumbs-up sign, and Daniela grinned.

When class was over, the girl introduced herself. "I'm April Kwan."

"Daniela—"

"Moreau. I know." She giggled, scooping up her notebook and gliding to her feet. She was slightly taller than Daniela, and waifishly thin. Glossy black hair cropped in a pageboy skimmed high, sharp cheekbones. "Don't worry, he has that effect on everyone with an X chromosome."

"So I see," Daniela murmured, eyeing the group of female students surrounding Caleb Thorne. At any minute, she half expected him to produce a pen and begin signing autographs.

"He is *such* a hottie. I heard that his classes always have the longest waiting lists. No wonder." April issued a lusty sigh, then grinned. "See you next time. Don't be late."

Daniela hung around until the last of the groupies had reluctantly taken her leave before descending the stairs and approaching Caleb Thorne. Up close he seemed even taller, towering over her even in the stacked wedge sandals she wore.

"I need a syllabus," she told him as he stuffed papers into a well-worn leather satchel.

When he passed her the requested document, their fingers brushed. Something like awareness passed between them, and for one charged moment their gazes locked and held.

Daniela stepped back, feeling as if she'd been singed with a dangerous, seductive heat, the likes of which she'd never before experienced. She drew vital air into her lungs. "I know we, uh, got off on the wrong foot, Professor Thorne, but—"

His eyes, rimmed with dense black lashes that would have given him a boyish appeal were he not so darned *virile,* narrowed on her face. "What's your first name?"

"Daniela," she answered, because she and her brothers had decided it was safe to stick as close as possible to the truth.

Caleb nodded slowly. "What were you saying?"

"I just wanted you to know that I'm serious about being here, that I plan to take my studies very seriously." It wasn't a lie—not exactly. After all, she'd always prided herself on being the best at whatever she set out to accomplish. Why should this situation be any different?

"Never doubted it for a second, Miss Moreau." With an economy of motion, Caleb swung the satchel over his shoulder and indicated that Daniela should precede him from the room.

As she walked, she racked her brain, wondering if there was any way to detain him without arousing his suspicion. It was the first day of the semester, too early to request help with her coursework—although the lengthy reading assignment he'd given them was no laughing matter. Should she invite him for a cup of coffee? She knew for a fact that he didn't teach another class until twelve-thirty. Still, there was no pressing reason to push him so hard, so fast. Was there? Even Kenneth had said that winning Caleb Thorne's trust would take time.

Suddenly Caleb was staring past her, his mouth curving into a warm, relaxed grin that made her breath hitch and caused her to wonder who was the lucky beneficiary of such a bone-melting smile.

She turned her head to find a tall, willowy, Caribbean-looking woman with waist-length dark hair waving at him from the opposite end of the bustling corridor. "Wanna grab a cup of coffee at Java's?" she called to him in a smooth, lilting voice.

"Of course," he responded, and Daniela's heart sank. He glanced down at her, his face an impassive mask that convinced Daniela she'd only imagined that electrically charged moment back in the classroom. "My office hours are on the syllabus if you need to reach me. See you on Wednesday."

"Okay." As Daniela watched him saunter toward the Caribbean beauty, she realized she didn't have as much time as she'd thought to win over the sexy law professor.

It was time to step up her game or pack up her toys and go home.

"How'd the first day of classes go?"

The question greeted Daniela as she entered the one-story bungalow she shared with her mother. Balancing a purse, a backpack and a large plastic bag filled with the remaining supplies she'd had to purchase for school, Daniela kicked the door shut and divested herself of her baggage before sinking gratefully into the nearest armchair.

Sanjuanita Roarke, curled up on a sofa slipcovered in persimmon suede, smiled at Daniela over the paperback novel she'd been reading. "That bad, huh?"

Daniela groaned, throwing her head back against the chair. "I am so exhausted, Janie. Between Civil Procedure and Contracts, I have a ton of reading to do—and this was just the first day. God only knows how much more awaits me tomorrow."

Her sister-in-law chuckled, setting aside her chick-lit novel and scraping her thick, dark hair into a ponytail. "No one ever said law school would be easy. In fact, no one in their right mind would claim such a thing."

"You got that right. Tonight I'll probably wake up in a cold sweat after having nightmares about appellate briefs, pleadings and torts." She frowned up at the textured ceiling. "I must be insane to willingly put myself through this. After studying for the CPA exam, I swore I'd never subject my brain to that kind of torture again."

Janie snorted. "What are you talking about? You aced that exam, and Kenny says you hardly studied at all."

"Your husband greatly exaggerates." Daniela sat up and nudged off her wedge sandals, wiggling her toes against the Persian rug she'd practically plundered from an antiques dealer. "How's the patient doing?"

"Sleeping. Stayed awake long enough to take her meds and swallow a few spoonfuls of tortilla soup before it was lights-out again."

"No more fever? Nausea?"

"Not since this morning. Dr. Molina says the best thing for her is to get some rest—that's what her body is craving anyway."

"I know," murmured Daniela. "I wish there was some way to convince her to cut back on some of her extracurricular activities—like volunteering at the senior center or heading the women's ministry at church."

Janie grimaced, dark, thick brows furrowing together until they nearly touched. Her face was a soft oval characterized by high, round cheeks, full lips and a dimple carved into her chin, which lent an impish charm to her beauty.

"You know your mother," Janie said. "She figures as long as she's not earning a salary for what she's doing, then technically she's not violating the doctor's orders not to work."

Daniela scowled. "I've tried asking some of the church members to talk sense into her, but everyone seems to think 'doing the Lord's work' will only rejuvenate her. I'm sorely tempted to tell Pastor Wiggins that Mom and the organist are fooling around—*that* might persuade him to relieve Sister Roarke of her duties."

"*¡Ay dios!* You wouldn't dare!"

"I'm a desperate woman. Having my mother around for years to come is more important to me than preserving her reputation at church."

"But she's *not* having an affair with the organist," Janie pointed out, then frowned. "Is she?"

"Of course not." Daniela winked. "She thinks Deacon Hubbard is *far* more handsome."

Janie laughed and shook her head, dislodging a stubborn chunk of glossy hair from the scrunchie she wore. "Speaking of handsome men," she said, reaching up to repair the ponytail, "how'd it go with Professor Thorne?"

Just hearing the man's name made Daniela's mouth go dry. "Well, we sort of got off to a rocky start when I showed up ten minutes late for class." Grimacing, she told her sister-in-law about her ignominious arrival and Caleb Thorne's dry rebuke that had sent a rumble of laughter around the classroom. "If I could have melted through the floor, I would have."

Janie grinned sympathetically. "On the bright side, at least you got his attention."

"Yeah, but somehow that's *not* the strategy I had in mind."

"What *is* your strategy?"

Daniela frowned, biting her bottom lip. "To be perfectly honest with you, I don't know. I mean, I know Kenny and Noah spent weeks prepping me and giving me pointers on how to do undercover work, but none of that really prepared me for the real thing—the moment of truth, when I walked into that classroom and saw 'the mark.'" She shook her head, lips curving ruefully. "I sure wish I'd known what Caleb Thorne looked like beforehand. Kenny and Noah have photos, but I refused to see them. I didn't want to have preconceived notions about the man based solely on his appearance."

"I should have warned you. As soon as Kenny told me about the assignment—which, by the way, I had to pry out of him because he was being so darned secretive—I went online and looked up Caleb Thorne's picture on the university's Web site." Janie made a low, feline sound. "The man is positively scrumptious."

Daniela groaned. "Words can't begin to describe. And let's not even talk about his voice."

"No, let's," Janie urged.

Daniela grinned. "Deep, dark, smooth as honey. Like liquid sex."

Janie shrieked with laughter, then clapped a hand to her mouth, belatedly remembering that her mother-in-law was fast asleep in a bedroom down the hall.

"I don't know what I'm going to do," Daniela confessed when her own mirth had finally subsided. "Just between you and me, I already feel like I'm in over my head. You know I don't do the whole femme fatale thing."

"Bull. I've seen you bat those long eyelashes and toss that pretty hair when you want something badly enough—like that antique rug resting beneath your feet." She chuckled at Daniela's sheepish expression. "Seriously, El, I don't think you'll have to become a seductress in order to accomplish your mission. Think about it. Smart, good-looking men like Caleb Thorne get hit on all the time. He's probably been slipped more thongs and been the victim of more tawdry pickup lines than he can stomach. Stand out from the crowd. Be yourself. Something tells me Caleb Thorne won't be able to resist getting to know the real you."

"As much as that's possible, considering I came into his life under false pretenses." Daniela pulled in a deep breath, suppressing a pang of guilt over the duplicitous role she'd been asked, and had agreed, to play.

Janie gave her a sympathetic look, understanding her predicament. She glanced at the diamond-encrusted wristwatch that had been a tenth-anniversary gift from Kenneth, then rose from the sofa, stretching her limbs with the fluid grace of a gymnast—which she'd been in another lifetime. "I have to go pick up the kids from school. They won't appreciate Mommy being late on the first day—or any day, for that matter."

Daniela smiled softly, thinking of her seven-year-old niece and nephew, fraternal twins who'd both inherited their mother's intolerance for tardiness. "Give KJ and Lourdes my love. And thank you so much for coming to the rescue with Mom today, and for agreeing to come back tomorrow. I really appreciate it."

Janie waved off the gratitude. "Believe me, looking after your mom, flu and all, beats picking up after the twins *any* day of the week." A wistful note in her tone made Daniela wonder, not for the first time, whether Janie Roarke regretted her decision to quit her job in exchange for full-time motherhood. With an MBA from the Wharton School of Business, Janie had been climbing the ranks at a top advertising firm when she learned she was pregnant—with twins, no less. She and Kenneth had decided it was best for one parent to stay home with the children, and Janie had been the unanimous choice.

She hugged Daniela, retrieved her purse and paperback, then moved toward the front door. "Oh, that reminds me," she said over her shoulder, "call Kenny whenever you can. He's been trying to reach you all day—he wants to know, of course, how everything went this morning. He kept complaining because you weren't answering your cell phone. Guess that's because you accidentally left it on the kitchen counter this morning." Janie's wicked grin told Daniela that she'd enjoyed making her husband sweat it out.

Daniela chuckled, getting up to follow Janie to the door. "Serves him right. If he thinks I'm going to be checking in with him every minute of the day like we're on some episode of *Charlie's Angels*, he's got another think coming."

Janie laughed all the way to her white SUV parked in the driveway.

Long after she left, Daniela stood at the window thinking about Caleb Thorne and the impossible mission she'd embarked upon. She hadn't been lying when she'd told Janie that she felt like she was in over her head. A man like Caleb would *not* be easy prey, despite what she may have secretly hoped. He was shrewd, tough and powerfully seductive. When he looked at her with those midnight eyes, she could hardly remember who was supposed to be the hunter, and who the hunted. Her attraction to him was a weakness she couldn't afford.

One way or another, she'd have to find a way to keep sight of her goal. Buying a dream ranch for her mother was the goal. Falling victim to Caleb Thorne's animal magnetism was *not*.

As long as she stayed the course and remained focused, she would escape from this mission unscathed.

Failure was not an option—not when her mother's future happiness hinged on the successful outcome.

Chapter 3

It was after seven o'clock by the time Caleb Thorne steered his black Dodge Durango through the heavy iron gates of the C&C Ranch.

His last class had ended before two, and although today marked only the first day of the semester, his office had seen a steady flow of foot traffic from students seeking everything from academic counseling to career advice. There had been a few "suspect" visitors, girls who seemed more interested in perfecting their come-hither looks than actually tapping into Caleb's legal expertise.

Afterward he'd hung around a little longer than his scheduled office hours dictated, telling himself his reasons had nothing whatsoever to do with a certain dark-eyed, exotic beauty whose image had invaded his thoughts more times than he cared to admit.

Scowling, Caleb shoved aside the unsettling reminder and downshifted. The sturdy rig climbed uphill, the grind of wheels against gravel sending clouds of dust through the open windows. Once outside city limits, Caleb never ran the air conditioner. He preferred—no, *needed*—to soak it all in as he drove: the scent of earth and pine from the mountains, the call of elk grazing in pastures so lush and green they seemed artificial, the shimmering hues of ponds and lakes he knew firsthand were stocked with largemouth bass and black catfish.

Crandall Thorne had purchased the property years ago, long before South Texas brush country was discovered by out-of-state billionaires seeking a recreational paradise in what many considered the last frontier. The invasion of affluent buyers and investors had driven up the price of the ranches, so that even Crandall Thorne would have been hard-pressed to afford the Hill Country home he now claimed as his primary residence.

Caleb slowed the Durango as the road steepened in elevation, and after several more minutes his father's sprawling estate rolled into view. Built of stucco and covered with red-tiled Spanish roofs, the hacienda-style ranch was situated atop a five-hundred-foot bluff that boasted stunning panoramic views of the surrounding valley. The property included three barns, three silos specifically for storing grain and feed, two outbuildings and a large roping arena. The main house had six bedrooms with wood-burning fireplaces, a large great room, a guest wing separated from the family living areas and featuring its own private porch and three detached garages.

Caleb nosed his truck into an unoccupied unit and killed the engine. Bypassing the front door entirely—and knowing he'd catch hell for it from his father's longtime housekeeper, Rita—Caleb headed straight toward the covered patio spanning the rear of the house.

He knew Crandall Thorne would be waiting for him, seated in his favorite Adirondack chair facing east of the mountain range, where he wouldn't miss the setting sun. After twenty-five years of pouring blood, sweat and tears into building a successful law practice, Crandall Thorne had finally learned to appreciate sunsets.

It was amazing how a brush with mortality could change a man.

"Didn't know if you'd be coming today." Crandall Thorne spoke without glancing over his shoulder.

Caleb crossed the stained-concrete patio to claim the chair next to his father's. "Might be the only chance I'll get this week," he replied, "now that the semester has started."

Crandall nodded slowly. His profile displayed craggy brows sprinkled with salt and pepper to match the full thatch of hair on his head. Dark eyes the color of bittersweet chocolate revealed the shrewdness of a man who missed nothing and had seen just about everything in his lifetime, a shrewdness that had served him well both in and out of the courtroom. His nose was strong, almost aristocratic, and a neatly trimmed mustache framed firm, no-nonsense lips. Whether seated at the head of a boardroom or lounging on his patio, Crandall Thorne exuded an innate confidence and power that was hard to reckon with. Few tried.

Caleb had always been the exception.

"How many classes are you teaching this semester?" his father asked. A thick afghan was draped across his lap to ward off the evening chill, a concession he'd made only to keep the women of his household—the housekeeper, cook and a private nurse—off his back while he enjoyed the outdoors.

"Three," answered Caleb, stretching out his long, booted legs. "Two civil procedure classes three days a week, and a two-hour advanced criminal law course on Tuesdays."

"I see. And what do you do with the rest of your time?"

Caleb slanted his father an amused look, knowing where this particular line of questioning would lead. "I've been teaching at St. Mary's for five years. You know damned well what I do with the rest of my time."

A grim smile curved one corner of Crandall Thorne's mouth. "You don't belong in academia, son. You belong in the courtroom, challenging the system and taking no prisoners. Academicians don't have killer instincts. *You* do."

Caleb shook his head, chuckling softly. "I know you still find this hard to believe, Dad, but I actually enjoy teaching."

"You enjoy playing God," Crandall corrected. "You enjoy dispensing your knowledge and wisdom and holding the fate of those kids' futures in your hand."

"And where would *you* be without the law professors who shared their 'knowledge and wisdom' with you?"

"Touché," the old man murmured in a voice tinged with admiration for the adept comeback. He turned his head and studied Caleb's face in the lengthening shadows of twilight. "You need a shave."

Absently Caleb stroked a hand down his stubbled chin. "I'll get around to it. Eventually." A lifetime ago, when he'd worked at his father's law firm, he'd prided himself on his impeccable appearance. *That* Caleb, with the knife-blade creases in his trousers and professionally pressed shirts, would never have gone a full day without shaving, because his father had always drilled into him the importance of setting a tone from the moment he stepped foot in the courtroom.

"You only get one shot at making a good first impression," Crandall Thorne had lectured on numerous occasions. "You'd be surprised how much damage an untucked shirt or a cheap pair of shoes can do. Don't do your clients a disservice by showing up to court looking any ol' kind of way. Dress for success, and others will sit up and take notice and know that you mean business."

Caleb's walk-in closet at home was filled with three-piece Armani suits he hadn't worn in years. Five years, to be exact, when he'd walked away from the firm, a lucrative career and the only way of life he'd ever known.

"I never thought I'd live to see the day when I would be reduced to running the firm from afar. Not now, not at the age of sixty-two." Crandall's voice was laced with the bitterness that had plagued him since being diagnosed with acute renal failure three months ago. The severity of his condition had necessitated a complete lifestyle change—the first "casualty" had been his workaholic schedule. In virulent denial, he'd sought second, third and fourth opinions, consulting the best physicians money could buy in the vain hope of receiving a different verdict. But each time he was given the same prognosis: either scale back on the workload or face the very real possibility of developing end-stage renal disease, which, in most cases, led to death.

Crandall had grudgingly submitted to his doctor's decree, as well as the prescribed dialysis treatments, but not a day passed that he didn't bemoan the cruel blow fate had dealt him.

"My father worked until he was eighty-five," Crandall sullenly continued. "Never missed a day of work in his life. What would he say if he could see me now, reduced to running board meetings through a video monitor and conducting business from the confines of my own home?"

"Where I come from," Caleb drawled sardonically, "what you've just described is called videoconferencing and telecommuting. Some people actually appreciate the modern conveniences made possible by living in the twenty-first century."

"Well, I ain't one of 'em." A large fist clenched on the arm of the cypress chair as Crandall's familiar anger and frustration thrummed in the air around him.

Caleb said nothing, knowing better than to offer any words of solace that would only make his father feel coddled or patronized—two things Crandall Thorne would never tolerate.

Silence lingered between father and son as daylight eased into night. From a treetop somewhere above, an eagle took flight, its piercing cry cutting across the fabric of the evening like a razor. From somewhere else, another bird of prey responded.

At length, Crandall spoke again. "I don't have to tell you how much it would mean to me if you considered returning to the firm," he said quietly. "Your mother would want the same thing, too."

A muscle tightened in Caleb's jaw. "Don't go there, Dad," he warned in a low voice. "You and I both know that was the last thing she would have wanted."

Crandall turned his profile to Caleb once again and stared off into the distance at the lush, rolling terrain that surrounded them from their high perch on the mountain. His impassive expression gave nothing away and at the same time hinted at many deeper truths than those on the surface of his next words.

"You're right," he said simply.

Caleb made no reply, instead steering his thoughts away from the painful memories that threatened to shatter the peaceful calm of the evening.

After a few more minutes, he rose from the chair, stomping dirt and gravel from his scuffed leather boots. "I'm going inside to say hello to everyone. I know you have them under strict orders not to disturb you while you're out here, but they won't appreciate finding out that I was here for an entire hour without greeting them."

"You're right about that." Crandall gazed up at his only son with an imploring expression he didn't bother to disguise. "You'll stay for dinner, won't you? Gloria made enough food to feed an army. I think she was hoping you'd stop by."

Caleb hesitated, then nodded slowly. "I'll stay. Got nothing but cold leftovers at home anyway."

Daniela should have known she was making a mistake when she decided to walk back to her car between classes on Tuesday. The late-morning sky had turned a gunmetal-gray and the clouds seemed swollen with the threat of rain. But there'd been no mention of showers in the weather forecast, and she wanted to retrieve her cell phone from her car in case her mother, or Janie, needed to reach her for any reason.

She'd barely locked the car door behind her when she felt the first fat drops of rain. Hoisting her backpack over her head, she began sprinting for cover. But by the time she reached the Sarita Kenedy East Law Library, where she'd been headed next anyway, her fitted T-shirt and dark jeans were half-soaked. Her hot pink flip-flops made a loud squishing noise as she ducked inside the elegant, modern building.

"Excuse me, where's the restroom?" she asked the woman seated behind the wide circulation desk.

"Around the corner to your right."

Two boys standing nearby glanced over at Daniela and stared, their mouths hanging open before they exchanged lewd grins.

Daniela looked down at herself and grimaced. Her pink T-shirt was plastered to the front of her body, and the black lacy bra she wore was no match against the rain and the frigid temperature of the library. Her nipples puckered rebelliously against the now-translucent fabric.

Clutching her backpack protectively to her chest, Daniela headed in the direction the librarian had indicated. Head bent, shoulders hunched forward in an attempt to conceal her dilemma, she hurried around the corner and ran headlong into something solid and immovable.

Her backpack dropped to the floor as she lost her balance and stumbled backward. A pair of steely arms came up to steady her as she lifted her eyes, embarrassed, to mumble an apology. Her breath lodged in her throat when she found herself staring into the darkly handsome face of Caleb Thorne.

The apology died on her lips, and her hands stilled against his wide chest, where they'd landed during the collision. The warmth and solidness of muscled flesh beneath her splayed fingers sent heat crashing through her body.

"Miss Moreau," he murmured in that deep, hypnotic voice that had whispered through her dreams all night long.

She swallowed hard and silently ordered herself to get a grip. She'd never be able to carry out her mission if she got tongue-tied every time the man was near. "Sorry about bumping into you, Professor Thorne. I was sort of in a hurry."

"You don't say." Slowly he knelt and picked up her backpack. As he straightened, his midnight-black eyes slowly raked over her, taking in her wet T-shirt and the outline of full, rounded breasts protruding against a flimsy layer of cotton. His gaze darkened for a moment, coaxing a shiver from Daniela that had nothing to do with the cool air circulating through the building.

"Thank you," she murmured, accepting her backpack from him. This time their fingers did not touch during the transfer.

Daniela didn't know whether to be relieved or disappointed.

Caleb glanced over the top of her head toward the windows at the front of the library. His sensuous mouth quirked at the corners. "Guess it's raining outside."

"Yeah," she grumbled, cradling her soggy backpack to her chest. "You'd think those meteorologists could have given us a little warning."

His amused gaze returned to hers. "No umbrella?"

"Left it at home." She pushed at a lock of wet hair that fell into her right eye, and wondered if she was only imagining Caleb's reluctance to part company with her.

As if reading her mind, he took a step backward. "I'd better let you go…dry off. See you in class tomorrow."

"Um, yeah. Sure." *Wait! Don't go! It'll only take me a few minutes to lose the drowned-rat look and make myself presentable again.*

But she only turned and continued on her way to the restroom, telling herself she'd have better luck next time.

Caleb stood watching as Daniela walked away from him, damp black curls hanging heavy between her shoulder blades, clothes plastered against her hourglass body to flaunt a tiny waist that flared into an eat-your-heart-out-Beyoncé rump. The sight of her apple-round bottom and long, curvy legs poured into painted-on denim made Caleb's mouth water. He drew in a deep, ragged breath and slowly made his way back to the table in a private corner of the library where he'd been studying before the encounter with Daniela Moreau.

No matter how hard he tried to dislodge it, her sultry, fallen-angel image was seared into his brain. As if she still stood before him, he saw the long-lashed dark eyes that tilted exotically at the corners, the lush mouth that begged to be kissed, the finely carved cheekbones and the delicate chin that hinted at a stubborn streak. Her hair was parted halfway down the center, and soft black curls molded the sensual contours of her face before cascading down to her shoulders.

His eyes hadn't deceived him yesterday. She was beautiful. Half temptress, half innocent.

"Mind if I join you?"

For a moment Caleb wondered if he'd only imagined hearing the soft, husky voice of the woman dominating his thoughts. But when he glanced up from the table, she stood there in the flesh, remarkably drier than she'd been twenty minutes earlier. Idly he wondered if she'd patted herself dry with a ream of paper towels, or positioned herself in front of one of those automatic hand dryers in the restroom. His groin tightened at the image of her tugging off the clingy T-shirt to expose a flat belly and high, voluptuous breasts spilling from a scrap of black lace.

"Do you mind?" she repeated, sculpted black brows arched inquisitively as she awaited his response.

Against his better judgment, Caleb shook his head and gestured toward the seat opposite his own. She lowered that luscious rump into the chair, and he suffered a pang of envy toward the lucky piece of furniture.

That's when he should have known he was in deep trouble.

Forcing normalcy into his tone, Caleb asked, "What are you working on?"

"An assignment for my legal research and writing class. We have to prepare a case brief by the end of the semester." Daniela stepped out of her pink flip-flops and tucked her bare feet beneath her legs, sitting Indian-style in the chair. There was something so earthy, so bohemian, about the pose that Caleb almost smiled. There they were, seated in a richly appointed law library that boasted the largest collection of legal information in San Antonio. Around them were scholarly-looking people roaming up and down rows of mahogany-paneled bookcases filled with tomes on every legal subject conceivable.

And there was Daniela, seated across the table from her law professor, looking as wholesome and appealing as a barefoot contessa. Her scent wafted into his nostrils, rain mingled with something exotic that conjured images of lush Texas wildflowers.

Just the essence of the woman could inspire even the most hardened misanthropist to spout poetry—long, flowery sonnets of angst and devotion.

With a supreme effort, Caleb reined in his thoughts. "A case brief, huh?"

She nodded, removing a spiral notebook from her backpack. "Got any pointers for me?"

"Yeah," he said, returning to his own work, "be as brief as possible."

She chuckled, a low, throaty sound that sucker-punched him in the gut. He lifted his head to look at her. "Seriously. A case brief should be precise and get to the point of the issues that have been raised. It should be coherent, focused, well organized and properly cited. You don't want—" He broke off, frowning as Daniela scribbled furiously in her notebook. "What are you doing?"

She glanced up, blinking those dreamy dark eyes at him. "I'm taking notes. This is good stuff."

His mouth twitched. "I'm sure your instructor provided the same information. But if you want," he heard himself saying, "I can look over your case brief before you turn it in."

Daniela beamed a smile at him that made him feel twenty feet tall. "I'm going to take you up on that offer, Professor Thorne. Thank you very much."

"Who do you have, by the way? For legal research and writing."

"Adler."

Caleb nodded approvingly. "Shara's a good friend of mine. You'll like her—she definitely knows her stuff."

"I'll bet," Daniela murmured, and Caleb thought he detected a double meaning in those two words. And then he remembered that Daniela had been with him yesterday when Shara invited him for coffee. She had probably reached the conclusion that he and Shara were involved. Not that it mattered one iota what Daniela Moreau had assumed. She was his student, one of many under his instruction.

He'd do well to remember that.

She hitched a chin toward the pile of books spread before him on the table. "What about you, Professor Thorne? What brings you to the library this rainy morning?"

"Research."

"You have homework, too?" she teased.

Caleb smiled a little. "Sort of. I'm writing a book on criminal procedure, specifically as it pertains to race and racism in American law. But I won't bore you with the details."

"Doesn't sound boring at all," Daniela said, and the sincerity in her soft voice caught him unaware and made him want to share everything about the project with her, as if she were his trusty editor in New York.

Or a woman in whom he found it wholly natural to confide.

Scary thinking, Thorne. You're charting dangerous territory. Better come back before you lose your way.

"Maybe another time," he said, dismissing her invitation to expound on the book. "You need to work on your case brief, and I need to get some research done."

Daniela, to her credit, took the hint. "Yeah, I need to get on one of those computers over there and access FindLaw," she said, unfolding her long legs and rising from the table. As she stuffed her notebook inside her backpack, a lock of damp hair glided across one smooth brown cheek to catch in the corner of her mouth. She swept it away with a finger and tucked the errant curl behind one ear.

God, she was beautiful.

She swung her backpack over one shoulder and smiled at him. "See you in class tomorrow, Professor Thorne."

Caleb nodded slowly. "See you then."

This time, as Daniela walked away, he forced himself not to watch.

He'd already punished himself into enough cold showers to last a lifetime.

Chapter 4

Although the rain had stopped by the time Daniela left campus that evening, the humidity clung stubbornly to the air, as unwelcome as toilet tissue stuck to a pair of Prada pumps.

As she drove through the tree-lined streets of the King William District, she fantasized about taking a long, relaxing shower and unwinding with a glass of Pinot Grigio and a good book—something that didn't include lengthy discussions of torts and statute of limitations. After a day spent researching case briefs and how best to write one, Daniela had reached *her* statute of limitations. Not for the first time, she wondered what on earth had possessed her to agree to go undercover as a *law student,* of all things.

If all else failed, she supposed she could always plead temporary insanity.

The thought made her grimace. Two days into law school, and she was already thinking like a lawyer.

Around the corner from her house, Daniela slowed to a stop sign and watched as an elderly couple meandered across the street with a gray-bearded miniature schnauzer in tow. They smiled at her, and she waved at them and thought how refreshing it was to be on friendly terms with her neighbors. Not like before, at the apartment building where her neighbors had blasted music at all hours of the day and regularly stole her parking space. Daniela had patiently bided her time, saving up enough money to buy a house in the historic King William District, where she'd dreamed of living ever since attending an art show at the Blue Star Arts Complex as a teenager.

The historic town ran parallel to the San Antonio River, and featured grand old Victorian houses and quaint bungalows painted in sedate hues of surrey-beige, Sèvres blue, hawthorn-green, frontier-days brown and Plymouth Rock–gray. Several years ago, the city's most famous literary personality had caused an uproar in the community by painting her house a shocking shade of periwinkle-purple. Many of the town residents had protested her decision, claiming that the house's contemporary color scheme was inappropriate for the historic district. The controversy had drawn the attention of the local media, who printed a flurry of articles on the topic. In the end, the author won the battle against her neighbors, and her purple house now drew almost as many tourists as the town's other attractions, which included a charming array of tiny shops and restaurants, two museums and more bed-and-breakfasts than Daniela could count.

Twenty minutes after leaving St. Mary's University, she pulled up in front of her house, a one-story beige bungalow shaded by large pecan trees and boasting a wraparound porch. The lawn was a tidy swath of green, the shrubs meticulously trimmed by her own hands.

But as Daniela steered her car into the driveway behind a black BMW, she was too distracted by the sight of the vehicle to pause and admire her landscaping skills, as she often did. Grabbing her purse and backpack, she hurried from the car and into the house.

She skidded to a halt at the arched entryway to the kitchen.

Seated at the breakfast table, shirtsleeves rolled to his elbows as he feasted on a plump piece of fried chicken, was Kenneth Roarke. The plate before him was piled high with candied yams, collard greens and macaroni and cheese.

At Daniela's appearance, he glanced up and froze, midchew. His dark eyes flickered with guilt, then slid away at the murderous look on his sister's face.

"The rolls are almost ready, baby," Pamela Roarke announced, oblivious to Daniela's arrival as she leaned down to peer into the oven. "Do you want one or two?"

"As many as you can fit into a glass," Daniela muttered, advancing on her brother like an enraged lioness, "because when I get done with him, he'll be sucking his food through a straw!"

Eyes wide with alarm, Kenneth lurched from his chair as Daniela charged him, teeth bared, fists raised and ready to do damage.

"Daniela!" With a speed that belied her sixty-one years, Pamela Roarke crossed the room and planted herself squarely in front of Kenneth just as his sister came within striking distance.

Wearing a mint-green chenille robe and matching bedroom slippers, Pamela Roarke stood at just over five-two. Skin the color of mocha cream maintained an elasticity that defied gravity. Her short, silvered hair had been cropped into stylish layers that accentuated her fine-boned features.

She wagged a reproachful finger at her daughter. "Stop this! What has gotten into you?"

"Me?" Daniela cried in disbelief. "I'm not the one who has you slaving over a hot stove when you're supposed to be in bed resting!"

"Hey, I didn't ask Mom to cook for me!" Kenneth protested over his mother's head.

"That's right. He didn't," Pamela affirmed. "I *wanted* to cook. Beats lying around in bed all day feeling sorry for myself."

"You have the flu, Mom," Daniela pointed out, exasperated.

"*Had* the flu. Sister Jenkins came by this morning and prayed over me. I'm all better now. Prayer works—isn't that what I've always taught you and your brothers?"

"Mom—"

"Not another word about it, Daniela. Who's the RN in this room, me or you? Now, why don't you have a seat and let your brother finish his meal in peace? I'll fix you a plate too, if you'd like."

"I'm not hungry," Daniela grumbled, reluctantly allowing herself to be ushered into a chair at the antique cedar table. Kenneth eyed her warily as he sat down and picked up his abandoned chicken breast.

Pamela gave her daughter's shoulder a gentle, conciliatory squeeze before shuffling away to check on her rolls.

"Oh, good, they didn't burn," she murmured, removing the pan from the oven. The mouthwatering aroma of honey rolls saturated the air, mingling with the other delicious scents that had greeted Daniela upon entering the house. Her stomach growled loudly, drawing a knowing grin from Kenneth.

She skewered him with a look. "You could have at least *tried* to stop her from cooking," she accused, her voice pitched low so their mother wouldn't hear and come to his rescue. "But I guess your appetite takes precedence over her health."

Kenneth frowned. "That's not true, El. I left the office early just to check up on her. I was worried about her."

"Oh yeah?" Daniela glared pointedly at the smorgasbord on his plate. "Sure have a funny way of showing it."

With a shrug, he shoveled a forkful of collard greens into his mouth and chewed in impenitent bliss.

Daniela sucked in her breath to keep her traitorous stomach from rumbling again. Okay, so maybe she was a *little* hungry.

"How was school today, baby?" Pamela asked, materializing at her daughter's side with a plate laden with food. Before Daniela could utter a word of protest, Pamela slid the plate under her nose and handed her a fork.

"Eat," she ordered in a tone that brooked no argument—the same tone she'd once used to inform Daniela that under no circumstances could she wear a gown with a plunging neckline to her prom.

Daniela obediently dug into her meal.

"I was just telling your brother that I'm so proud of you for going back to school," Pamela remarked, filling two glasses with sweet tea and serving the drinks to her children. She pulled out a chair and sat down beside Daniela. "I remember how unhappy you were at that CPA firm, the long hours you worked, the vacations you accrued but never took. No amount of money or company perks could compensate for how miserable you were at that job."

Daniela frowned, fork halfway to her mouth. "I never told you I was miserable, Mom."

Pamela gave her a quiet, intuitive smile. "You didn't have to tell me anything, darling. A mother knows these things." She pursed her lips, her hazel eyes narrowing thoughtfully on Daniela's face. "Just as I can tell now that something is weighing on your mind."

Daniela thought of Caleb Thorne, and resisted the urge to squirm in her chair like a second grader caught cheating. Everyone at church, both young and old, believed Pamela Roarke had the gift of prophecy.

Sometimes Daniela wondered if they weren't on to something.

She stalled for time by biting into a hot, moist roll and savoring the burst of honey in her mouth. Across the table, Kenneth ate with gusto, but she knew that he, too, was awaiting her response. She and her brothers had decided not to tell their mother about the undercover assignment, knowing she would never approve of the deceptive scheme.

"The only thing weighing on my mind," Daniela said, "is all the reading I have to do between now and tomorrow morning. And *that's* just for CivPro."

Her mother's finely arched brows furrowed together. "CivPro?"

"Civil Procedure."

Pamela chuckled. "My baby, the law student. I must admit that when you first told me you were enrolling in law school, I was a little worried. I didn't want to see you jumping into another stressful career. But Kenny assured me that your law degree would come in handy for the agency, since you guys often work with the courts." She gently patted Kenneth's arm. "It was awfully sweet of you to give your sister this opportunity, and to allow the business to cover the cost of her tuition. Thank you, baby."

"No thanks necessary, Mom," Kenneth said gallantly. "Daniela walked away from a very profitable career to help me and Noah establish the detective agency. She's been invaluable to us and our clients. As far as I'm concerned, sending her to law school is the least we can do."

Pamela beamed proudly at her son, and Daniela did a mental eye roll.

"And to think you wanted to hurt your brother when you walked through that door," Pamela lightly scolded her daughter. "Shame on you."

Daniela scowled. "He had it coming."

"Nonsense. There's nothing wrong with my wanting to have a hot meal ready for you after a long day of classes. Did you get much studying done at the library?"

"Mmm-hmm," Daniela answered vaguely. Another image of Caleb Thorne's sexy face intruded upon her thoughts, bringing warmth to her cheeks.

She glanced up from her plate and met Kenneth's dark, watchful gaze.

Inwardly she groaned. She knew it was only a matter of time before he'd be grilling her for information.

Her mother drew closer and brushed her palm over Daniela's hair in a soothing, maternal gesture. "Don't you worry about a thing, darling. You'll do just fine in law school. I believe in you. We *all* do."

"Thank you, Mom," Daniela murmured, feeling like the biggest fraud that ever walked the face of the earth.

"You look a little tired, Mom," Kenneth said, all gentle concern. "Maybe you should go lie down. I don't want you to overexert yourself."

"Oh, I'm fine." But even as Pamela spoke, a telltale yawn escaped. She chuckled sheepishly, covering her mouth with her hand. "Goodness, maybe I *am* a bit peaked."

"Of course you are," Daniela said with a trace of censure. "You cooked a full-course meal three days after coming down with the flu."

"I told you I'm healed," Pamela reminded her, rising from the table as Kenneth came around to meet her. She reached up and patted the lean curve of his cheek. "Be sure to take home some food to Janie and the twins. I made enough to feed an army."

"Yes, ma'am, I will. You know how much they enjoy your cooking. It'll be a real treat for them. Now come on, let me tuck you into bed the way you used to tuck us in."

Pamela laughed. "Oh, go on with you, boy!" But she happily linked her arm through his and allowed herself to be escorted from the kitchen.

When Kenneth returned a few minutes later, Daniela had cleared the table and was filling the sink with hot, sudsy water to wash the dishes. To preserve the Victorian charm of the small kitchen, she'd refrained from buying a dishwasher. So far, she'd never needed one, since it was just her and her mother, and Pamela Roarke—a compulsive neat freak—scarcely allowed two forks to accumulate in the sink between meals.

"How'd things go with Thorne yesterday?" Kenneth asked, propping a hip against the center island and crossing his arms.

"Ahh, now we get down to the *real* reason behind your visit. Let's get something straight, big brother. I'm not going to be calling you every hour on the hour to provide a detailed report of what I'm doing. If I'm going to do this thing, you have to give me some breathing room."

"No one's asking you to call every hour," Kenneth retorted. "But yesterday was the first day of classes, El. I would have at least expected you to call to let us know you'd established contact."

"I established contact. There, are you satisfied?"

"Hardly. A few details would be nice."

Daniela shrugged, filling Tupperware containers with food. "Not much to tell. I arrived to class ten minutes late and got called out for it—so much for making a good first impression. The next time I ran into him wasn't much better. I got caught in the rain today and *literally* ran into him at the library." She grimaced at the memory. "I looked like a drowned rat."

When Kenneth said nothing, she glanced over her shoulder to find dark eyes critically assessing her from head to toe. "Is that what you were wearing?" her brother asked.

"Yeah. Why?"

A slow, devious grin curved his mouth. "Wet T-shirt,

tight jeans. Trust me, baby girl, the *last* thing on Caleb Thorne's mind was rats, drowned or otherwise. What're you wearing to class tomorrow?"

Daniela wanted to clobber him over the head with the gleaming copper pots suspended from a rack above the island, or strangle him with the Burberry silk tie tugged loose around his collar. She settled for a withering look. "Don't even *think* about giving me tips on what to wear, Kenny, or I swear—"

He laughed. "Relax, sweetheart. Your taste in clothes has come a *long* way from the high-water pants you used to call fashionable. I trust your judgment."

"Gee, thanks."

Kenneth paused a beat, his eyes twinkling with mirth. "Of course, if you happen to have any leather bustiers lying around—"

Daniela shoved a stack of hot Tupperware containers against his chest, making him grunt in surprise.

With stinging sweetness, she said, "Don't let the door hit you on your way out, *sweetheart*."

After Kenneth left, grumbling under his breath about temperamental females, Daniela washed the dishes and cleaned the kitchen. When she was finished, she poured herself a glass of Pinot Grigio, settled down at the table with the San Antonio *Express-News* and worked on crossword puzzles. Half an hour later, knowing she could not put it off any longer, she got up and went in search of her textbooks to begin what promised to be a long, grueling night of reading.

On her way out of the kitchen, she passed her mother's bedroom and paused in the half-open doorway. A tender smile touched her lips as she gazed across the room at Pamela Roarke, fast asleep in the heavily quilted sleigh bed. The curtains were drawn closed on the waning light of early dusk, casting the room and its antique oak furnishings into deep shadows.

Sleep had softened the lines of worry and fatigue etched into her mother's face. For as long as Daniela could remember, Pamela had always worried—about her children, about working enough hours at the hospital to keep a roof over their heads and food in their bellies, about caring for the sick and elderly at church—about everyone but herself.

She'd been widowed when her husband was killed in a machinery accident at the textile factory where he worked. Daniela was less than a year old, barely weaned off her mother's breast milk, when a grief-stricken but resolute Pamela Roarke embarked on a nursing career to help raise her three children. They'd all been forced to grow up quickly—Pamela included. The young widow learned how to clip coupons and stretch a dollar at the grocery store, and Daniela and her brothers soon learned how to fend for themselves during the long evenings when their mother couldn't be there to fix dinner and check homework assignments.

Although Kenneth was the eldest, it was Noah Roarke who had stepped in to fill his father's shoes, assuming responsibility for Daniela when Kenneth's only concern was running in the streets with his friends. It was Noah who fed and bathed his baby sister, who dispensed the horrid cough syrup she'd swallowed only after he threatened to turn off her favorite cartoon. It was Noah who'd exclaimed over her stick-figure drawings and taped them to the refrigerator for their mother to coo over when she got home in the morning.

And it was Noah, not Kenneth, who'd always comforted Daniela after a nightmare by reassuring her that their mother would *not* leave them, as their father had.

Although Daniela didn't remember her father, she'd always lived with a keen understanding of the transcendent bond her parents had shared. She knew that they'd both dreamed of someday buying a little ranch in the Hill Country and enjoying their golden years surrounded by frolicking grandchildren and wet-nosed puppies. While it had been years since Pamela Roarke spoke of it, Daniela knew her mother still secretly clung to that dream. It whispered in her eyes every time she and Daniela drove through the scenic countryside on an antiquing excursion, or to pick peaches at their favorite orchard outside town.

More than anything, Daniela wished she could reverse the hand of fate and bring back Nelson Roarke so that he and Pamela could grow old together. But since Daniela couldn't resurrect her father, the next best thing was to give her mother something of the future she'd always envisioned.

Hoyt Philbin was willing to shell out the kind of money that would turn their mother's dream of owning a ranch into a reality.

It was a once-in-a-lifetime opportunity Daniela couldn't pass up on.

Even if it meant deceiving an innocent man.

Caleb stayed at the office late to catch up on paperwork and work on a law review article that was due at the end of the week. At six-forty-five he called it quits and headed home to his downtown apartment.

Twenty minutes later, he pulled off Houston Street

and swung into the parking garage connected to the Towers of the Majestic—or the Towers, as the high-rise building was known to its residents. As he rode the elevator to the sixteenth floor, he was grateful that at that hour, most of his neighbors were already ensconced in their luxury apartments, or out for a night on the town along the Riverwalk.

The moment he crossed the threshold of his penthouse, he knew he was not alone.

Without turning on the lights, Caleb dropped his satchel by the door and crossed a gleaming expanse of hardwood floor to reach the wet bar. Calmly, deliberately, he filled a glass with whiskey and lowered himself onto one of the bar stools that ran the curved length of the counter. Fifteen-foot windows with custom-designed wrought-iron bars provided a panoramic view of the San Antonio skyline, now awash in flame from the setting sun.

As Caleb sipped his whiskey, he quietly contemplated the stunning view he took for granted every day.

"I take it you're not going to offer me a drink." A coolly amused voice spoke from the shadows of the living room.

Caleb didn't spare a glance over his shoulder. "Only invited guests receive that kind of hospitality."

There was a low chuckle. "Testy, aren't we?"

"Can you blame me?" Caleb drawled sardonically. "You'd think for all the money I pay to live here, I could count on better security."

"Now, Caleb, you of all people should know that for the right price, no door remains closed to me. Which brings me to the purpose of my visit." There was a deliberate pause. "Your old man is still refusing to take on Lito's case."

"That's his prerogative, isn't it?" Caleb said in mild unconcern. "Last I checked, the firm's not exactly hard up for business. Besides, I think they've already met their monthly quota of representing embezzlers."

"Come now," came the smiling rejoinder, "there's always room for one more."

Caleb shrugged, keeping his back turned on his visitor. "Guess the old man doesn't think so."

"Apparently not. However, I'm of the opinion that he can be persuaded otherwise." When Caleb showed no reaction to the veiled threat, the voice continued, "We both know, Caleb, that I can make your father take Lito's case."

"So what're you doing here?"

"I came to reason with you, man to man."

"By breaking into my apartment and skulking in the shadows until I return? I don't think so." Shaking his head, Caleb downed the rest of his whiskey and reached for the crystal decanter to refill his glass. Despite his cavalier tone, every muscle in his body was rigid, primed for the unpredictable.

Experience had taught him such preparedness.

"I don't have to remind you, Junior, that all it takes is one phone call to bring all of Crandall Thorne's dirty laundry to light. And I know for a fact there's one particular item you'd do anything to keep safely tucked away." Soft, triumphant laughter razored along Caleb's nerve endings, making his gut clench in instinctive outrage.

In a deceptively bored tone, he drawled, "You of all people should know that Thornes don't respond to blackmail."

"Don't they? I beg to differ." But the man was angry now, impatience lacing his next words. "Talk to your father, Caleb. Appeal to his common sense. This doesn't have to get ugly, unless you want it to. Tell Crandall to take Lito's case."

"Even if I were to do that, what makes you so sure he'd agree?"

"Don't insult my intelligence, Junior. We both know how much influence you have over your father. One word from you and the old man is on his knees, eager to make amends for his past sins. If anyone can make him see reason, *you* can."

Caleb had had enough. He wasn't in the mood for this. He was tired and edgy, filled with a restlessness that had plagued him all afternoon, tracing back to the library encounter with Daniela Moreau.

Forbidden fruit had a way of making a man more ravenous.

And more reckless.

With an economy of motion, he reached beneath the counter and grabbed the semiautomatic tucked away for just such an occasion. Quick as a snake striking, he was on his feet, the nine-millimeter cocked and aimed at the man's chest with unerring precision.

"Get out," he said, low and controlled.

The man faltered a moment before a slow, self-assured smile curved his mouth. "You won't shoot me, Thorne. Not with my men parked outside the building, waiting for my safe return."

"I'd have a round of bullets between your eyes before they even suspected a thing. You know that."

"Ah, but you'd never get out of here alive."

One shoulder lifted in a shrug. "I'll take my chances. Now for the last time, leave before my finger starts to twitch."

The visitor got slowly to his feet, one elegant hand smoothing a nonexistent crease from his expensively tailored suit coat. Pale blue eyes assessed Caleb in shrewd silence. "I remember an idealistic kid fresh out of law school—bright-eyed, bushy-tailed and ready to take on the world. Your father stole that innocence from you. Wouldn't you give anything to get a little of it back?"

A solitary muscle ticked in Caleb's jaw. He said nothing, keeping the nine-millimeter trained on the intruder.

"You need something to live for, Junior. We'll have to find it for you, before it's too late." He gave a thoughtful pause. "You should seriously consider returning to the courtroom. You were one helluva lawyer, a rare talent. I know Lito would be thrilled to have you represent him."

"Not gonna happen," Caleb said flatly.

"Never say never. I suggest you give it some thought." The man offered a benevolent smile, then tipped his head. "I'll be in touch."

And then he was gone, leaving only a subtle scent of Dior as proof that he'd been there.

Slowly Caleb walked back to the bar and returned the semiautomatic to its hiding place. Picking up his drink, he swallowed the rest of the whiskey, then set down the glass with a thud. Suddenly his hand tightened around the base, then lifted and hurled the glass against the nearest wall. Shards of crystal exploded, showering across the floor in a violent storm.

Simmering with fury and something else—something he didn't want to identify—he grabbed his car keys and slammed out of the apartment.

Chapter 5

"Hey, look who's early."

Daniela glanced up from checking e-mail messages on her laptop computer to find April Kwan sliding into the chair beside her in the third row.

"Yeah, I learned the hard way not to be late for this class," Daniela admitted with a rueful smile. "Looks like we both made it before Professor Thorne."

"Good. I love to watch him walk into a room." The girl's full lips curved in a wicked grin. "What am I saying? I love to watch him *period*."

Daniela chuckled, turning her head to observe the students filing into the lecture hall, bleary-eyed from a long night of studying—or partying.

First-year law students were assigned to a section, which was a large group of students who had the same courses with the same professors at all the same times.

After spending two days in the company of these kids, most of whom were fresh out of college, Daniela already had a pretty good idea which of her peers were the scholars and which were the boozers.

As if to prove her point, one scraggly blond boy staggered and fell into a seat near the back, drawing laughs from his classmates. He grinned sheepishly and let loose a loud burp, this time eliciting disgusted groans.

Watching him, April predicted, "*He* won't be around much longer."

Daniela wondered if the same could be said about *her*. How long would it take her to win Caleb Thorne's trust and accomplish her mission?

Would she win Caleb's trust?

"Here he comes," April murmured, sotto voce. "The reason God made denim."

Amen, thought Daniela, watching as Caleb Thorne entered the lecture hall wearing a white T-shirt and a pair of faded jeans that clung to the strong, corded muscles of his thighs. A shiny black-and-silver helmet emblazoned with the Harley-Davidson emblem was tucked beneath one arm, completing the whole rebel-without-a-cause look he managed so effortlessly. He walked with a controlled stride, unhurried yet deliberate, a cross between a strut and a prowl. As he started down the wide stairs, Daniela could almost hear the collective female sighs that swept around the room.

"Good morning, Professor Thorne," cooed a pretty brunette seated at the opposite end of Daniela's row.

Caleb inclined his head in tacit greeting. By the time he reached the lectern at the front, all conversation ceased, and an air of hushed expectancy settled over the room. Daniela silently marveled at the transformation. Nearly ten minutes remained until the start of class, yet the mere appearance of Caleb Thorne was enough to bring the students to attention. She remembered what Kenneth had told her about Caleb's prowess as a criminal defense attorney. No doubt he'd commanded the courtroom as easily as he did a classroom of sixty-five.

As Caleb placed his motorcycle helmet behind the lectern and began pulling course materials from his satchel, April leaned close to whisper, "Why aren't we sitting in the *first* row?"

"Because we don't want to be so obvious," Daniela whispered back.

As if he'd picked up on her words, Caleb glanced up, his dark eyes sweeping the crowded room before coming to land on hers. Her breath hitched, her skin tingling as if he'd physically reached out and touched her.

But a second later his gaze shifted away, leaving Daniela to wonder if he'd noticed her at all.

April seemed to think so, seizing Daniela's arm in sudden excitement. "Did you see that? He looked right at you!"

"We're seated in his direct line of vision," Daniela said drolly.

"And yet, *you're* the only one he looked at."

Daniela felt a tiny thrill of pleasure. Maybe there was hope after all.

She half listened to a series of announcements made by Caleb's research assistant, Emma Richter, a mousy-looking brunette in desperate need of a makeover. As she began distributing handouts, Daniela wondered, not unkindly, if she could earn extra credit by offering fashion-emergency services to the poorly dressed young woman.

"Emma is passing out copies of the seating chart," Caleb informed the class. "Study it, memorize it. Starting Friday, and for the rest of the semester, sit in your assigned seat. This not only helps me connect names with faces, but gives me a way to track attendance. I will circulate an attendance sheet every class period. If you don't sign the sheet, I'll mark you as absent. As stated on the syllabus, you may miss up to six classes this semester, for whatever reasons you deem necessary. But if you miss more than six classes, you will have missed more than thirty percent of the class, which means that you will fail this course, regardless of how you perform on the final exam. Understood?"

The students murmured in docile agreement. April whispered out of the corner of her mouth, "Anyone dumb enough to miss six of *his* classes deserves to fail."

Daniela chuckled, then wished she hadn't.

Caleb's dark, piercing eyes homed in on hers, and this time there was no mistaking that she was the focus of his gaze. "Let's recap what we discussed on the first day of class. Miss Moreau, why don't you tell us what you've learned about civil procedure so far."

Daniela took a deep breath as she found herself in the proverbial hot seat, a rite of passage dreaded by all first-year law students. "Well, basically, civil procedure consists of the rules used by the courts to conduct civil trials. Civil trials, of course, being the judicial resolution of claims by one individual or group against another. As I understand it, civil procedure is sort of like the 'blueprint' for litigation."

"Yes, but why the heavy focus on the federal rules of civil procedure in this class?"

"Because most states model *their* rules of civil procedure after the federal rules of civil procedure."

"And?"

She gave him a quizzical look. Hadn't she answered the question correctly? But then again, she'd heard horror stories about law professors deliberately trying to trip up their students, sometimes subjecting them to sadistic interrogations, all in the name of teaching legal reasoning skills and stimulating "lawyerly" thinking.

Before she could formulate a response, Caleb segued to the next line of questioning, leaving Daniela feeling unbalanced—which, she supposed, had been his intent.

"Talk to me about the *United States v. Hatahley.* Who are the parties, and what are the facts of the case?"

Daniela racked her brain, mentally sifting through the myriad cases she'd read the night before. "Um, the plaintiffs are members of the Navajo tribe. Their livestock was grazing on federal land, and they were sued to have the livestock removed. But before the suit was decided, the feds unlawfully sold the plaintiffs' livestock to a glue factory. As a result, the plaintiffs were awarded damages of almost $200,000 by the federal district court and the U.S. Court of Appeals."

Caleb nodded, leaning against the table in front of the podium and folding his arms across his wide chest, as if he had all the time in the world to grill her. "So, what is the rule of law here, Miss Moreau?"

"The injured party needs to be put in the position it would have been in were it not for the wrong of the injurer."

"Which means?" he prompted.

Daniela moistened her lips with the tip of her tongue. Her mouth felt dry as dust. "If we apply this rule to the case at hand, the plaintiffs should get the market value of the livestock, as well as the loss of use in the time before they could have reasonably replaced the livestock."

Caleb nodded slowly, those fathomless dark eyes fastened on hers in a way that made it increasingly difficult for her to concentrate. "If the facts of the case were changed so that, say, the Navajo lost a herd of cats instead of highly trained horses, would the court rule the same?"

"That depends," Daniela hedged.

"On what, Miss Moreau?"

"On whether the judge was a cat lover, thereby placing greater importance on the loss of cats over livestock."

Her classmates, who'd been heretofore watching the spirited exchange like spectators at a hotly contested Wimbledon match, now erupted into laughter.

A ghost of a smile played around the edges of Caleb's mouth. He straightened from the table and sauntered around the podium to turn a page in his textbook. "Good job, Miss Moreau," he said in a deep voice tinged with humor. "Although you probably should have quit while you were ahead."

Daniela grinned sheepishly as more laughter rumbled across the room.

After class, Daniela was approached by two male students inviting her to join their study group.

"Nice work briefing the *Hatahley* case," they complimented her, gazing at her with frank male appreciation. She wore a fitted red shirt with a scooped neckline and a pencil-slim skirt made of stretch denim that hugged her body like a glove.

"How many people are in your study group?" Daniela asked, leaning over the table to unplug her laptop.

"Four so far," answered the taller of the pair, a good-looking Hispanic boy who couldn't keep his eyes off her butt. "We're trying to keep it at six, like they suggested in orientation over the summer."

"Good," Daniela said briskly. "April and I will make it six, then."

Two pairs of eyes shifted toward April, who stood almost shyly beside Daniela.

"Cool," said the other student, a cute redhead with clear green eyes and a smattering of freckles across his nose. "Do you guys want to meet now? We've got some time before Contracts at eleven."

"Can't," said Daniela, with a surreptitious glance toward the front of the room where Caleb stood talking to a group of students. "I've got something to take care of first. Maybe after class on Friday."

"Sounds good. Catch you ladies later."

As the pair moved off, April giggled. "This is going to be a great year. With you by my side, I'll get to meet all the hotties on campus."

Daniela grinned, but there was only one hottie on her mind at the moment.

"Hey, did you check out the seating chart?" April asked, thrusting her copy forward for Daniela's inspection. "It's in alphabetical order, but look where it places you. Smack-dab in the middle of the second row, right in front of Professor Thorne's lectern. He'll have an up-close-and-personal view of you *all* the time."

"Hmm," Daniela murmured, both pleased and terrified at the prospect.

"I, on the other hand, have been banished to the far end of the second row, to languish in obscurity." April gave a wistful sigh. "You lucky woman."

Daniela laughed. "Maybe not. Being in that seat puts me in his crosshairs, and we all know how *that* goes."

"Yeah, but he's already called on you, so theoretically, you should be safe for a while. Besides, you did great. I think he was really impressed. I know the rest of us were. Anyway, I'm going to the library to get some reading done before class. I'm nowhere near as prepared as you obviously are." Stifling a yawn, the girl stepped into the aisle and headed up the stairs. "See you at eleven."

Daniela stayed behind and waited for Caleb to finish talking to students. She couldn't afford to let him out of her sight, knowing that Shara Adler was probably camped outside the classroom waiting to invite him for coffee.

This time Daniela would beat her to the chase.

Gradually the last of her classmates dispersed, and Caleb and his assistant, Emma, started up the stairs together. As they conversed, the woman gazed up at him with pure adoration, leading Daniela to wonder if *any* female on campus was immune to the man.

As the pair drew nearer to where she stood, Caleb's dark eyes locked on hers, making her mouth go dry.

Immune she was not.

"Do you have a minute?" she asked when he reached her.

He nodded, then glanced at Emma. "Thanks for your help today. We'll talk later."

"All right," she said, smiling shyly. She eyed Daniela curiously before continuing up the stairs and out of the classroom.

"What can I do for you, Miss Moreau?" Caleb asked, his tone formal.

Shoring up her courage, Daniela said, "I was wondering if I could buy you a cup of coffee."

She saw the refusal in his eyes even before he opened his mouth. "Thank you, but—"

"I was hoping to pick your brain about the case brief I'm working on. I know it isn't due until the end of the semester, but I could really use some help."

"I'm sure Shara would be more than happy to answer any questions you have."

"I know, but..." She gave him what she hoped was her most beguiling smile. "Well, you *did* offer your assistance yesterday in the library. Do you remember?"

"Of course I remember." By the look on his face, though, she could tell he probably wished *she* hadn't remembered. Fortunately, he was too much of a gentleman to renege on the deal. "Why don't you stop by during my office hours this afternoon? We can talk then."

"Can't do it this afternoon," she lied. "I'm meeting with my study group. Besides, I really want to start working on the case brief as soon as possible. One cup of coffee, Professor Thorne. That's all I ask. Please?"

He hesitated, flicking a glance at his wristwatch. "Coffee, huh?"

She grinned, tasting victory. "And maybe a beignet, too. What the heck. I'm feeling generous."

He chuckled, and her stomach bottomed out at the low, sexy rumble. "In that case," he drawled, "how can I refuse?"

Chapter 6

Daniela was surprised, and more than a little relieved, when they made it out of the building and to the parking lot without encountering Shara Adler.

"We can take my car," she told Caleb. She glanced at the helmet tucked beneath his arm, then added hopefully, "Unless you want to take me for a spin on your Harley?"

He looked down at her tight-fitting skirt, and his eyes darkened. "You're not exactly dressed for it," he said gruffly.

Daniela swallowed, tingling from the heat of his brief perusal. "Guess not."

They reached her car, a silver Mustang that gleamed in the morning sunlight. Caleb ran an appreciative eye over the sleek, classic contours of the vehicle. "Nice whip."

"Thanks. I like it, too." She unlocked the doors and dropped her laptop and backpack into the backseat next to Caleb's helmet and leather satchel. As she slid into the car beside him, she saw that his legs were too long in the confined space, his knees colliding with the dashboard.

"Sorry about that," she said, grinning as he adjusted the seat. "The last person who rode in the passenger seat was my mother, and she's only five-two."

He smiled a little. "How tall are you?"

"Five-seven." She started the car and reversed out of the tight parking space. "From what I understand, my father was very tall, and that's where I get my height from. He passed away before I turned one."

"I'm sorry to hear that," Caleb said quietly.

"Thanks. In a way it was both a blessing and a curse that I was too young to remember him."

Caleb nodded. "I can understand that."

Daniela maneuvered through the parking lot bustling with students and faculty, and turned left at the first intersection. "How long have you been teaching at St. Mary's?" she asked, though she already knew the answer. Might as well get used to pretending not to know certain details about him.

"Five years." Out of the corner of her eye, she saw him studying her profile. "Are you originally from San Antonio?"

She nodded. "You?"

"Born and raised."

"Ever wanted to live anywhere else?"

"Can't say that I have. You?"

"Not a chance." She slanted him a whimsical smile. "Guess we're kindred souls."

He chuckled low in his throat and shifted in his seat,

heightening her awareness of him. She drew in a breath of his clean-scented male warmth and fought to keep her mind on the road, and not the way his jeans molded the hard, sculpted muscles of his thighs.

"You *do* know that there's a coffee shop on campus," he commented. "And a Starbucks right around the corner."

"Yeah, but I figured you might prefer to go somewhere less...populated by your students and colleagues."

His mouth twitched with wry humor. "If I was afraid to be seen in public with you, Miss Moreau, believe me, I wouldn't be here. Maybe *you're* the one who's afraid to be seen with me."

"No way," Daniela said quickly—too quickly.

A lazy smile was his only response.

Two minutes later, she pulled into the parking lot of Anthony O's Coffeehouse and killed the engine. Together they climbed out of the Mustang and walked toward the restaurant.

Caleb held the door open for her and she brushed past him, the brief contact raising a prickly set of goose bumps along her skin. When she looked over her shoulder to thank him, she found his hooded gaze on her mouth. She trembled, actually *trembled,* and somehow forced her legs to keep moving toward the hostess station.

At that early hour, the café wasn't crowded. Natural light poured in through floor-to-ceiling windows, and soft jazz wafted throughout the dining room that featured an inviting turquoise color scheme.

They were shown to a booth near the back and presented with menus. Caleb ordered a cup of the house blend along with the beignet Daniela had promised.

"I'll have an espresso," she told the young blond waitress, "and a small serving of vanilla ice cream."

When the waitress slipped away to fill their orders, Caleb cocked an amused brow at Daniela. "Coffee and ice cream?"

She grinned. "Ever tried it?"

"No."

"You should. It's one of those simple pleasures everyone should experience at some point in their lives. Like watching a sunset…or riding a motorcycle."

Caleb chuckled, leaning back in the booth. His T-shirt stretched across his wide chest, displaying the solid muscle structure that bunched and rippled beneath. "Still lobbying for that free ride, huh?"

Her grin widened. "Can't blame a girl for trying. I'm nothing if not persistent."

"I'll be sure to remember that." With his arms spread over the back of the leather cushions behind him, he looked relaxed and content, not to mention heartthrob-sexy. "Why do you want to be a lawyer, Miss Moreau?"

"Please, call me Daniela." At his guarded look, she hastened to add, "At least outside the classroom. It feels weird to be on such formal terms over a friendly cup of coffee. Please?"

He hesitated, then gave a slight nod. "All right. Now, tell me why you want to be an attorney. Were you a prelaw major in college?"

"No, accounting." It was another detail, like her first name, that she and her brothers had decided not to fabricate. The less she lied about, the less risk she ran of blowing her cover. Theoretically, anyway.

"I earned a bachelor's degree in accounting, became

a CPA and went to work for a large accounting firm. But, after just three years, I knew it wasn't for me."

"How did you know?"

Something in his gentle tone made her want to tell him everything—about the long nights, demanding clients, unscrupulous bosses. About the tears of frustration she'd shed on the way home, then quickly scraped away before going inside the house so her mother wouldn't notice and worry even more.

"I was unhappy," she said simply. "The reason I became a CPA was that I'd always been good at math, so it seemed the natural choice for me to go into accounting. And, quite honestly, I wanted to make a lot of money—and I did."

"But it wasn't enough for you," Caleb said softly.

"No, it wasn't." A sardonic smile curved her mouth. "When the whole Enron scandal broke, I realized that what had happened to those employees could just as easily happen to me. The next day, I walked into my boss's office and handed him my resignation letter."

"That took a lot of guts," Caleb said in a voice laced with admiration.

She shrugged. "Not really. I should have done it a lot sooner."

Caleb nodded slowly. "So, what have you been doing since then?"

"Freelancing. Preparing taxes, doing bookkeeping—stuff like that."

The waitress materialized with their orders, setting each item carefully on the table. "Is there anything else I can get for you?" she inquired, looking at Caleb.

He shook his head, and Daniela asked, "May I have a spoon?"

"Oh. Sorry." The girl fumbled out a set of linen-wrapped silverware from the front pocket of her apron and passed it to Daniela without ever taking her baby blues off Caleb. "Can I get you anything else, sir?"

His mouth twitched. "I'm fine, thanks."

"Okay. Well, just let me know if there's anything else you need. Anything at all."

"Will do," he said with a wink that made the girl blush. "Thanks."

Daniela shook her head at Caleb as the waitress moved on to the next customer. "Is it just me," she muttered, "or have you ever noticed the effect you seem to have on every female that crosses your path?"

He took a sip of steaming coffee, dark eyes glinting with amusement over the rim. "How would you know that? We've been acquainted all of, what, two days?"

"Three days. I met you bright and early on Monday morning."

"Not so early," he pointed out dryly. "You were ten minutes late to my class."

"Semantics."

He laughed, a strong, deep sound that rumbled up from his chest and made Daniela's toes curl inside her wood-heeled Jimmy Choo sandals. "You're going to make a fine lawyer someday, Miss Moreau," he drawled.

"I'll choose to take that as a compliment," she quipped, enjoying the repartee so much that she didn't bother correcting him on the formal address. She spooned vanilla ice cream into her mouth, then followed up with a sip of espresso.

A deep, languorous sigh escaped her lips. "*Mmm-mmm.*"

Caleb was watching her, cup halfway to his mouth. "That good, huh?" His voice sounded rough, tight.

Daniela nodded, grinning. "It's a sensory thing. You know, the combination of rich, hot coffee mixed with sweet, cold ice cream. Mmm, heavenly. You should try it."

He shook his head. "No, thanks."

"Come on, try it," Daniela coaxed, holding out a spoonful of ice cream to him. "I think you'd really like it. Try it. I insist."

Caleb hesitated, then leaned forward to accept the sweet offering. As she slid the spoon into his mouth, she was caught off guard by the sudden heat that bloomed in her belly and spread outward like a slow, thick liquid.

Her heart thundered at the very male look that filled his eyes as he watched her watching him. Slowly he ran his tongue over the sensuous curve of his bottom lip, removing traces of the creamy concoction.

"You're right," he said silkily. "It is good."

Her breasts felt tight and achy against the lace bra she wore. Without thinking, she drew the spoon into her own mouth and licked off the remainder of vanilla ice cream, imagining she could taste *him*. It was the most erotic experience she'd ever had. The only thing that'd be more erotic would be Caleb licking ice cream from her body.

She shivered convulsively.

"You, uh, were supposed to take a sip of coffee right afterward," she said huskily. "To, uh, get the full effect."

His eyes darkened, stoking the flames already building inside her. "I think I did."

Her pulse accelerated, and she felt a thrill of wicked pleasure at his words. Another minute of this, and she'd be begging him to take her into the bathroom and do unspeakable things to her.

Fortunately, Caleb chose that moment to glance at his watch. "Let's talk about your case brief."

As opposed to having hot, kinky sex in a public restroom.

Biting back a sigh of regret, Daniela reached under the table for her purse. As she rummaged around for a pen and the small notepad she'd brought to take notes, Caleb's gaze wandered to the flat-screen television mounted in a nearby corner of the restaurant. A KSAT-12 news anchor was reporting on the early-morning indictment of a local labor union boss. Carlito "Lito" Olivares, president of the Oil Refineries Workers Union, had been charged with embezzling over one million dollars from various employers represented by his union.

Shaking her head in disgust, Daniela was about to make a scathing comment when something in Caleb's demeanor stopped her. A muscle worked in his tightly clenched jaw, and he gripped his coffee cup so hard, she worried it would shatter in his big hand.

With mounting curiosity, she looked at the television, then back at Caleb. What was going on here?

One of the waiters turned up the volume on the television. "…is also charged with defrauding the union by submitting false entertainment vouchers, using union funds to purchase personal airline tickets and billing the organization for $30,000 in personal telephone calls made on a union-issued cell phone. Olivares is expected to enter a not-guilty plea at the arraignment next week. We're also getting word, from sources close to the Olivares camp, that legal heavyweight Crandall Thorne may soon step in to represent Olivares on this case."

Daniela snapped to attention. Crandall Thorne was going to defend the corrupt labor union boss? Was that why Caleb looked so ominous? Did he have a problem with his father representing Olivares? Or did he disagree with Olivares's indictment?

When Caleb returned his gaze to hers, his face was devoid of expression. Calmly he took a sip of coffee and set the cup back down on the table.

Daniela studied him carefully. "Crandall Thorne is your father, isn't he?"

"Yes." He inclined his head toward the notepad in front of her, making it clear he didn't want to discuss the matter further. "What can I help you with?"

Daniela wanted to press him for more information, but she knew she wouldn't get very far.

Reminding herself once again that it would take time to win his trust, she launched into a detailed explanation of the problems she was having with her case brief.

It was, Caleb admitted to himself later that afternoon, one of the stupidest things he'd ever done in his life.

He'd had no business having coffee with Daniela Moreau.

Not when thoughts of her had taunted him for the past three days.

Not when he'd found himself seeking her out almost from the moment he stepped foot in the classroom that morning.

And definitely not when, in the middle of drilling her on a case, he'd found himself imagining her silky-soft skin against his own, imagining her warm, lush body writhing beneath his as he made love to her.

He'd had no business having coffee with her.

His first mistake had been getting into her car. The eight-minute ride to the restaurant had been pure torture. Every time Daniela shifted in her seat, the high slit in the side of her skirt exposed the shapely curve of a milky-brown thigh. Every time her slender hand palmed the gearshift, working the manual transmission with the skilled ease of a pro, his imagination—along with his libido—kicked into overdrive.

By the time they reached the coffeehouse, he'd been half out of his mind with lust.

Was it any wonder he'd put up little resistance when Daniela offered him a taste of her ice cream, holding out the sweet sampling like Eve beckoning to Adam with the forbidden fruit? Against his better judgment he'd accepted the offering, and the answering hunger in Daniela's dark, sultry eyes had sent need rushing straight to his groin.

Who would've thought that something so simple, so seemingly innocent, could be so mind-numbingly erotic? When Daniela turned around and slid the spoon back into her own mouth, Caleb just about lost it. It took a monumental act of willpower not to haul her across the table and into his lap, onlookers be damned.

Even now, five hours later, the memory of that encounter heated his blood, causing an uncomfortable straining at his zipper. Caleb bit back a savage oath and scrubbed a hand over his face as if to erase the torturous images from his mind—*all* of them, including the one of Daniela's luscious rump encased in skintight denim.

Why couldn't he have included some sort of dress code on the syllabus, something that would keep every enticing curve and inch of Daniela Moreau's body concealed?

It was bad enough that the alphabetical seating chart placed her right in front of the lectern, making it impossible for him not to notice her. When his assistant, Emma Richter, gave him the chart yesterday, he'd been half tempted to rearrange the seating assignments, sending Daniela all the way to the back of the lecture hall where she couldn't torment him.

Swearing under his breath, Caleb stared at the blinking cursor on his computer screen. In the hour since he'd sat down to work on his law review article, he'd typed all of three sentences. *Three*. At this rate, he wouldn't be finished until Christmas.

"Does that scowl mean things aren't going well?"

Caleb looked up as Shara Adler appeared in the doorway, a teasing smile on her face.

"Hey there," he said warmly, welcoming the distraction. Perhaps what he needed was a few minutes of stimulating conversation with a colleague to get those cerebral juices flowing again. God knows he'd done enough thinking with the wrong head that day.

Pushing away from his desk, he leaned back in the swivel chair and folded his arms behind his head, giving Shara a lazy smile. "How's your day going?"

"Can't complain. But judging by the look on your face a minute ago, you can't say the same. What are you working on?"

"Law review article."

She shook her head at him. "It isn't enough to be the faculty advisory chair of the *Law Journal*, is it? You just have to add your two cents to every issue."

Caleb chuckled. "I'm narcissistic enough to think

my two cents are what makes our journal among the most frequently cited law reviews in the country," he drawled. "Leave me to my illusions, woman."

She smiled, but it didn't quite reach her amber-colored eyes. With sun-kissed reddish-brown skin and dark, silky hair that hung to her waist, Shara Adler was a striking woman who drew her fair share of admirers. Her tall, lithe body was stylishly attired in a silk halter top and a pleated russet skirt that flared to midcalf length, and was accented by a woven leather belt and low-heeled linen sandals.

"I haven't seen you all day," she said quietly.

"I was just about to say the same thing. Where've you been hiding?"

"*I'm* not the one who's been hiding," said Shara, a touch of reproof in her cultured tones. "You are."

Caleb lifted a brow. "I am?"

"Yes." Without waiting for an invitation—knowing she didn't need one—she stepped into his office and walked toward the window overlooking the courtyard nestled between the Law Classroom Building and library. As she passed his desk, Caleb caught a hint of the light, tropical fragrance she wore, a scent that often reminded him of the week he'd spent at her beachside house in the Caribbean, where he'd retreated to escape the turbulence of his own life. Shara had generously opened her home, and her arms, to him, and for that he'd always be grateful to her.

Absently he picked up a round crystal paperweight his father had once given him. Embedded inside was a small acrylic globe because, as Crandall Thorne had explained, he'd always known Caleb would take the world by storm.

The paperweight was the only memento Caleb had taken from his plush corner office suite when he left the law firm.

"How's Devon?" he asked Shara, who stood utterly still at the window with her back turned to him. "Enjoying his final year in middle school so far?"

"Of course. He and his friends already have bets going about who can charm the prettiest incoming sixth-grader. Isn't that the most ridiculous thing you've ever heard? Why should they spend all their time chasing younger girls?" She gave a mirthless laugh. "But I guess that's something men never outgrow."

The subtly launched missile hit its intended target. Without missing a beat, Caleb continued transferring the crystal paperweight from one hand to the other. When he spoke, his voice was remarkably calm. "What's on your mind, Shara?"

She turned around slowly to face him. "Was that Daniela Moreau I saw you leaving campus with earlier?"

He inclined his head. "It was."

Shara frowned with disapproval. "Do you really think that's a good idea, Caleb? Fraternizing with your students?"

"She invited me for coffee. I accepted. End of story."

"You know very well it's not that cut-and-dried. You can't be seen going out on dates with—"

"I'd hardly call what we had a date," he countered dryly.

"Maybe not this time. But what about the next time, and the time after that?" Shara's nostrils flared in anger. "Can you really afford to risk your career by getting involved with Daniela Moreau, or any other student? You've got a good thing going here, Caleb. You're greatly admired and respected by your students and colleagues. The administration thinks you walk on water—*despite* your maverick attitude toward policies and procedures and your outright refusal to attend faculty networking events. My God, Caleb, they even let you get away with showing up to class looking like the poster boy for a motorcycle gang!"

"You know I hate wearing suits," he growled.

"I know. *Everyone* knows. It's your legacy around here—Professor Thorne, the dark, brooding bad boy with the soulful bedroom eyes and sin-inducing voice."

His lips twitched with barely suppressed humor. "*Sin-inducing?*"

"Don't mock me! If you heard what these girls whisper about you, you'd understand exactly what I mean by that expression. All I'm saying is, no student is worth losing your job over. I don't care how pretty she is." She paused, then added snidely, "And honestly, Caleb, you've had prettier—students *and* girlfriends."

His eyes narrowed on hers in silent appraisal. "This isn't really about my job security, is it, Shara?" he queried softly.

She averted her gaze, her mouth tightening. "Don't make this about us."

"Is it?"

"No," she snapped. "It's about me looking out for a colleague, someone I also consider a good friend. I don't have to remind you that there aren't too many of us in this department, Caleb. If the three of us—you, me and Bernard—don't watch one another's backs, who will?" With a glance at her slim gold wristwatch, she started toward the door. "I have a class in five minutes."

"Shara."

She turned back, one finely shaped brow arched. "Yes?"

Caleb searched her tense face. "You know I've never crossed the line with any of my students before. What makes you so sure Daniela Moreau will be the exception?"

Shara gave him a sharp look. "What makes you so sure she *won't?*"

With that terse challenge hanging in the air between them, she spun on her heel and strode out of the office.

Caleb was left to mull over the question, already knowing the answer.

When it came to Daniela Moreau, the only thing he *could* be sure of was that he was in trouble.

Just how much trouble remained to be seen.

Chapter 7

When Daniela stepped through the doors of Roarke Investigations that afternoon, the phone was ringing off the hook. The secretary, Carole Hightower, was frantically trying to keep up with the rapid succession of incoming calls while entering information into the computer in front of her.

Daniela quickly surveyed the reception area, which had undergone a radical transformation with the purchase of rustic pine tables and chairs artfully arranged around the large room. The seat cushions were upholstered in earthy shades of orange, red, salmon and turquoise that added to the Southwestern motif, and wood-framed Native American prints graced walls painted the color of papaya. The new and improved decor—courtesy of Daniela—was a marked departure from the sparse, no-frills private detective offices characterized in hardboiled mystery novels.

In one chair, a short, balding Hispanic man barked rapid-fire Spanish into his cell phone while puffing away on a cigarette.

Daniela walked over to him. "Excuse me, sir."

When he glanced up at her, she pointed toward the sign prominently displayed above the large oak reception desk. "We don't allow smoking in the building."

"Sorry," he mumbled sheepishly. He glanced around the room for an ashtray, then, finding none, stubbed out his cigarette against the sole of his leather loafer.

"Would you like some coffee, Mr.—?"

"Rodriguez. Luis Rodriguez. Yes, thank you very much."

"Coming right up."

Daniela made her way toward the reception desk, where the secretary was juggling multiple calls. She sent Daniela a flustered look as she approached. "Kenneth Roarke is not in at the moment," she spoke into the receiver. "Can I transfer you to his voice mail? All right, please hold." She pressed a flashing button on the phone, then groaned. "Oh, no. I hung up on him. Again."

Daniela inwardly cringed. "Why don't you take a break and get Mr. Rodriguez a cup of coffee?" she suggested.

The woman was only too eager to vacate her station in exchange for a less demanding task.

Daniela spent the next fifteen minutes answering and forwarding calls with a swiftness and efficiency borne from years of practice. Three years, to be exact.

That was how Noah Roarke found her when he emerged from his office followed by another man. After escorting his client to the door, Noah doubled back to the reception desk, one dark brow raised at his sister.

"Where's Carole?" he asked.

"Making coffee."

Noah grimaced. "Have you *tasted* her coffee?" he muttered under his breath, so as not to be overheard by those waiting in the reception area.

Leaning forward, Daniela whispered back, "It can't be much worse than her skills as a receptionist."

"Don't be too sure about that." Noah turned and gestured for Luis Rodriguez to follow him back to his office.

Carole returned a few minutes later carrying a disposable cup filled with a dark, sludgy brew masquerading as coffee. "Where's Mr. Rodriguez?"

"With Noah. I'll take him the coffee," Daniela promised, knowing she'd do no such thing as she accepted the cup from the woman and rose from the chair.

The phone rang, and while Carole was preoccupied, Daniela dumped the coffee into a giant potted plant and tossed the cup in the trash before heading to her own office in the back.

Her office was actually a windowless cubbyhole that doubled as the supply room. The space was dominated by a wooden antique desk and bench, and black metal filing cabinets that marched along one wall. The basic functionality of the room was offset by soft, feminine touches interspersed throughout—a ceramic vase here, a cluster of decorative candles there, a multicolored wool serape that hung on a wall.

Ignoring a mound of paperwork that awaited her attention, Daniela dropped her purse onto the desk and turned on the computer to check her e-mail messages. Although she was on assignment and technically "out of pocket," she couldn't stay away entirely. For the past three years she'd ate, slept and breathed Roarke Investigations, serving as secretary, bookkeeper and part-time private detective as she helped her brothers establish the business. It was as much a part of her as it was part of Kenneth and Noah Roarke.

Noah stuck his head in the doorway just as she was responding to her last e-mail message. "What're you doing here, anyway? Not that I mind seeing you around, kiddo, but I thought we all agreed that you should avoid this place as much as possible, in case Thorne gets suspicious at some point and starts having you followed."

"I know, I know," Daniela muttered, sending off her reply. "I had a ton of e-mail messages to respond to."

"You can check your e-mail from home," Noah reminded her dryly. "That's why we set you up with remote access."

Grinning at her brother, Daniela leaned back in her chair, propped her long legs on the desk and crossed her feet at the ankles. "One message was from a client who wanted to thank me for proving that her husband *wasn't* cheating on her. What do you have to say about that?"

Noah chuckled, stepping into the tiny office and causing it to shrink even more by the sheer breadth of his wide shoulders. He wore a gray polo shirt that showed off his muscular physique, tucked into loose-fitting black gabardine trousers. He could have stepped from the cover of *GQ,* though he'd sooner wrestle tigers than suffer such a compliment.

"What I have to say," he grumbled good-naturedly, dropping into the chair opposite her desk, "is that you're in the wrong line of business, El. You're supposed to *want* spouses to be guilty. How else are we supposed to make any money around here?"

Daniela made a face at him, but she knew that Noah, like her, took no pleasure in chasing down cheaters, especially when children were thrown into the equation. He loathed being the bearer of bad news almost as much as he loathed the act of infidelity itself.

"Not that we're hurting for business around here," Daniela said. "The phone's been ringing off the hook all afternoon. What gives?"

"We took out an ad in today's *Express-News*. Guess it's already starting to pay off."

"Not for long though, if Carole keeps hanging up on people."

Noah scowled. "Tell me about it. She's the *third* secretary we've hired in a month. After the first two disasters, we figured we couldn't go wrong using a temp agency—especially since Carole came so highly recommended."

Daniela gave a mock shudder. "I'd hate to see what they consider *incompetent*."

"We have to get rid of her before she puts us out of business."

"Hey, don't look at me," Daniela said quickly. "I'm not even supposed to be here, remember? I only stopped by to see how you're doing, and to commend you for not accompanying Kenny yesterday on his quest to pry information out of me."

Noah chuckled. "You know I don't operate that way, baby girl." He paused, searching her face. "But since you're here, why don't you fill me in on how things are going?"

"Didn't Kenny tell you?"

"He did," Noah said carefully, "but I guess what I'm asking is, how do *you* feel things are going?"

He was asking her, without really asking her, whether she still had reservations about her role in the undercover investigation. The fact that he cared at all was what set him apart from Kenneth Roarke.

And it was for this reason that she readily confided in him, telling him about her coffeehouse excursion with Caleb—minus the vanilla ice cream incident. *That* would be something she kept to herself, savoring the delicious memory like...well, like ice cream and espresso melting on her tongue.

Only better.

"By the way he reacted to the news," she explained, shoving aside the wicked thought, "I knew something was wrong, even before I heard that his father might be representing Olivares on the case. Why do you think that would bother Caleb so much?"

"Well, based on what Philbin told us, Caleb and his father don't see eye to eye on the type of clients Crandall Thorne chooses to represent. Obviously this labor union boss is no exception."

Daniela frowned, unsatisfied with the simple explanation. "But there was something else, something that went beyond disapproval. It was more of a...quiet rage."

Noah gave her a long, measuring look. "Do you think it was directed at his father, or Olivares?"

"I'm not sure. And I know it may sound crazy, but I think he's hiding something."

"I guess that'll be your job to find out," said Noah, rising from the chair and walking to the door. He turned back to look at his sister, his expression unreadable. "Just promise me you'll be careful, Daniela. There's a lot at stake here."

She nodded slowly. "I know."

Noah didn't have to tell her how much was at stake. She knew as well as anyone how much they all stood to gain if she successfully completed the mission.

But a funny thing was starting to happen, something she hadn't admitted to herself until that very moment.

The more time she spent with Caleb Thorne, the less she found herself eagerly anticipating what she and her family would gain at his expense. Instead, her thoughts were increasingly dominated by what she, alone, stood to *lose.*

Chapter 8

Late Thursday morning, Daniela was on her way out of the classroom after Legal Research and Writing when she was stopped by Shara Adler's voice. "Miss Moreau, may I speak to you for a minute?"

April, walking beside Daniela, arched a questioning brow at her.

"I'll catch up to you later," Daniela told the girl, then turned and made her way to the front of the lecture hall where Shara stood, stuffing files into an expensive-looking leather briefcase. She was understated elegance in a teal silk blouse worn over tan linen slacks, and her long, dark mane gleamed under the room's warm, recessed lights.

"Is something wrong?" Daniela asked, stopping in front of her.

"Depends on whose perspective you're talking

about," the woman answered without looking up from her task. "What I may consider wrong, you might find perfectly acceptable."

Daniela frowned. "I'm afraid I don't understand," she said, though she had a sinking feeling she understood perfectly.

Amber eyes lifted and bore into hers with arctic intensity. "I understand you and Caleb Thorne had coffee together yesterday."

"That's right. He was kind enough to answer some questions I had about an assignment." She didn't add that the assignment was for Shara's class. Why add fuel to the fire?

"Oh, I'm sure kindness had little to do with it," Shara said in a voice laced with cynicism. "And I would imagine you both had more on your minds than coffee and homework."

Daniela bristled. "Is there something you want to say to me, Professor Adler?"

"Yes," Shara snapped. "I've been around a long time, Miss Moreau, long enough to know how things work around here. Every semester, I watch pretty young things throw themselves at Caleb—some are subtle, some not so subtle. For the most part, Caleb pays these girls no mind, enduring their advances like minor annoyances. But there's always that one who sneaks beneath the radar, the one he simply can't resist." Her smile was cold and narrow. "I guess you've drawn the winning lottery ticket this semester, Miss Moreau. Congratulations."

Daniela kept her features carefully schooled, though inside she was shaking with anger and an emotion that came too close to disillusionment. Raw, gut-twisting disillusionment. Which was ridiculous. Why should she care that Caleb engaged in meaningless flings with his students? Given that the success of her mission *depended* on his susceptibility to temptation, she should be relieved.

She wasn't. Far from it.

Looking Shara Adler squarely in the eye, she said coolly, "It must be very difficult to watch the man you love drift from one affair to another right in front of your face."

Shara flinched, then inclined her head slowly, conceding the match point to Daniela. "How astute of you, Miss Moreau. I *do* love Caleb. Indiscretions aside, he's a wonderful man, and great with my thirteen-year-old son, who adores him. I'm idealistic enough to believe that someday, when he's finished sowing his wild oats in an attempt to escape his demons, Caleb will be ready for a serious commitment. And when that day comes, Miss Moreau," she said with absolute certainty, "you'd better believe *I'm* the one he'll come running to, not one of his starry-eyed students."

Daniela could feel the blood rushing through her veins, making her skin hot. Mustering a smile etched in steel, she said, "In that case, I guess I'd better enjoy him while I can. And I trust you won't hold it against me when it's grading time?"

Shara's expression hardened with contempt. Without waiting for her response, Daniela turned on her heel and strode out of the classroom.

She fumed all the way to the library, where she retreated to a table in a remote corner of the reading room and hoped she wouldn't run into any of her classmates.

She wasn't in the mood for small talk, or to play the role of overstressed law student.

Her emotions were in turmoil, and she needed time alone to sort through them and regain her equilibrium.

It shouldn't have stunned her to learn of Caleb's exploits with his students. As Shara Adler had told her, and as she herself had witnessed firsthand, Caleb didn't lack for opportunities to indulge his sexual needs. He was a handsome, virile man who was constantly ogled, admired and—apparently—propositioned by women. Experience had taught Daniela that few men could resist that kind of temptation. Certainly not the losers she'd dated in college, or the one on whom she'd wasted two good years of her life, only to discover he had a fiancée waiting for him in Dallas.

After that disaster, Daniela had thrown herself into work like never before, climbing her way through the ranks at the large accounting firm where she'd worked since graduating from college. Still, she hadn't exactly lived like a puritan. On the few occasions when she surfaced from calculating balance sheets and escrow accounts, she'd sought male companionship, someone with whom to explore a new restaurant or enjoy a night at the symphony, or to share courtside tickets to watch the Spurs. And although she'd always told herself otherwise, in the back of her mind lingered the hope that she was one candlelight dinner away from meeting Mr. Right. That hope grew dimmer and dimmer with each passing year, after each outing with attractive, intelligent men who failed to interest her on any meaningful level. The sexual relationships she'd had had run the gamut from disappointing to satisfactory, but nothing had ever ventured close to being the stuff of fantasies. After one too many go-nowhere dates, Daniela had finally declared a moratorium on dating, which, she'd come to decide, required too much effort for the nonexistent return-on-investment.

Now, at the age of twenty-seven, she'd all but resigned herself to the idea that she would never find her soul mate—if indeed such a person existed.

She'd filled her life with other, more important things, like taking care of her mother and helping her brothers establish the detective agency. She didn't have time to do much more than daydream about Prince Charming, and on those rare occasions when she did daydream, it was almost always about kissing. A simple yet powerful thing that few men, at least in *her* experience, had taken the time to master.

Caleb Thorne was probably a great kisser, she thought, which was followed by an image of his full, sensuous lips glistening with moisture after he'd sampled her ice cream.

Daniela scowled, even as she crossed her legs under the table.

She wondered how many eager female students Caleb had kissed, caressed, then taken home to seduce. And how many times had he and Shara made love? If Daniela was foolhardy enough to sleep with Caleb, would she become just another notch on his bedpost? Was he rogue enough to take from her, without giving anything of himself in return? He'd obviously done a number on Shara Adler, who'd heretofore struck Daniela as a smart, savvy, no-nonsense woman who would *never* be reduced to waiting on the sidelines for a man to finish sowing his wild oats.

Daniela frowned.

Somehow she'd thought Caleb Thorne was different from the other men she'd encountered in her life. And although she knew it shouldn't matter that he wasn't, it did.

Mattered more than it should have.

Crandall Thorne grimaced as two needles were inserted into his vein, then connected to a plastic tube suspended from the dialysis machine beside his chair. Lights blinked on the machine that monitored and maintained his blood flow while administering dialysate, a clear fluid used to draw waste products from his blood. For four hours he would be chained to the detested machine, with nothing more to occupy his mind than reviewing the case files his associates had couriered to him that morning.

And then Caleb sauntered into the room, and suddenly the required four hours of treatment became a great deal more bearable.

Caleb saw the way his father's face lit up when he entered the sunroom that doubled as Crandall's home treatment center. But by the time he sat down in a wicker armchair beside him, Crandall was wearing his typical poker face.

"You know you didn't have to come all the way up here," he said gruffly. "I don't need my hand held."

"Do you see me holding any hands?" Caleb retorted. He grinned at the woman standing beside Crandall, adjusting levers on the dialysis machine. "How ya doin', Ms. Ruth?"

"I'm doing just fine, Caleb. And don't you pay your father any mind. You know he's happy to see you. He's just too proud to say so."

Ruth Gaylord had been hired as Crandall Thorne's private nurse over the summer, shortly after he was diagnosed with acute renal failure. Although she'd only been around for three months, she already seemed like a member of the family.

Her skin was the color of melted brown sugar, her black hair liberally woven with strands of gray that she claimed had been put there by her ornery employer. But, as she told it, thirty years of marriage to a temperamental man had been her proving ground for working with the likes of Crandall Thorne. Widowed three years ago and retired from a stressful career in oncology nursing, she'd been working as a home healthcare provider as a way to keep herself occupied between visits from her four grown children, who were scattered around the country.

"Are you done fooling with that machine?" Crandall groused at her.

"Calm down, or you'll get your blood pressure up." She made one final adjustment, then patted his arm, gentle despite his brusqueness with her. "I'll be back to check on you in a little bit. Caleb, would you care for something to drink? I believe Gloria made a fresh batch of sun-brewed iced tea this morning before she left. Sweet, the way you like it."

Caleb smiled at her. "Maybe later, Ms. Ruth. I drank nearly a gallon of water on the way up here. But thanks anyway."

After the woman left the room, closing the door behind her, Caleb shook his head at his father. "I don't know why anyone puts up with you."

"They put up with me because I pay them more than they've ever received anywhere else," Crandall asserted. "That includes everyone who works at the firm, right down to the administrative assistants."

Caleb considered it, then gave his head another shake. "Nah, I don't think that's it. Hard as it is to believe, I think they genuinely like you, old man."

"Old man, nothing. I may be hooked up to this confounded machine, but I can still take you across my knee, boy."

Caleb chuckled, stretching out his long legs. "You heard Ms. Ruth. Don't get your blood pressure up."

Crandall scowled without any real rancor. With his free arm, he set aside the paperwork he'd been preparing to review and slowly removed his wireless reading glasses. He regarded his son in silence for a prolonged moment. "You didn't tell me you had a visitor on Tuesday."

Caleb stiffened at the reminder, then said levelly, "I didn't think it was worth mentioning. Besides, you obviously didn't need to hear it from me."

"Still, it would have been nice."

"Why?" Caleb challenged. "Would it have changed your mind about taking Lito's case?"

Crandall's lips flattened with displeasure. "I haven't agreed to take his case."

"But you will. I know you will."

"What choice do I have? If I don't, we both know what will happen."

"Then let it happen," snarled Caleb. "Maybe it'll put an end to this senseless feud once and for all."

Crandall's nostrils flared. "There's nothing 'senseless' about any of this. Your mother died—"

"That's right, Dad, she *died!* Died because of a horrible secret you kept from her, from us, until it was too late!" Angrily he sprang from his chair and thrust his hands into his pockets to keep from smashing his fists through the wall and bringing the glass roof down on their heads.

Crandall watched as his son paced the floor, a caged panther dressed entirely in black—black T-shirt, black jeans, black boots. "We both know Philbin is bluffing," Caleb growled. "If he really knew anything, he would've gone public a long time ago."

"Be that as it may," Crandall said tersely, "I can't afford to take any chances. My sources tell me he's digging for information again."

"He's been *digging* for years."

"Yes, but now he may have employed the services of a private investigator. I have my people looking into it."

Caleb's harsh crack of laughter reverberated around the glass-walled room. "When does it ever end?" he bitterly demanded. "You have *him* investigated, he has *you* investigated, back and forth, so on and so forth. When does it ever end?"

"Dammit, Caleb—" Beside Crandall, the dialysis machine beeped loudly in protest.

Half a moment later, the door swung open and Ruth strode into the room, her brisk, purposeful strides carrying her swiftly to Crandall's side. She checked the machine, then made an adjustment that quieted the alarm.

In the ensuing silence, father and son glowered at each other like a pair of gunslingers facing off in an old Western.

Ruth frowned, holding Crandall's wrist and checking her watch. "Your blood pressure's skyrocketing," she scolded. "What on earth have you been doing in here?"

"Nothing," he grumbled, sounding like a recalcitrant child.

Ruth sent a stern look over her shoulder at Caleb, who stood with his hands braced on his hips, vibrating with restrained fury. "If this were a clinic, you know I couldn't allow you more than ten minutes an hour with him. Do I need to escort you out, Caleb?"

"No, ma'am," he mumbled, shamefaced. "It won't happen again."

"Be sure that it doesn't." With one final warning look at her patient, she stalked out of the room—this time leaving the door wide open.

For several moments neither man spoke.

At length Caleb scrubbed his hands over his face and shoved out a deep, weary breath. "Look, I'm sorry. I didn't come here to argue with you."

"I know that," Crandall said gruffly, "and believe me, I don't want to argue with you, either. Truth be told, I'm glad you stopped by today. You're a sight for sore eyes, son."

Caleb walked back to the armchair he'd vacated, sat and propped his elbows on his knees, the fight drained out of him.

"How's the first week of classes going?" Crandall asked, making an attempt at safe conversation.

"Fine, thanks."

"And what about your pretty lawyer friend? Does she still teach with you? You haven't mentioned her name in quite a while. Any particular reason?"

"No," Caleb answered dryly, knowing his father was fishing for information that wasn't there. "And, yes, she still teaches at the university. I'll tell her you asked about her."

Crandall gave him a long, appraising look. "When are you going to marry her?"

A grim smile curved Caleb's mouth. "How'd I know that question was coming?"

"Because you've been avoiding it for years."

"Shara and I aren't getting married, Dad. We're just friends."

Crandall lifted a dubious brow. "Does *she* know that?"

"Of course," Caleb retorted, even as an image of Shara's furious expression flashed across his mind. Since their confrontation yesterday, he'd told himself that the anger she'd displayed was nothing more than that of one concerned friend looking out for another.

But deep down inside, he knew better.

His father cut him a look that said he knew better, too. "I won't presume to give you advice on your love life—"

"Then don't."

"But women can be very unpredictable and unstable creatures," Crandall continued as if Caleb hadn't spoken. "If you have no intention of making a commitment to this woman, you'd better make darned sure she knows it."

"She knows it," Caleb said shortly, then expelled a long, exasperated breath. "Look, I care for Shara a whole lot. We connect on many levels—intellectually, professionally and, yes, physically. We could probably make one helluva couple someday."

Crandall grinned. "Sounds like the beginnings of a marriage proposal to me."

Caleb shook his head, frustrated with his father's relentless prying, but even more frustrated with his own inability to articulate the reasons he and Shara could never work.

Maybe because he hadn't quite sold himself on the reasons, nebulous as they were.

Crandall brushed an invisible fleck of lint off the knife-blade crease of his trousers. Though mostly confined to the house, he still got up every morning and dressed as if he were heading to the office. "If you and Shara don't work out," he said casually, "you know Ruth's youngest daughter is moving back to San Antonio next month. You could—"

"Nice try, Dad."

Crandall scowled. "Can't blame a man for wanting to see his only son happily married off while he's still around to witness it. And while we're on the subject, I wouldn't mind having some noisy grandchildren running up and down these lands, either."

Caleb couldn't help chuckling. "You're getting sentimental in your old age," he drawled, but his thoughts had strayed, inexorably, to Daniela Moreau.

Earlier that day, he'd been working in the offices of the *Law Journal,* which were housed in the library, when he'd glanced out the window and seen Daniela charging toward the building, looking mad enough to spit nails. Curious, he'd paused in his task to watch her, wondering who, or what, had made her so angry. He'd been sorely tempted to go to her—just to find out if everything was all right, he told himself. It had taken sheer willpower to stay right where he was. But his concentration was shot, knowing she was in the same building. Finally, when he couldn't take it anymore, he'd packed up his stuff and left campus, driving until he found himself on the way to his father's Hill Country ranch.

He'd spent the whole ride alternately thinking about her, and calling himself all kinds of a damned fool for letting her get under his skin so easily. In the five years he'd been teaching, this was the first time he'd ever been so affected by a student. Sure, there had been a few beautiful girls whose sultry smiles had made him wonder how anyone could possibly maintain a celibate lifestyle. But he'd never been tempted to cross the line with any of them. His will where temptresses were concerned had always been strong, if not ironclad.

Until now.

Until Daniela Moreau stepped through the door of his classroom on Monday morning, shattering all precedents. Just being around her was like being trapped in a seductive spider's web, sticky and warm and exciting, but infinitely dangerous. Caleb was determined to keep himself from being ensnared, no matter how enticing this particular temptress proved to be.

Chapter 9

"You're going *where?*"

"You heard me. I'm going to Houston to visit your Aunt Phyllis."

Daniela frowned into her cell phone. "I don't think that's such a good idea, Mom. You're recovering from the flu. Less than a week ago you were sick as a dog and bedridden, and now you're talking about traveling to *Houston?*"

"First of all," came the indignant response, "stop referring to Houston as if it's on the other side of the country. It's two and a half hours away. Second of all, you don't have to keep reminding me how sick I was. I'm all better now, as you've seen with your own two eyes. Third, I am *not* a child, and I would appreciate not being treated like one."

"Sorry," Daniela mumbled, suitably chastened. She

threw a surreptitious glance around the scenic courtyard bustling with students, then lowered her voice. "I'm not trying to tell you what to do, Mom. I'm just a little worried about you, that's all. What if you get sick again?"

"Then Phyllis will take care of me," Pamela said blithely. "Considering she used to look after me when we were growing up, I think she's got a bit more experience than you do."

"Be that as it may," said Daniela, striving for patience, "I still don't understand the sudden urgency to visit your sister. You didn't say a thing about this last night over dinner." She paused, her frown deepening. "Is Aunt Phyllis sick?"

"No, darling, she's not sick. But when you get to be our age, you don't take anything for granted, least of all time. I haven't seen your aunt since last Christmas. I miss her, and I'd like to see her again. Is something wrong with that?"

"Of course not. But if you'll just wait until tomorrow, I can drive you myself."

"It's not necessary. Besides, you need to use your weekends to study and get your coursework done. Deacon Hubbard has offered to let me catch a ride with him to Houston, since he has to be there for a conference. He'll bring me back with him next Saturday."

A slow, knowing grin spread across Daniela's face. "Deacon Hubbard, huh?"

"Don't you go taking that sly tone with me, young lady. I'm not one of your little chit-chat girlfriends. Deacon Hubbard is taking me to Houston, and that's all I'm going to say about the matter. We're leaving in an hour, so I won't be here when you get back from class.

I wanted to call and let you know." Her tone softened. "Take care of yourself, you hear? You didn't seem like yourself last night. I know you've got a lot on your mind with law school, but everything's going to work out just fine, you'll see."

Daniela smiled into the phone. "Call me when you arrive in Houston, and give Aunt Phyllis my love."

She flipped her cell phone shut and tucked it inside her backpack, then rose from the stone bench and headed toward the library to meet her study group.

Before making her way to the rooftop terrace where they awaited her, she stopped first in one of the reading rooms to search for a book she needed for her torts class. She wandered down rows of mahogany-paneled bookcases filled with leather-bound tomes before finally locating the right aisle.

Unfortunately, it was already occupied. By none other than Caleb Thorne.

She felt a fresh spurt of anger, though she'd just spent the past hour in his class trying her best to pretend what he did in his private life mattered not one iota to her.

Squaring her shoulders determinedly, she started down the aisle, scanning thick leather spines as she went, praying she would find what she needed before she reached him.

No such luck.

"Professor Thorne," she greeted him, as if she'd just noticed him standing there.

He barely glanced up from the book he'd been thumbing through. "Miss Moreau," he murmured.

Was it just her imagination, or was there an edge to his deep voice?

"Excuse me," she said, hitching her chin toward a segment of books at his midsection.

He stepped aside, but not by much.

Biting back a sigh of irritation, Daniela moved in beside him and knelt in front of the bookcase. She ran her fingers over the spines until she found the volume she was looking for, pulling it off the shelf and cracking it open.

"Is everything all right?" Caleb asked without looking up from his book. "You left rather abruptly after class."

She felt a surge of feminine satisfaction to know he'd been watching her. "Everything's fine," she told him. "I had to take a personal call."

Let him think it had been her boyfriend, she mused. Let him care.

His next query, nonchalantly posed, brought a tiny, triumphant smile to her lips. "Nothing dire, I hope?"

"Mmm, I guess that depends on your perspective," she all but purred, and let her gaze deliberately wander up the muscular length of his denim-clad legs, past the impressive broadness of his chest, over the strong column of his throat and the hard line of his jaw, to his unsmiling, sensuous mouth.

She allowed her gaze to linger there for a moment before lifting her eyes to meet his, shivering at the piercing intensity in those dark, magnificent pools. "You know how it is," she murmured silkily.

His jaw tightened. "You might want to make your boyfriend aware of the hours you're in class," he said in a voice edged in steel.

Daniela swallowed another smile. "Yes, sir," she promised sweetly. She thumbed through the contents of her book a minute longer, then decided she'd better go find her study mates before they came looking for her.

As she began to straighten from her crouching position, Caleb moved at the same time, reaching around her to return his book to the shelf. The sudden shift was uncalculated.

And potent.

Without warning Daniela found her back flush against the solid warmth of his body.

She looked over her shoulder at him, and their eyes met. She felt his body tense, felt the tremor of response in her own. Her pulse quickened, her breasts tingled.

As she slowly rose to her full height, the resulting friction between their bodies was so charged, so *intense,* that she nearly moaned aloud.

Caleb stepped back from her, his handsome face an impenetrable mask.

Suddenly the aisle seemed too narrow, the space too confining. They held each other in a locked gaze for a long, tense moment. Then, without a word, Daniela turned on legs that shook and beat a hasty retreat.

Caleb stood watching as Daniela walked away from him as quickly as if the devil were on her heels. And maybe he was. God knows there was nothing saintly about the thoughts racing through Caleb's mind, or the raw hunger rampaging through his body. How could something as simple and fleeting as the accidental brush of their bodies wreak such havoc on his senses? When he'd unexpectedly found himself pressed against Daniela's lush body, the temptation, the want, stunned him. Her eyes, at once starkly innocent and boldly alluring, had bewitched him. He couldn't breathe, couldn't think, couldn't move. Staring at her slightly parted lips, he'd been struck with a fierce urge to kiss her, to plunge his tongue into the sweet depths of her mouth, to devour her. As she'd slowly risen to her feet, the unhurried pace of the movement had intensified his awareness of the soft, dangerous curves of her body. He'd wanted nothing more than to grab her by the waist and crush himself against the ripe swell of her buttocks.

Shaken, Caleb took a deep breath that burned in his lungs. As he blinked, his surroundings slowly came back into focus. He was in the library, for God's sake. He'd been on the verge of seducing one of his students in the *library,* where at any moment another student, or one of his colleagues, could have stumbled upon them.

Caleb swore under his breath, filled with shame and self-loathing.

Somehow, some way, he had to resist this forbidden craving he had for Daniela Moreau, before his slick grasp on control slipped away completely.

If it wasn't already too late.

Daniela slid a tube of deep-red lipstick over her lips and finger-combed her glossy black curls before turning away from the mirror. As she bent to retrieve a pair of strappy high-heeled sandals from the floor, she felt the onset of a migraine behind her eyelids. For just a moment she wished she could crawl into bed and sleep it off, both the headache and the growing fatigue that had dogged her all afternoon. But she'd promised April that she would attend tonight's art exhibit at the Blue Star, where some of April's photography would be on display for the first time ever. As the girl had spoken of little else during their study session that morning, Daniela would have felt like an ogre if she didn't make an appearance.

Besides, she needed a diversion, something to get her mind off the library encounter with Caleb Thorne. It was all she'd thought about for the rest of the day, torturing herself with mental images of being pinned to the bookcase while he kissed her hungrily, his strong, capable hands roaming across her body until she arched against him in mindless surrender.

No wonder she felt so hot and bothered.

Daniela slipped on her sandals, swallowed two aspirin, then grabbed her black clutch purse and left the house. It was a mild summer evening, perfect for the five-minute stroll to her destination.

The Blue Star Arts Complex was nestled on the outskirts of the historic King William District, and boasted an eclectic cluster of old warehouse buildings that were divided into galleries, artists' performance spaces, design offices and studio apartments. The Blue Star's most popular event was First Friday, a community-wide art walk held the first Friday of every month that drew crowds from all over San Antonio for art openings, theater productions, shopping and dining. Rain or shine the event was held, which meant that every so often the turnout was low, as people opted for some other form of nighttime entertainment, knowing that First Friday would be there next month, like an ever-faithful lover.

Such was the case this evening, Daniela noted as she drew near to the brightly lit complex. The parking lot was only half-full, though it was well past seven o'clock. On a busy night, the valets were usually turning motorists away by six. Lively jazz music beckoned to visitors from the Blue Star Brewing Company, a charming pub located in what was once an old beer storage warehouse.

Passing the brewery, Daniela climbed a steep set of metal stairs to reach the gallery dedicated to showcasing the works of new and emerging artists. Because she was a regular at First Friday, she did not flinch at the stifling heat that greeted her upon entering the building.

At the end of the long corridor and wearing a chic black pantsuit, April stood at the entrance to one of the small exhibit rooms, talking animatedly to a middle-aged white couple dressed for a night on the town. Her grin widened at the sight of Daniela.

Giving the girl a wink, Daniela stepped into the narrow confines of the room and wandered from one mounted photograph to the next while she waited for April to finish with her customers. She was pleasantly surprised by what she saw on display, rich candids that captured the essence of San Antonio. A wide shot of a tourist-packed river barge drifting lazily down the sun-dappled Riverwalk; a close-up revealing the crumbling, faded glory of the Alamo; a festively attired mariachi band; a vibrant blanketing of wildflowers along a Texas highway; the historic Majestic Theatre framed against a glittering night skyline.

She turned as April approached, her dark eyes shimmering with excitement. "I made my first sale!" she squealed, throwing her arms around Daniela's neck.

Daniela laughed, hugging her back. "Oh, April, that's wonderful!"

The girl drew away on a breathless giggle. "I was so worried that I wouldn't sell anything," she confessed.

"I don't know why. You're very talented. These photos are amazing, every last one of them."

April beamed. "Do you really think so?"

"I know so. You have a real eye, April."

"Thanks, Daniela." The girl's proud gaze swept across the photos displayed around the room. "I see life in frames, captured in the blink of an eye for all eternity."

Daniela grinned. "Hey, that's pretty deep, Kwan. Are you sure you want to become a lawyer?"

April's expression clouded. "I don't really have much of a choice," she said somewhat wistfully. "Everyone in my family expects me to become an attorney. The day I graduate from law school will probably be the first time I ever see my father cry. But don't worry," she added quickly at the concerned look on Daniela's face, "I've got a plan. I'll use my salary as a lawyer to support my photography habit until someday my work is on exhibit at the Guggenheim, and then I can quit the day job and travel around the world."

Daniela chuckled. "Sounds like a plan, kiddo. In the meantime, allow me to do *my* part to hasten those plans along. I want to buy the Majestic, and the photo with the hauntingly beautiful Native American mother and child."

Blinking back tears, April wrapped her in another tight hug. "Thank you so much, Daniela," she whispered fervently.

While April rang up her purchases, Daniela wandered around the corner to check out the works of other exhibiting artists. When she returned, she discovered that April had lured two new potential customers.

Daniela's heart sank when she recognized the couple: Caleb Thorne and Shara Adler.

Shara was elegantly coiffed and resplendent in a silk sheath dress that accentuated the sleek curves of her body, but it was Caleb who drew Daniela's eye. He was dark and devastatingly handsome in a black polo shirt that molded the powerful contours of his broad chest, and expensively tailored charcoal trousers that hung low on his trim waist and rode his long legs in a way that would make Giorgio Armani weep with pride. He exuded such raw magnetism and sex appeal that it was all Daniela could do to keep from rushing over and pouncing on him.

April saw her and waved her over excitedly. "Daniela, look who's here! Not one, but *two* of our law school professors!"

Daniela wanted to disappear through the floor as both Caleb and Shara turned to watch her slow approach. While Shara's eyes narrowed in displeasure, Caleb's impassive expression betrayed no emotion.

Daniela forced herself to smile civilly at each of them. "Good evening."

Caleb inclined his head. "Miss Moreau."

Shara linked her arm through his, staking her claim. Her cool, measuring gaze ran the length of Daniela, taking in the simple black cocktail dress that flared slightly above her knees and the black sandals with four-inch stiletto heels. "You look nice, Miss Moreau," she said, a malicious gleam in her amber eyes. "Hot date tonight?"

"Afraid not," Daniela murmured. "You?"

Shara's laugh had all the warmth of a polar ice cap. She cast a demure look at Caleb beneath her lashes. "We shall see."

Cheerfully oblivious to any undercurrents between the threesome, April said to Daniela, "I was just thanking Professor Thorne for coming out tonight. After class today I was telling him about my photography exhibit. I had no idea he would actually show up."

Humor threaded Caleb's deep voice as he said, "I think you mentioned the time and location at least three times during our conversation."

April grinned unabashedly. "Never underestimate the power of subliminal messaging."

Caleb chuckled, drawing away from Shara and stepping inside the room. "Why don't you come talk to me about your work? Sell me something."

"With pleasure," April said, eagerly leading him to the first wall.

Daniela started to follow, when Shara's low, mocking voice stopped her. "You really *do* look nice tonight, Miss Moreau. I like that dress—Chanel, isn't it?" At Daniela's brief nod, her lips curled derisively. "A bit of a change from your usual jeans-and-miniskirt look, isn't it?"

Daniela feigned a wounded look. "You don't approve of the way I dress, Professor Adler?"

Shara pointedly ignored the sarcasm. "When I attended law school," she said haughtily, "we were more mindful of the way we dressed for class. But then, most of us weren't there to seduce our instructors in order to earn an easy *A*."

Daniela's face flushed. Before she could muster a comeback, Shara gave the dagger in her chest another vicious twist. "As I was saying, dear, it's a shame you don't have any special plans this evening. Caleb is taking me to dinner, and then to the symphony for a late performance. After that," she said coyly, "who knows where we'll end up?"

Daniela had a pretty good idea just where *she* wanted Shara to end up. Gritting her teeth, she pasted on a saccharine smile. "Thanks for sharing your evening plans with me, Professor Adler. As much as I'd love to hear more, I really think we should save it for our next bonding session, say, when hell freezes over."

With a curt nod, she sidestepped the scowling woman and walked over to where April stood, explaining to Caleb the creative inspiration for her photography. "Sorry to interrupt," Daniela said, directing her apology to April. "I'm going to head down to the main gallery to check out some of the other exhibits. I'll be back in a little while."

"Okay. Oh, hey, guess what, Daniela? Professor Thorne really liked the same two photos you bought. You both have the same taste. Isn't that funny?"

"Hilarious," Daniela murmured, meeting Caleb's dark gaze for the first time that evening. At the memory of their earlier encounter, forbidden heat curled through her blood. As if he, too, remembered, his ebony lashes flickered, his eyes touching her mouth like a whispered caress. It was so subtle she could have imagined it.

"In fact," April continued merrily, "he wants to buy the Majestic from you. He lives in those cool high-rise apartments that are built above the Majestic Theatre, and he was telling me how his parents used to take him to shows at the theater back in its heyday."

"Is that right?" Daniela drawled.

Caleb nodded, a trace of wry humor in his expression as he gazed down at her. "How much?"

"That depends," Daniela said. "How much is it worth to you?"

"How much is it worth to *you?*" he countered in a low, enigmatic voice that made Daniela wonder if they were still talking about the photograph.

She swallowed, her heart thumping hard. "It's not for sale. But I'm sure if you go easy on April in class, she'd be more than happy to take another photo of the Majestic for you."

April laughed, dividing a wary look between the two. "Hey, don't put me in the middle of this. I will *not* be an accessory to bribing a professor."

Daniela shrugged, backing out of the room. "Suit yourselves. See you in a little bit, April."

Once outside, she took a moment to draw deep, cleansing breaths of the cool night air. When she felt steadier, she began making her way toward the main gallery in a connecting building. It wasn't so much that she was dying to check out the other exhibits, though the works of some of San Antonio's finest would be on display. She'd simply needed to get away—quickly.

Seeing Caleb again had rattled her cage. Seeing him on a date with Shara Adler made her want to draw blood. An image of the couple gazing at each other across a romantic candlelit table, or holding hands at the symphony, brought a sick feeling to Daniela's stomach. Knowing she had no right to be jealous didn't stop her from being jealous anyway.

She reached the main gallery and smiled absently at the attractive, well-dressed man who held the door open for her on his way out. As she stepped into the high-ceilinged room with its pristine white walls, gleaming hardwood floors and recessed lighting, she sent up a silent prayer of thanks that this building, at least, was air-conditioned. Not that heat generated by a large crowd would be a problem tonight. Less than a dozen art-goers milled about, and half were people she'd seen in the other gallery.

The works on display featured an eclectic blend of traditional, contemporary and experimental art. As

Daniela wandered from one exhibit to the next, she was not surprised when the courteous stranger, who'd apparently changed his mind about leaving, doubled back and began following her around the room. He maintained a discreet distance at first, casting surreptitious glances at her when he thought she wasn't looking. When Daniela paused long enough to admire a sepia-toned photograph of a seventeenth-century Mexican cathedral, he made his move.

"Powerful, isn't it?" he remarked, materializing beside her as if by pure accident. The heavy spice of an expensive cologne tickled her nostrils. "Makes you feel reverent in the face of all that holy splendor."

Holy splendor?

Daniela murmured noncommittally and moved on to the next display. She hid a knowing smile as the stranger pretended to linger over the photo, studying it with his head tipped thoughtfully to one side, before following her.

"I don't think I've ever seen you here before," he said. "Is this your first time at First Friday?"

"I've been here a few times," she answered vaguely. In truth, she'd been coming to the event since she was a teenager, accompanied by her mother and brothers. Pamela Roarke had been a staunch advocate of exposing her children to the arts, arranging her schedule at the hospital so that she was off the first Friday of every month. Although Kenneth and Noah had to be dragged to the event and spent the entire time alternately yawning and complaining of boredom, Daniela had always looked forward to each excursion. Some of her favorite memories included trips to the Blue Star, and feasting on hot Frito Pies from Sonic afterward.

"I think it's a wonderful way to showcase the talents of our local artists," the stranger was saying. "A lot of people don't realize just how much San Antonio has to offer. We're so much more than the Riverwalk and a championship basketball team."

"Well said," drawled an amused voice behind them.

Daniela and her companion turned in unison to find Caleb standing there, hands thrust deep in his pockets, a lazy smile on his handsome face. Automatically Daniela's pulse spiked.

The stranger looked startled, his pale green eyes widening in surprise. "Th-Thorne," he stammered. "What're you doing here?"

"Same thing everyone else is doing," Caleb murmured, gazing at Daniela until she glanced away. "Admiring art."

"Of course that's what you're doing here. I didn't mean—"

Caleb chuckled dryly. "I know what you meant, Stuart. I see you've met Miss Moreau."

"Not quite," Stuart said. "We hadn't gotten around to introductions yet."

"Allow me," Caleb offered smoothly. "Stuart Epps, I'd like you to meet Daniela Moreau, a student of mine at the university."

Daniela wondered if she'd only imagined the possessive note in his voice when he introduced her as "a student of *mine*."

"A pleasure to meet you, Daniela," Stuart said, reaching forward to grasp her hand eagerly. "Daniela. What an absolutely beautiful name."

"Thank you," Daniela said, giving her hand a discreet tug when he held on a little longer than etiquette necessitated. She forced a pleasant smile. "And how are you and Professor Thorne acquainted?"

"Caleb and I went to UT together," Stuart explained. "We had a bit of a friendly rivalry going back then—with academics, sports. Girls," he added with a wink at Caleb.

"Ahh, yes," Caleb murmured, nodding. "Stu married the girl we all wanted, the lovely president of the Alpha Kappa Alpha sorority. Where *is* Nicole tonight, by the way?"

Stuart's copper-toned face reddened. "Uh, she had to work late. We're, uh, supposed to be meeting for dinner at—" He glanced at his Rolex and started in surprise. "Damn. I didn't realize how late it was."

"Better not keep Nicole waiting," Caleb warned softly. "She always did have quite the temper."

With an embarrassed look at Daniela, who was biting the inside of her cheeks to keep from laughing, Stuart Epps turned and beat a hasty retreat.

"Poor Stuart," Caleb lamented with a mournful shake of his head.

Daniela covered her mouth with her hand to muffle a peal of laughter, but it spilled forth anyway.

Caleb chuckled, watching her. "Aren't you going to thank me?"

"For what?" she gasped between giggles.

"For rescuing you from the clutches of a notorious womanizer."

At that she sobered, the laughter dying on her lips like a flame that had been suddenly doused. Her chin went up. "Well, *you* would know."

Caleb frowned. "What's that supposed to mean?"

"You're the brilliant professor," she said, moving on to the next display. "I'll let you figure it out."

Caleb followed her. "Is there something you're trying to tell me, Miss Moreau?"

"Where's Shara?" she answered with a question of her own.

He hesitated. "On her way home. Her son called to say he wasn't feeling well. Seems there's a flu bug going around."

"That's too bad," Daniela murmured. "You two had *such* a romantic evening ahead of you."

Dark eyes narrowed on her face. "I fail to see," he said, drawing each word out carefully, "how that could possibly be any concern of yours."

Her cheeks heated. "It's not."

Caleb arched a brow. "If I didn't know better, Miss Moreau, I would think you were jealous."

Her temper flared. Before she could respond, he turned and sauntered over to an exhibit on the facing wall. This time *she* followed him.

"I'm not jealous of you and Shara," she snapped, reaching his side. "If you think I am, think again."

Caleb said nothing, his arms folded across his wide chest as he studied the black-and-white photograph mounted before him. It was an edgy, experimental piece, a portrait of a nude man and woman locked in a passionate embrace against the backdrop of French doors. The photo had been skillfully retouched, the background softly blurred to bring the couple into sharper focus, creating an image that was at once artistic, and shockingly erotic. Beneath the photo, the caption read Voyeur.

How apropos, thought Daniela, feeling as if she were intruding upon an intimate moment between two strangers. As a slow flush crept over her body, she wondered whether it was a reaction to the provocative portrait, or to the silent, brooding man beside her. Even in her anger she was acutely aware of him. His utter maleness beckoned to her, wreaking sheer havoc on her senses.

She stole a look at him beneath her lashes, covertly admiring his profile—straight nose, strong jaw, the curve of those masculine, sensual lips. Obsidian eyes rimmed with a thick fringe of black lashes, matched to the slash of his brows. He was beautiful, wickedly so.

And she wanted him. Wanted him like no other man she'd ever wanted before.

"This thing between us," he said suddenly, his voice low and controlled. "It can't happen."

Fresh anger swept through her, though she didn't know whom she was angrier with—herself or Caleb. Spurred by a recklessness she didn't question, she stepped directly in front of him, forcing herself into his line of vision. She might as well have thrown herself before a ravenous wolf.

"Is that what you came all the way down here to tell me?" she challenged hotly.

His dark eyes flashed a warning. "Don't do this."

"Don't do what, Professor Thorne?" she taunted, knowing she was playing with fire, too far-gone to care. "Don't cause a scene? Or don't call you a liar?"

Before she could react, Caleb grabbed her by the wrist and strode purposefully from the room.

Chapter 10

Caleb felt dangerously out of control as he hauled Daniela into a tiny room located off the main gallery. Once, on a previous visit to the Blue Star, he'd made a wrong turn on his way to the men's room and had stumbled upon the closet, which was used to store old props and photography equipment.

Daniela stared up at him as if he'd lost his mind as he kicked the door shut behind him and advanced on her. She took three steps backward and he matched her step for step, until only a hairsbreadth separated them.

Nervously she passed her tongue over her lush bottom lip. "What are you—"

He never let her finish. Before he could help himself, or stop to consider the consequences of his actions, he cupped her face in his hands and slanted his mouth possessively over hers. The moment their lips touched, he was lost. All thought and reason fled, leaving only need, an all-consuming need that pounded through his body and made him greedy for more.

At the first intrusion of his tongue, Daniela gasped a little, and he took full advantage, thrusting deeply into the honeyed warmth of her mouth. She tasted sweet, even sweeter than he'd imagined. She was heaven on earth, and the exotic scent of her was as sexy and alluring as the fevered mating of their tongues. When her hands slid up his chest and wreathed around his neck, he groaned low in his throat and pressed closer, deepening the kiss.

He kissed her because he wanted—no, *needed*—to feel the softness of her lips, because he had been driving himself crazy thinking about her since the day they met. He kissed her because he hadn't been able to take his eyes off her tonight, exquisitely breathtaking in the low-cut black dress that clung to her lush curves and fueled his imagination with thoughts of sliding it off her milky-brown body, one strap at a time, and watching it fall in a heap at her glorious feet. He wanted her a hundred different ways, under him, over him, any part of him inside any part of her.

His hands roamed down her back, spanning her tiny waist before, at long last, cupping the exquisite swell of her bottom. Her soft moan of pleasure joined his own, making his loins tighten in a rush. He braced his legs apart and crushed her body to his, fire shooting through him as his thighs brushed the outside of hers and his erection nudged her belly. He wanted her so bad, he ached. It was crazy to want like this.

"Caleb..." The sound of his name on her lips gradually penetrated the thick fog of desire clouding his brain. Sanity returned in slow degrees, along with a healthy dose of self-disgust over the way he'd lost control with her.

Daniela's long raven lashes flickered open as he stepped away. Like a woman in a daze, she lifted a hand and touched her fingertips to her swollen lips.

Caleb watched her, his eyes hooded. "I didn't mean to kiss you," he said huskily. "But if you stand there a minute longer, I won't be responsible for what happens next."

Wide, dark eyes lifted to meet his gaze. She opened her mouth to speak, but the look on his face undoubtedly made her reconsider.

Without a word, she turned and left the room, walking out on him for the second time that day.

And not a minute too soon.

Daniela did not remember returning to the first gallery, collecting her purchases from April and saying good-night, then walking the short distance home.

Inside the moonlit darkness of her bedroom, she unzipped her dress and let it slide slowly from her body, imagining the silk was Caleb's big, warm hands. She stripped off her black lace underwear and stepped out of her high-heeled sandals, then slid, naked, beneath the bedcovers.

The memory of Caleb's mouth on hers, hot and demanding, made her belly quiver in wanton response. She'd known the man would be an incredible kisser, but never in her wildest dreams could she have imagined how far reality would surpass the fantasy.

She felt a thrill of wicked pleasure, remembering the way he'd lost control and dragged her out of the main gallery. If any other man had pulled a stunt like that, Daniela would have been livid, and she certainly wouldn't have gone without a fight. Resisting Caleb had never crossed her mind. Instead she'd felt a heady mixture of alarm and excitement, fear and arousal.

She'd pushed him to the edge, and he'd snapped.

And, oh, how he'd snapped, she mused with a naughty smile.

She thought of the blazing intensity in his coal-black eyes as he'd backed her into the room, one deliberate step at a time. A delicious shiver ran through her.

She wanted him.

And one way or another, she was going to have him.

But when she awakened at the crack of dawn burning up with fever, she knew it had nothing to do with her exploits of the night before.

She had the flu, which would explain the headache and fatigue that had plagued her the day before. She'd caught the virus from her mother.

Great. Just great. Of all the years to skip my flu shot.

She stumbled out of bed, struggled into a thick chenille robe from her walk-in closet and staggered down the hall to the bathroom. Assiduously avoiding her haggard reflection, she opened the medicine cabinet and rummaged around for the flu medication she'd forced upon her mother less than a week ago. To her dismay, the bottle was nearly empty. She unscrewed the cap anyway and chugged down the remaining drops of cherry-flavored liquid, then tossed away the container with a disgusted grunt.

She couldn't afford to be sick. She had way too much to do, such as work on her case brief, outline her class notes, wash two loads of laundry. Oh, and devise the perfect scheme for seducing Caleb Thorne. She couldn't seduce anyone looking as if she belonged in a commercial for a cold/flu medication.

Since it was Saturday, her doctor's office was closed, which meant she wouldn't be able to get a prescription for Tamiflu until Monday. In the meantime, she'd have to run to the store and buy more flu medicine. But as she leaned over the bathtub to turn on the shower faucet, her head spun dizzily. With a groan, Daniela sank weakly onto the edge of the clawfoot porcelain tub and dropped her aching head into her hands. She was in no condition to walk or drive anywhere.

When the dizziness had passed, she got up and shuffled back to her bedroom, where she crawled under the covers and fell asleep once again.

Three hours later she awakened feeling worse than before. Having no other choice, she reached for the phone on her nightstand.

"Janie?" she croaked out when her sister-in-law answered on the second ring. "Sorry to bother you, but I need a huge favor."

Janie Roarke arrived an hour later bearing an armload of groceries and a steaming pot of tortilla soup. She whisked into the house using her spare key and headed straight for the kitchen, tsk-tsking at the piteous sight of Daniela curled up on the living room sofa dressed in her bathrobe, her hair in wild disarray.

"I'm going to have to start charging your family a co-pay," Janie teased.

Daniela made a face, getting slowly to her feet and trailing her sister-in-law into the kitchen. She slumped into a chair at the breakfast table while Janie set down the grocery bag, then fished out a bottle of flu medicine and passed it to Daniela.

When Daniela had swallowed four teaspoonfuls of cherry-flavored syrup, she shook her head at the pot of tortilla soup now warming on the stove. "What, you always have a fresh batch on hand to feed the sick?"

Janie grinned, walking back to the table. "But of course." She laid the back of her hand against Daniela's forehead. "Yep, you've definitely got it," she announced with a grimace. "You're burning up."

Daniela scowled. "Why haven't *you* caught it?" she demanded, half-accusingly. "You spent just as much time with my mom as I did when she had the flu."

"I don't get sick," Janie stated matter-of-factly, pouring orange juice into a tall frosted glass and handing it to Daniela. "I have 'Mommy Immunity.' Looking after the twins through all their childhood illnesses helped build my resistance to viruses."

Daniela took a small sip of juice, wincing as it hit the back of her sore throat. She set the glass aside. "Speaking of KJ and Lourdes, where are they?"

"With my parents. I dropped them off on my way over here. Mom and Dad are taking the twins to Dave & Buster's this afternoon, so they were both pretty excited about that. But you'll be happy to know that your niece and nephew stopped celebrating long enough to send you their love and wish you a speedy recovery—and Mom provided the tortilla soup, much as I'd like to take credit for it."

Daniela smiled wanly. "Your mother is too good to me."

"No kidding. She adores you. Every time I see her,

she asks me what's wrong with the men of our generation, allowing a smart, beautiful girl like you to remain single. And then she just looks at me, an indignant expression on her face, as if she fully expects me to answer on behalf of all men between the ages of twenty-one and forty."

Daniela wrinkled her nose. "No twenty-one-year-olds," she grumbled. "I have a hard enough time dealing with men my own age."

Janie laughed, stirring the soup on the front burner. The fragrant aroma of chicken, onion and avocado filled the room, a scent Daniela would have welcomed any other day. Today it only made her nauseous.

Janie turned, and, seeing Daniela's sickly expression, frowned sympathetically. "Go lie down on the sofa. I'll bring you a cup of chamomile tea."

Daniela obeyed, and a few minutes later Janie carried a silver serving tray into the living room and set it down on the cedar coffee table. Daniela emerged from beneath a thick comforter to accept a steaming cup of tea.

"I'm really sorry for taking up your Saturday like this," she murmured, taking a grateful sip of the hot, soothing brew.

"Girl, please," said Janie, waving a dismissive hand. "Even if you hadn't called, I still would have dropped the twins over at my parents' house. And then I would have gone back home and cleaned the house, washed and folded laundry, sorted clothes to be donated to the Salvation Army, putted around in the garden and *maybe* grabbed a power nap before picking up the twins this evening." Her smile was overly bright. "As you can see, it's not like you interrupted any exciting plans."

"Where's Kenny?" Daniela asked quietly.

"Where else? At the office, catching up on paperwork. He left first thing this morning and said he probably wouldn't be back until dinnertime."

Daniela fell silent, hearing the pain in the other woman's voice, a pain she'd tried to conceal from the rest of the family for years. But everyone knew that Janie and Kenneth Roarke were unhappy, that their marriage was in trouble and had been for a very long time. Gone was the carefree couple who'd fallen madly in love when their eyes met across a crowded dance floor one night, the couple who'd once shared such chemistry that anyone within a fifty-foot radius felt singed by it. That couple had been replaced by two polite strangers who shared a big, beautiful house and parenting duties, and not much more.

No one could pinpoint when the change in their relationship had occurred, though Daniela had her own suspicions.

"Daniela, I need a favor from you."

The quiet request interrupted Daniela's grim musings. Her eyes snapped to Janie's face. "Anything," she said quickly. "Just name it."

Janie stirred sugar into her tea, then lifted the cup and took a sip. She swallowed carefully, then pinned Daniela with a resolute look. "I want you to help me get a job at the detective agency."

Daniela's brows furrowed together. "At Roarke Investigations?" At Janie's nod, her confusion grew. "Sure, but...what kind of job?"

"Noah tells me you're going to have another vacancy in the secretary position."

Daniela nodded, grimacing. "We've had rotten luck

so far. The first one we hired called in sick every week, the second one couldn't type a lick, and now..." She trailed off suddenly, gaping at Janie. "Wait a minute! Are you saying *you* want to be our new secretary?"

"That's exactly what I'm saying."

Daniela blinked, nonplussed. "I'm sorry," she mumbled, lifting a hand to her forehead. "I think this fever is starting to make me delirious. I'm hearing the *strangest* things."

Janie chuckled. "You're not delirious, El, and you heard me right. I want to be hired as your secretary."

"Why?"

"Why not? This *is* a family business, isn't it? Besides, you said it yourself. You've had a string of bad luck with the people you've hired thus far. What've you got to lose by taking a chance on me?"

Daniela rolled her eyes heavenward. "I'm not worried about your *competence,* Janie. You have an MBA from the Wharton School of Business, for goodness' sake."

"And while I earned my stripes," Janie interjected, "I made coffee, answered phones, typed memos, created spreadsheets, filed papers and did anything else the senior managers demanded. And let me tell you, they were *very* demanding."

"They've got nothing on Kenny," Daniela drawled. "Speaking of your husband, do you really think he's going to agree to having you as our secretary? He's the one who insisted that you stay home with the twins in the first place. How's he going to feel about you returning to the workforce—as our secretary, at that?"

Janie made a face. "Now that the twins are in school and involved in so many extracurricular activities, we both know that they don't need me around nearly as much as they used to. Besides, I could arrange my schedule so that I come into the office early, then leave early enough to pick them up from school. We can make it work."

Daniela chuckled dryly. "*I'm* not the one you need to convince. Your husband is, and something tells me he'll never go for it."

Janie sat forward in the armchair. "He will if you ask him."

"What do I have to do with this?"

"You're the only one he'll listen to."

"What!" Daniela exclaimed. "Okay, this time I'm *definitely* hearing things. Since when does Kenneth Roarke listen to anyone but himself?"

Janie smiled cryptically. "I know you may find it hard to believe, El, but Kenny *does* value your opinion. Whenever something happens in the family, he's always worried about what you'll say, or think or do. Oh, he tries to pretend otherwise, put up a macho front, but I know better. He cares what you think of him."

Daniela scowled. "If he spent less time worrying about my opinion and more time concentrating on your feelings, maybe he wouldn't—" Seeing Janie flinch, she snapped her mouth shut, but it was too late. Shame engulfed her at once.

Wishing she could take back the harsh words, she said, "I'm sorry, Janie—"

Janie held up a hand, looking grim. "It's all right. I know there's no love lost between you and your brother, and I know you blame him for the problems in our marriage. But just remember, Daniela, that there are two sides to every story, and you shouldn't allow your personal issues with Kenny to cloud your objectivity where he and I are concerned. You're bigger than that."

"I know," Daniela murmured, suitably chastened.

"Want to talk about it?" Janie gently prodded.

An awkward silence ensued, the silence of two people who wanted to move forward but were afraid to take the next step. This was uncharted territory for them. In all the years they'd been friends, they had never discussed Janie's marriage, or Daniela's strained relationship with her brother.

At length, Daniela drew a deep breath and prayed she was doing the right thing by speaking her mind. "As you well know, Kenny can be an incredibly selfish person. For as long as I can remember, he's always put his own needs above everyone else's. Whenever we needed him, he was nowhere to be found. He caused my mother a great deal of stress and heartache, and I grew up resenting him for that." She stared into the golden contents of her teacup. "I guess I've never really forgiven him. Sadly enough, whenever he acts like a bonehead, it reinforces my opinion of him and justifies the way I feel. I'm not saying that's right or wrong. It's just the way it is."

Janie gazed at her with an expression of gentle understanding. "I think you and your brother have a lot to talk about and work through. Knowing him the way I do, I can tell you that he probably doesn't have a clue where to begin to make things right between you two. I think he feels a lot of guilt over the way he let you guys down in the past, but instead of facing that guilt, he pretends it doesn't exist."

Daniela nodded slowly. "That's probably true." She gave Janie a long, measured look. "So you hope that by working in the same office, you and Kenny will see more of each other, giving you a greater opportunity to work through some of your own issues."

Janie nodded, her eyes dark and earnest. "I love your brother, and I know he loves me. We both have our shortcomings, and God knows we've each played a hand in the situation we now find ourselves in. But I'm willing to do whatever it takes to make sure we don't lose each other, once and for all. If working as a secretary at the agency helps me save my marriage, then so be it. Will you help me, Daniela?"

Daniela felt a constriction in her throat that had nothing to do with her sickness. "Of course I'll help you," she said, gruff and tender.

"Thanks, El," Janie murmured gratefully.

"Don't thank me. I only agreed because I was afraid you'd turn into Nurse Ratched if I didn't."

The two women laughed, until a violent coughing spasm overtook Daniela. With a tortured groan, she set aside her unfinished tea, then dragged her aching body from the sofa and down the hall to her bedroom.

She climbed into bed, and as she willed herself to sleep, it was an image of Caleb Thorne that permeated her thoughts. The memory of his kiss—the hot brand of his mouth upon hers, the searing possession of his embrace—made her temperature spike several degrees, which was the *last* thing she needed in her current condition.

She had to get better quickly. It was now a matter of personal safety, because if she didn't have Caleb soon, she was going to burst into flames.

Chapter 11

Rita Owens had spent the better part of thirty years working for Crandall Thorne. In that time, she'd helped organize birthday and anniversary parties, had chauffeured carloads of youngsters to and from various school functions and had played gracious hostess to visiting dignitaries, politicians and mobsters alike. She'd shamelessly eavesdropped on closed-door conversations, and had refereed more than a few nasty brawls. Twenty-one years ago, she'd witnessed the untimely death of Crandall's wife, a sweet, tortured soul Rita had grown to love more than her own flesh and blood. The sorrow of that unspeakable tragedy had been eclipsed only by the joy of watching Caleb, who'd been a shy five-year-old when Rita first joined the household, come into his manhood. A finer, more upstanding son you couldn't find, and Rita took a certain amount of pride in knowing she'd had a hand in that. She'd never married, and the two children she'd birthed had never amounted to much, drinking and cavorting with the wrong crowd until their wild ways landed them in prison up north. As far as Rita was concerned, the only son she'd ever known was Caleb, and that was just fine with her.

Now, gazing out across the rolling expanse of green land that Saturday afternoon, a deep frown marred the smooth line of her brow. "Have you ever seen anything like it?" she murmured, half to herself.

Standing beside her in the large, sunlit kitchen, Ruth Gaylord shook her head. "Never."

Mounted on a big sorrel horse, Caleb herded cattle through the pasture gate. The brim of his black Stetson shaded his eyes, but his mouth was set in a grim line as he attended to his task. His bare, muscled chest was covered in sweat and grime to the low waist of his filthy jeans. The jeans, along with his mud-caked boots, would never cross the threshold of the main house, if Rita had anything to say about it—which she always did.

The day was winding down, the sun sliding toward the far side of the mountain range and casting the ranch yard into long shadows and tall silhouettes. Most of the ranch hands had called it quits for the day, dispersing to their rustic lodgings for dinner and much-deserved rest.

Only Caleb and the Native American foreman, Wyome, remained behind, corralling the few wayward steers and heifers into the holding pen. In the pasture beyond, the cattle that had been herded in during the course of the long day grazed quietly.

"What are you two gawking at?" Crandall Thorne demanded upon entering the room and seeing the two women huddled together at the bay window.

"Come see for yourself," Rita answered, with barely a glance over her shoulder.

Frowning, Crandall walked over and deliberately wedged himself between the two women. If they were gossiping about one of his laborers, he'd soon put a stop to it. Gossiping was one of the many things Crandall had little patience for.

The sight of his son astride the sleekly muscled black sorrel made his chest swell with pride. It was branding season at the ranch, and Caleb, his only heir, had arrived to lend a helping hand. To Crandall's way of thinking, it was a sure sign that his son understood, and accepted, that one day these lands would belong to him.

Now if only he could convince Caleb to claim ownership of the law firm, as well.

As Crandall watched, Caleb shifted in the saddle and urged his mount into a canter, moving as one with the magnificent animal as if he'd been riding horses all his life.

"Well, what's the problem?" Crandall demanded, dividing an impatient look between the two women.

"He's been at it since before the crack of dawn," Rita informed him in hushed tones. "Vaccinating, clipping ears, branding the cattle. Working nonstop, like a man possessed."

"Hasn't stopped for more than a water break," Ruth chimed in. "I know, because *I'm* the one who took the water to him. Gave him a good tongue-lashing, too, about the dangers of becoming dehydrated and suffering a heatstroke. I don't even think he heard me," she added with a sad little shake of her head.

"A man gets henpecked enough," Crandall griped, "he learns to tune a woman out." But he, too, was a bit worried about his son, who'd arrived unexpectedly last night, and without uttering a word to anyone, had headed straight for the guest wing of the house, where he resided whenever he spent an extended amount of time at the ranch.

In silence the threesome watched Caleb for another long moment. "Must be a woman," Rita concluded.

"I think you're right," Ruth agreed, and the two women exchanged looks of unconcealed delight.

Crandall scowled. Though a secret hope sprang to life in his chest, he had to be the voice of dissent. "Thorne men don't obsess over women," he informed his meddling housekeeper and nurse in an imperious tone. "Never have, never will."

Ruth and Rita traded knowing looks again. "Well, you know what they say," Rita began in a singsong voice.

"Never say never," Ruth finished smugly.

Caleb spent the weekend at his father's ranch hoping, through hard, honest labor, to purge the memory of a forbidden kiss. When he arrived on campus bright and early Monday morning, he told himself he could handle the sight of Daniela, could hear her soft, husky voice without wanting to drag her into the nearest janitor's closet to have his way with her.

But as he would soon discover, his newfound resolve was not to be put to the test that morning.

At first he thought she was merely late for class again. But as the hour progressed without an appearance from her, he found himself distracted as he went through the motions of teaching class, calling students at random to recite cases—all the while taunted by one particular empty chair. As the minutes ticked off the clock and she remained a no-show, he went from feeling relieved to irritated, concerned and then, again, irritated.

When class was over, he detained April Kwan to casually inquire about her friend's whereabouts.

"I haven't spoken to her since Friday, Professor Thorne," the girl informed him. "When I called her at home yesterday, a man answered the phone and told me she was sleeping."

Caleb kept his expression neutral. "If you happen to see her before Wednesday," he said in a deceptively mild tone, "tell her she might want to rethink the wisdom of skipping my class as early as the second week of the semester."

April nodded, biting her lip worriedly as she backed away. "I—I'll let her know, Professor Thorne."

He gave a short nod, finished shoving lecture notes into his satchel, then headed from the classroom.

Shara caught up to him in the bustling corridor. "Hey there," she greeted him above the noisy din of conversation and laughter. "I tried to reach you all weekend."

"I was at the ranch," he said somewhat distractedly. "How's Devon doing?"

"Not so great. When I left home this morning, he was sleeping like a baby, poor thing. I'm going home to check on him after my next class."

Caleb nodded, holding the door open for her, then following her from the building.

"When he's feeling better," Shara said, "I was

thinking we could reschedule our evening plans. Are you free on Friday?"

Caleb inclined his head toward a student who called a greeting to him across the courtyard. "Let me check my schedule and get back to you," he told Shara.

"All right," she murmured, looking a little deflated.

When they reached the law faculty building, Caleb walked unerringly to his office and shut the door behind him. Dropping his satchel to the floor, he sank into the chair behind his desk and logged on to the computer.

His mouth was set in a grim line as he opened a file he'd been working on that morning. He had a lot of things to do, more than enough to keep his mind off beautiful, troublesome women who skipped class in order to play house with their boyfriends.

Daniela stepped from the steamy shower and wrapped her body in a thick cotton bath towel.

She'd spent the entire weekend in bed, alternately sleeping and tossing fitfully between the sheets. On Sunday, Noah had shown up to relieve Janie of duty. Heedless of his sister's protests, he'd planted himself on the living room sofa and become immersed in mounds of paperwork while his "patient" slept in the next room. Pamela Roarke had called from Houston, and upon learning of Daniela's illness, had promptly decided to cut her trip short. Daniela, not wanting to cheat her mother of spending time with her sister, had talked Pamela out of returning home by agreeing to let Sister Jenkins stop by the house and pray over her.

She'd been barely lucid as the sweet, diminutive churchwoman stood at her bedside, eyes squeezed shut, hands clasped tightly together while Noah hovered in the doorway, head bent in reverent silence, the ghost of a smile curving his lips.

What Magdalena Jenkins lacked in stature, she more than made up for in volume. As she prayed over Daniela, her deep voice resonated with authority, booming so loudly through the house that Daniela feared the neighbors would call the police to report a domestic disturbance. Once Sister Jenkins had finished petitioning God for His healing mercies, she smiled sweetly at Daniela and Noah, then left with barely a whisper.

Daniela fell asleep afterward, and didn't awaken until five o'clock on Monday evening—eight hours later. As she climbed from bed and made her way to the bathroom to take a shower, she felt noticeably better than she had all weekend. Although she automatically attributed her improved condition to the long hours of rest she'd gotten, she couldn't help but smile at the memory of Sister Jenkins's morning visit and wonder if, indeed, her mother was right about the woman's intercessory prayer gift.

Daniela towel-dried her freshly washed hair and dressed in a pair of high-cut cotton shorts and a matching tank top emblazoned with the famous quote Well-Behaved Women Rarely Make History.

She threw on her chenille robe, then made her way to the kitchen. Noah had checked her mail and stacked the letters neatly on the breakfast table before leaving for the office that morning.

While Daniela was listening to her phone messages and sorting through junk mail, the doorbell rang. Thinking it was Janie, who'd promised to stop by that evening to check on her, Daniela went to answer the door.

"What, you lost your key or some—"

The teasing admonition died on her lips when she saw who stood on her doorstep.

Not Janie, as she'd expected, but Caleb Thorne. Caleb. At her house.

Her eyes widened in shock. "W-What are you doing here?" she stammered.

Hands thrust into the pockets of low-slung Levi's, he arched a dark brow at her. "Expecting someone else?"

"Well, yes, as a matter of fact, I was." Self-conscious, she tugged the lapels of her robe together. "What are you doing here?"

"You missed my class," Caleb said, deadpan.

"So I did." Mouth curving, Daniela leaned in the doorway and crossed one ankle over the other, drawling, "Are you the truancy officer?"

He frowned slightly. "I came to see if you were all right."

"How sweet. I'm touched, *Professor Thorne*." She slid him a look beneath the dense sweep of her lashes. "Do you extend this courtesy to all of your absentee students, or just the ones you kiss?"

A muscle ticked in his jaw. He held her gaze for a long moment, then turned abruptly and started away.

"Wait!" Daniela called, realizing she'd unintentionally pushed him too far. She hurried onto the porch after him in her bare feet. "I was only teasing you! Thank you for being concerned about me. I really do appreciate it."

"Good night, Miss Moreau," he said over his shoulder.

She reached out, grabbing his arm before he could take another step. Hard muscles bunched and flexed beneath her fingers, sending heat pulsing through her veins. He stopped, but didn't turn around.

"I didn't blow off your class," Daniela said softly. "I have the flu. I've been sick all weekend."

He turned then, dark, assessing eyes roaming across her face. "Now that you mention it," he murmured, "you *have* looked better."

Daniela grinned. "Touché. You should have seen me on Saturday, when my head *wasn't* in the toilet."

His mouth twitched. "Have a good evening, Miss Moreau," he said quietly. "I hope you feel better."

"Would you like to come inside for a cup of coffee?"

His gaze darkened, and Daniela knew he was remembering their coffeehouse excursion. A slow flush crawled up her neck. "Or, um, I could make you tea instead?"

When he hesitated, she warned half-seriously, "The longer we stand out here, the better the odds that old Mrs. Flores across the street will call the police to report you as an intruder. She's ninety-eight years old and somewhat senile. Last year she called the cops on the mailman. The year before that it was the garbageman. Don't look now—she's staring out the window at us."

Caleb scowled, but without any real rancor. Daniela tugged gently on his arm, and after another moment he followed her into the house.

Daniela swept a quick look around the living room, searching for anything that might betray her identity. Thankfully, *P.I. for Dummies* was not among the rows of assorted books lining the built-in cypress bookshelves, nor was her monogrammed leather briefcase anywhere in sight. Even if she could justify an interest in learning about private investigators, she'd have a hard time explaining to Caleb the reason she owned a briefcase stamped with the initials *D.R.*

"I was about to brave my first meal in two days," she told him, closing and locking the door behind him. "Do you like tortilla soup?"

"Sure," Caleb answered, dipping his hands into his jeans pockets as he glanced around the living room with its overstuffed sofa and chairs, and lush canvas oil paintings on walls papered in gold leaf. "You have a very nice home."

And you, sir, have a very nice tush, Daniela thought naughtily. Aloud she said, "You like my shabby chic look? See, I knew you were a man of discerning taste."

He sent her a bemused look over his shoulder. "My judgment can be flawed on occasion," he said in a tone that suggested he wasn't just talking about her decorating skills.

Daniela gave him a guileless smile. "I'll try not to hold it against you," she quipped, brushing past him to head into the kitchen. She waved him into a chair at the breakfast table, then lunged for the stack of mail she'd been sorting through when he rang the doorbell—mail addressed to Daniela Roarke.

He raised a puzzled brow at her, but said nothing as she hastily tucked the letters inside one of the cabinet drawers. *Close call,* she thought.

"Do you live here alone?" he asked as Daniela busied herself with dinner preparations, which consisted of heating up the tortilla soup and uncorking a bottle of Pinot Grigio.

She shook her head, filling two long-stemmed wineglasses. "My mother lives with me. She's in Houston visiting her sister for the week."

"Thanks," Caleb murmured, accepting a glass from her. He took a sip, watching her over the rim. "You two must be close. You and your mother, I mean."

"We are." As Daniela walked over to the stove to check the simmering tortilla soup, she grinned ruefully. "I must confess to being somewhat of a mama's girl. When I bought this house three years ago, I had to convince my mom to move in with me, offering the explanations that I wanted to help look after her, and that it made economic sense to combine our two households and save money on rent and utilities. While both of those reasons are true, the simple fact of the matter is that I wanted her around. I enjoy her company." She glanced over her shoulder at Caleb. "Does that make me a loser?"

A gentle smile curved his mouth. "Not at all. I think it's very sweet, actually."

Smiling, Daniela picked up her glass and took a sip of wine, though she knew it wasn't wise to drink alcohol on an empty—and as yet unstable—stomach. "What about you and your father?" she casually probed. "Are you two close?"

Just as she'd expected, Caleb's expression grew shuttered. "Not as close as you and your mother," he answered abstractedly. He nodded toward the stove. "Soup smells great."

"Wait till you taste it. It's my sister-in-law's mother's secret recipe." Daniela ladled tortilla soup into two ceramic bowls, then carried them over to the table. "Don't worry about catching my germs," she joked as she served Caleb. "I didn't cough or breathe into the pot."

He chuckled. "I'll take my chances."

She settled into a chair beside him. It wasn't exactly

a romantic candlelight dinner at Le Rêve, but it was as good a start as any.

"What did I miss in class today?" she asked as they began eating.

"Get the notes from April," Caleb told her. "I don't do encore lectures."

"Not even for the sick and shut-in?"

"Nah." Dark eyes glinting with amusement, he gave her a long, considering look. "Come to think of it, you don't look all that bad for someone three days into the flu."

She laughed. "That's not what you said when we were standing on the porch."

"What I mean is, when I had the flu, I was laid up for a week."

"That's surprising. You don't strike me as the type of person who gets sick very often."

"I don't. The last time I had the flu was in tenth grade."

She grinned. "In that case, you should be totally immune to me."

He bent his head over his bowl. "Not quite," he said, his voice pitched so low she couldn't be sure she'd heard right.

Except she knew she had.

Hiding a private smile, she swallowed another mouthful of soup. "I have Sister Jenkins to thank for my speedy recovery," she informed Caleb.

"Yeah?" He eyed her curiously. "Who's Sister Jenkins?"

"A woman who attends my mother's church. She's this tiny, demure, soft-spoken lady—until she opens her mouth to pray. And then it's like she's calling down the heavens in this loud, hellfire-and-brimstone, Southern Baptist preacher voice. It's a little scary, I tell you."

Caleb chuckled. "Sounds more comical than scary."

"That's what my brother Noah said. The whole time Sister Jenkins was praying over me, he could hardly contain his laughter."

"Your brother was here with you?"

Daniela nodded, wondering if she'd only imagined the note of relief in Caleb's voice. "He came over yesterday to take care of me. It was just like old times," she said with a reminiscent smile.

Caleb sipped his wine, watching her with a quiet, focused absorption that made Daniela feel as if they were the only two people in the world. No other man had ever made her feel that way, as if every word she spoke was of paramount interest to him.

"How many siblings do you have?" he asked.

"Two older brothers."

"They must be mighty protective over you."

She shrugged, idly toying with the crystal stem of her wineglass. "Sometimes. But they know I can take care of myself."

Humor lifted one corner of Caleb's mouth. "I can only imagine," he murmured.

Her eyes narrowed on his face. "What's that supposed to mean? How am I supposed to take that?"

"Any way you like, Miss Moreau," he said with a slow, lazy grin that made her pulse accelerate. "Thanks for dinner. I think that was the best tortilla soup I've ever had."

"Janie's mother will be thrilled to hear that," Daniela said, rising from the table with their empty bowls. "Janie is my sister-in-law, by the way. Would you like seconds?"

"No, thanks. I'm good."

"How about coffee, and some dessert? My mom made her award-winning peach cobbler before she left for Houston. Unless Noah devoured it all while he was here, there should be some left."

Caleb glanced at his watch. "I really should be going."

"Are you sure? Not many people can turn down my mother's famous cobbler, baked with the sweetest, juiciest peaches she handpicks from the orchard herself."

He hesitated. "Award-winning, huh?"

Daniela grinned. "Six years in a row at the annual church bake-off."

"In that case," Caleb drawled, "how can I refuse?"

He should have refused. Really, he should have. But refusing Daniela Moreau was fast becoming a foreign concept to him.

So he agreed to a slice of peach cobbler, and when Daniela asked innocently, "À la mode?" he shook his head, and forced his body not to react to the memory of the last time she'd offered him ice cream.

He polished off the cobbler in three bites, not because he was in a hurry to leave—as should have been the case—but because it was so damn good. When he'd finished eating, a laughing Daniela poured him a cup of coffee and led him into the living room. He couldn't help but admire the sensual, hypnotic sway of her hips as she walked, and his mouth watered at the way the plush fabric of her robe molded the delectable roundness of her bottom.

When Daniela joined him on the sofa, he realized, too late, that he should have sat in one of the armchairs. When she leaned forward to slide a coaster beneath his coffee cup, her robe gaped open, tempting him with an eyeful of lush cleavage.

He swallowed hard, feeling like a horny teenager on his first date.

He didn't know whether to be relieved or disappointed when she moved back, settling against the overstuffed cushions and tucking her long legs beneath her. She gave him a smile of relaxed contentment. "So you live in the Towers, huh? Pretty swanky."

He shrugged. "Believe it or not, my reasons for moving there had nothing to do with seeking a prestigious address."

"Ah, yes, you had sentimental reasons," Daniela murmured. "Your parents used to take you to see shows at the Majestic."

"That's right." A soft, nostalgic smile touched his mouth. "I saw *The Wiz* for the first time there. I'll never forget how excited I was to see an all-black cast in a live performance. It's all I talked about for weeks afterward."

Daniela chuckled. "I felt the same way when I watched *The Wiz* for the first time. I won't even tell you how long I pretended to be Dorothy. My brothers were ready to put me out of the house."

"My parents probably wanted to do the same to me," Caleb admitted wryly.

They exchanged teasing grins.

"What a little prince you must have been," Daniela ribbed, poking him playfully on the arm. "As the only child, I bet you were spoiled rotten."

"Think again. In fact, my father went out of his way *not* to spoil me, and he made damned sure my mother didn't, either. He said he didn't want to raise a soft, pampered rich boy, and I applaud him for that."

"You do?"

Caleb nodded, vaguely amused by her surprised tone. "One of the best things Crandall Thorne ever did for me was to make me work hard for everything I ever wanted. Whether it was money to attend football camp or to buy my first car, I had to earn it. I took nothing for granted, ever. And that's the way it should be."

"You're pretty adamant about this," Daniela observed. "Do you plan to raise your own children with the same tough love?"

"*If* I ever have children," Caleb drawled, "then, yes, I see nothing wrong with teaching them the value of a work ethic. I've watched too many of my childhood friends crap out because they never learned to fend for themselves."

"That's a shame." Dark, exotically tilted eyes studied him in silence for a moment. "How did your mother die, Caleb?"

He stiffened, his jaw hardening.

Seeing his reaction, Daniela hastened to say, "I'm sorry, that was too personal. You don't have to answer if—"

"She died of complications from lupus. I was fourteen."

"Oh, Caleb," Daniela murmured gently. "I'm so sorry."

"It was a long time ago," he said gruffly, suddenly awash with memories of his mother, a quiet, unassuming woman who'd struck him as a tragic figure long before her death. He remembered, as a child, wondering about the sadness in her eyes, the smiles she sometimes forced when Crandall spoke to her. Although his parents had never argued in front of him, Caleb had known that their marriage was unstable, fraught with a tension he hadn't understood until he was much older. That was when he'd learned about his father's extramarital affair with a woman he'd loved since childhood, a woman who grew up to become the wife of Crandall's worst enemy—Hoyt Philbin. Crandall's affair with Tessa Philbin had hastened his wife's descent into depression, making her more susceptible to the disease that eventually claimed her life. Because to this day, Caleb knew that what had killed his mother couldn't have been cured with medicine. She'd died of a broken heart.

"I guess we both know what it's like to lose a parent," Daniela said quietly. "But at least you had your mother for fourteen years. Does that make it better, or worse?"

"I don't know." He hesitated, then confided, "My mother and I weren't that close. I didn't know her very well."

Daniela fell silent for several moments, thinking. Then, "Can I ask you another personal question?"

He tensed, automatically bracing himself. "Go ahead," he said warily.

"Why did you stop practicing law, Caleb? I heard you were amazing."

Caleb frowned. "Don't believe everything you hear," he said grimly. Absently he realized she'd been calling him by his first name, but he didn't bother correcting her. What was the point? His behavior on Friday night, and his very presence in her home that evening, was proof that their relationship—or whatever it was—had progressed beyond the use of formal addresses.

"Don't be so modest," Daniela teased. "It's okay to

say you kicked butt and took names as one of San Antonio's most formidable attorneys."

"You have a flair for the dramatic, Miss Moreau."

"It's Daniela," she corrected. "And you're avoiding my question."

"No, I'm not." He rubbed a hand over his face and pushed out a long, deep breath. He could feel the dull edges of fatigue settling into his muscles. He'd overdone it at the ranch this weekend, trying to purge her from his system.

As if such a thing were possible.

"I stopped litigating because I got burned-out," he said finally. "Contrary to what you may have heard, there was no deep, philosophical reason behind my decision. I didn't wake up one morning and have an epiphany. The truth is, I didn't particularly like the people I was defending, and over time, I didn't like myself too much, either. So I got out."

"You make it sound so simple," Daniela said softly, watching him with eyes that saw too much. "I know it wasn't that simple."

Caleb shrugged, unnerved by her perceptiveness, but unwilling to show it. "No simpler than it was for you to walk away from your accounting career. But once you did it, you knew it was the right thing to do. Seems to me you should understand better than anyone my reasons for leaving the courtroom."

"I think I do," she murmured.

And somehow, Caleb knew she did. "Come to think of it, *you* never answered my question that day in the coffee shop. I asked you why you wanted to be a lawyer, and you never told me."

"I didn't?"

"No," he said succinctly, "you didn't." Why did he get the sense that Daniela was being deliberately evasive?

She shrugged, the edge of her teeth digging into the plump flesh of her bottom lip. "I don't know. Maybe I feel silly admitting to my law professor that I'm not really sure what I want to do with my law degree. I mean, I'm twenty-seven years old, too old not to know what I want to do with the rest of my life."

Caleb smiled, touched by this rare glimpse into her vulnerable side. "At the risk of sounding like a patronizing grown-up, there's nothing wrong with not knowing what you want to do with the rest of your life. At some point or another, everyone experiences that uncertainty about the future, no matter how old—or *young*—they are. You have nothing to be embarrassed about."

She beamed a smile at him, that beautiful, endearing smile that made his chest swell and caused him to feel twenty feet tall.

Gruffly he said, "But I would suggest that you come up with a game plan soon, because law school doesn't get any easier as you go along. And if you're in it for the long haul, you might as well have a clear idea what you expect to get out of it."

She grinned, giving him a mock salute. "Yes, sir."

He chuckled, reaching over to ruffle her hair playfully, as much to tease as to touch her. "Wise guy."

As he drew away, Daniela caught his hand in hers. Without releasing his gaze, she rested her cheek in the curve of his palm. His breath stalled in his lungs. As if in a trance, he watched her lips part and form the soft request: "Stay and watch a movie with me."

And though a warning bell went off in his brain, he felt himself nodding slowly. "All right."

Halfway through the romantic comedy, Daniela fell asleep, curled tightly into a fetal position in a corner of the sofa. As Caleb watched her, he had to force himself not to touch her, not to trace his fingers over the delicate arch of her brow or the lush fullness of her lips. Her cheeks were flushed, and there were faint dark smudges beneath her eyes from lack of sleep. As he gazed upon her, he felt a wave of tenderness wash over him. This Daniela, with the sweetly angelic face, posed no threat to him.

Or so he told himself.

Frowning darkly, Caleb rose from the sofa, reached down and swept her easily into his arms. She didn't awaken as he carried her down the hall and into the first bedroom, which he assumed, from the rumpled bedcovers, must be hers.

He laid her down gently in the queen-size bed, considered, then discarded the idea of removing her robe. He didn't think he could handle seeing whatever she wore—or *didn't* wear—beneath. Besides, he reasoned, it was probably best for her to stay covered up, in case she got the chills overnight. He drew the heavy comforter over her body and tucked it under her chin.

As an afterthought, he touched the back of his hand to her forehead. Her skin felt hot, almost feverish. He frowned, wondering if he should wake her and bring her some medicine or a cold, damp cloth.

As he stood over her, debating his next move, she tossed fitfully in her sleep, turning onto her side to face him. Caleb froze, holding his breath. But she didn't awaken.

Deciding he'd better get out of Dodge while he still could, Caleb turned and started for the door.

A soft, restless moan from the bed stopped him.

He turned his head, glancing over his shoulder at Daniela. In the soft wedge of light from the living room, he saw that her eyes were still closed. So he was unprepared, therefore, to hear the softly uttered plea, "Don't go."

He stood in the doorway, his pulse drumming in his ears. Every ounce of common sense warned him to pretend he hadn't heard her and to keep going until he'd put Daniela's cozy little bungalow in his rearview mirror. No good could come of him staying there a minute—hell, a *second*—longer.

His mind heeded the logic of the warning.

His body was an entirely different matter.

Before he could stop himself, he was striding back across the room, removing his wallet from the back pocket of his jeans and depositing it on the nightstand before lowering himself gently onto the bed. He'd stay for a few more minutes, he told himself firmly, just to make sure she was all right. Never mind that he could just as effectively monitor her condition from the antique chair by the window, or from the safe distance of the living room. And never mind that, given how tired he already was, he could very well fall asleep in Daniela's bed, and awaken to God only knew what kind of temptation.

Careful not to disturb Daniela, who remained fast asleep, he clasped his hands behind his head and stared up at the darkened ceiling with a look of fixed determination.

Just fifteen minutes, he vowed, and then he would go....

Chapter 12

Daniela awoke some time later and blinked in the quiet stillness of her bedroom. For a moment she felt groggy and disoriented, and then, all at once, she became aware of the solid warmth of a body beside her.

A *male* body.

Her heart thudded. She sat up quickly, staring down in shocked disbelief at the man sleeping next to her. How had Caleb Thorne wound up in her bed? The last thing she remembered was inviting him to watch a movie with her, and being secretly thrilled when he agreed. She didn't remember falling asleep, and she *definitely* didn't remember luring Caleb into her bedroom.

A buttery shaft of light from the living room illuminated him, his breathing deep and even. The hard angles of his face were softened in sleep, his thick black lashes fanning out in perfect formation from his closed eyelids. One arm was clasped behind his head, the other draped across his flat, hard stomach. One long leg hung off the edge of her bed, as if he hadn't been able to decide whether to stay or go.

She glanced toward the bedside clock. It was 2:15 a.m.

He'd stayed this long, she reasoned. No sense in sending him home now.

Slowly, so as not to awaken him, she eased from under the covers and crawled toward the end of the bed. She unlaced one of Caleb's big leather boots and carefully removed it from his foot. Then, reaching over the side of the bed, she lifted his other foot and began to work the laces free.

When she'd finished her task, she glanced up—and found her guest awake and watching her intently.

Her nerve endings tingled with awareness as she stared into his heavy-lidded midnight eyes. "I was just, um, making you more comfortable," she murmured. "It's late. I figured you might as well spend the night."

"You figured, huh?" His deep, sleep-roughened voice did dangerous things to her pulse.

She nodded, her tongue snaking out nervously to wet her lips. "Only if you want to stay, of course."

Slowly, keeping her trapped in the heat of his gaze, Caleb eased himself into a sitting position. "Come here," he said, a low, husky command that sent a shiver through her.

She crawled over to him, and without a word he drew his arms around her waist and lifted her smoothly onto his lap. As she watched in breathless fascination, he brought his dark head toward hers. It was exhilarating, the way he asked her permission with only his eyes, and by bringing his lips just inches away from hers. She had never known such a sense of heightened anticipation as when they looked into each other's eyes, their mouths separated by a mere heartbeat.

"I might be contagious," Daniela whispered, her pulse racing as he sank his hands into the thick, curly tangle of her hair.

"I'll take my chances," he muttered softly, and crushed his lips to hers. She wrapped her arms around his neck and opened hungrily to him. The tip of his tongue played inside her mouth in sensuous sweeps of warmth that explored the edges of her teeth and the silken dampness beyond. He kissed her, deeply and provocatively, until a shaking moan rose in her throat.

Her heart hammered in her chest as his mouth slid along the arch of her throat, trailing a simmering pathway of pulsing nerves. His lips moved to her ear, and his marauding tongue traced and stroked the delicate shell, making her breath quicken sharply. He reached between their bodies, untying her robe and slowly dragging it off her shoulders, the brush of his warm, callused fingers against her bare flesh causing her to shiver convulsively. She couldn't breathe deeply enough, or fast enough, her lungs striving to accommodate a desperate need for more oxygen as he tugged the skimpy tank top over her head and impatiently cast it aside. He stared at the rapid rise and fall of her chest, the dusky tips of her high, swollen breasts, and uttered a ragged oath as his head lowered. When he drew a nipple into the hot silk of his mouth, her blood turned to liquid fire. She arched upward as he flicked his tongue against the taut peak and circled the edge of her nipple before suckling it, wringing a hoarse cry from her.

They undressed each other quickly, as if any parting of their bodies was too long to be separated. When they came together, flesh to flesh, it was in an explosion of heat and fierce desire. They held and kissed each other as if their very survival depended on it.

Flattening both palms against the solid wall of his chest, Daniela shoved Caleb back upon the bed and straddled him. Slowly, seductively, she kissed her way down the length of his body, over the sinewy cords of his shoulder and the sculpted planes of his muscular chest, reveling in the warmth of smooth male flesh that felt like granite wrapped in velvet. His body was a revelation, a marvel to behold. When she reached his long, thick erection, she lifted her lashes slowly to meet the burning ferocity in his obsidian eyes. Holding his gaze, she took him in her mouth, and he sucked in a sharp, tortured breath. Heady with her newfound power, Daniela laved and suckled him, using her tongue in ways she'd never imagined doing with another man. Caleb groaned deep in his throat, a sound of raw male pleasure that caused a delicious pressure to coil in her belly.

"No more," he growled thickly. He sat up, reached for his wallet on the nightstand and removed a foil-wrapped condom, tearing open the packet with his teeth.

"Let me," Daniela murmured, taking the condom from his hand. He watched with a heavy-lidded gaze as she sheathed him, smoothing the latex over his rigid arousal slowly and provocatively.

She'd barely finished before he cradled the back of

her head and drew her mouth down to his. Daniela closed her eyes as he parted her lips and slid his hot, silky tongue between them, plunging deep and retreating in a slow, tantalizing rhythm that made liquid heat pool between her legs. Gradually he deepened the sensual caress until swift, penetrating strokes filled her, causing the pressure inside her to build into a throbbing ache of need. A need only he had the power to satisfy.

"Now, Caleb," she demanded in a throaty whisper, her hips already undulating against him in wanton anticipation. "I want you inside me. *Now*."

Caleb drew back, his dark, smoldering gaze capturing hers in the dimly lit room. "This will change everything," he said huskily.

I'm counting on it, Daniela thought, then ceased to think at all as he guided her over him and impaled her in one long, erotically painful stroke. She cried out his name sharply and arched against him, already on the brink of release. She threw back her head and moaned in mindless ecstasy as Caleb lifted her by the waist and slid her back down on the rigid, engorged length of his arousal. Slowly, inch by exquisite inch, until she shuddered deeply.

One hand grasped the curve of her buttocks, while with the other he reached up and cupped the aching swell of her breast, tweaking and tugging at the sensitized nipple until she thought she would burst into flames. Bracing her palms on the chiseled surface of his abdomen, she began to move on him, slowly at first, then more rapidly, fueled by his low, guttural moans and a driving hunger that threatened to consume her. Faster and faster she rode him until they were both breathless, until the heat between them condensed to a slick sheen of perspiration on their joined bodies.

In a sudden blur of movement Caleb reversed positions, rolling her over and onto her back, then covering her with the delicious weight of his body. She wrapped her legs tightly around him, shaking violently with need. She couldn't remember ever needing someone as badly as she needed Caleb. And her desire went beyond sex, went beyond her body's cry for release. It went deeper, to a forbidden place she dared not venture—a place of no return.

Caleb lowered his head and seized her lips in a hot, openmouthed kiss, his face above hers dark and taut with passion. She dug her fingernails into the muscled hardness of his back as he grasped her buttocks and thrust into her, deep and hard, taking her almost savagely. She lifted her hips to match him, stroke for desperate stroke, until their bodies slapped together in a heavy, pounding rhythm that finally drove her over the edge.

She cried out wildly as she came, her orgasm erupting through her in a blinding wave that made her cling to his broad shoulders as if for dear life. The force of her release, combined with the helpless whimpers she made as her body convulsed around him, seemed to shatter what was left of Caleb's control. Bracing his weight on both arms, he dropped his head and buried himself to the hilt.

"Daniela," he rasped, his back stiffening beneath her hands. His eyes closed, and he groaned harshly as he reached his own climax, his penis throbbing palpably inside her. *"Daniela..."*

Her heart soared upon finally hearing her name on his lips. She wrapped her arms around his chest and clung to him tightly as they slowly drifted back to earth, their ragged breathing gradually returning to normal.

When Caleb lifted his head to gaze into her eyes, she braced herself to see guilt, remorse, even anger. What she saw, instead, was tenderness, and the unmistakable glint of masculine satisfaction.

Her lips curved upward in a wicked smile. “This must be what Marvin Gaye had in mind when he wrote the lyrics to ‘Sexual Healing.’ If *this* doesn’t heal me, I don’t know what will.”

Caleb gave a low, hoarse laugh, then slowly withdrew from her and rolled them over so that she was on top. She smiled against his chest, endeared by the gentle concern he displayed in not wanting to crush her.

He stroked a hand over her tousled hair, then down her back, and she felt herself relax under his lazy touch. With a contented yawn, she snuggled against him, savoring the warmth and protection of his arms around her. Heaven didn’t get any better than this.

“I should have done some reading tonight,” she mumbled drowsily. “I didn’t study all weekend. I don’t want to fall behind in—”

Caleb placed a gentle finger to her lips. “Sleep, baby,” he murmured huskily.

And she did, sliding into a deep, satiated slumber.

When she awakened later that morning to find herself alone in the bed, she felt a sharp ache of disappointment.

It wasn’t that she’d expected Caleb to linger around to rouse her with a romantic serenade, or to greet her with a bouquet of long-stemmed red roses. But after the incredible—no, earth-shattering—night of passion they’d shared, she wouldn’t have minded waking up in his arms, lifting her head to see tender warmth reflected in his dark eyes as he gazed down at her.

Easy, girl, she mused grimly. *That kind of thinking will only get you into trouble.*

Daniela stretched languorously in the rumpled bed, feeling deliciously sore in places she'd never known existed. The sheets were still warm, faintly scented with the musk of their lovemaking. And just like that, she felt a stir of longing, starting in her belly and spreading outward in a slow, tormenting burn.

She scowled. *The least he could have done was hung around for a quickie,* she thought sulkily, throwing back the covers and rising from the bed.

Fortunately, she didn't have time to dwell on her burgeoning sexual appetite. It was ten minutes to seven, and if she didn't hurry, she'd be late for her eight o'clock class. Although Caleb had encouraged her to take another day off to get some rest, Daniela didn't want to fall behind in her studies. She *definitely* couldn't afford to miss Shara Adler's class—the woman was just looking for a reason to fail her, and Daniela refused to give her one. But she knew that if Shara somehow learned that she and Caleb had slept together, there'd be hell to pay.

Bring it on, thought Daniela as she stood beneath the hot spray of the shower, allowing her mind to return to memories of how she'd spent the early hours of the morning. She remembered the hard planes of Caleb's body moving against hers as they made love, the consummate fit between them, the sliding flex of muscle and sinew beneath her hands. Her skin tingled with the memory of his touch, and the sensual explorations of his mouth and fingers that had reduced her to molten lava. He was, without question, the best lover she'd ever had, far surpassing her deepest, darkest fantasies. Being with him, she decided, was worth any price.

She just hoped she wouldn't be forced to pay the ultimate price: the surrender of her heart.

As the first blush of dawn spread across the western sky, Caleb left Daniela's house and drove home in a daze.

For the first time in his five-year tenure as a professor, he'd crossed the line with a student.

It shouldn't have surprised him. He'd been in trouble from the moment he laid eyes on Daniela, one week ago. His reaction to her had been swift, and visceral. From that moment on, every look that passed between them, every word they exchanged, every fleeting touch, had been building inexorably toward this outcome. When he left campus yesterday and drove across town to the address he'd looked up in her records, he knew he was courting danger. When he accepted her invitation to stay and watch a movie, he and danger were doing the tango. By the time he crawled into bed with Daniela, he was beyond the point of rescue.

Caleb grimaced, hooking a hard right at the next intersection. He'd never left a woman's bed without saying goodbye, but when he'd awakened that morning to find Daniela's warm, exquisite body curved against his, as if they were two halves of a perfect whole, he'd panicked. Even as he eased away from her sleeping form, he felt a sharp surge of lust, his groin heating rapidly as he carefully untangled himself from the silken snare of her leg. The effort to keep from pushing her onto her back and mounting her made his entire body shake as he dressed hurriedly in the shadowed darkness of the bedroom. To his immense relief, Daniela remained fast asleep—even when, unable to resist, he knelt by the bedside and drank his fill of her fresh morning beauty.

Caleb frowned darkly. Before meeting Daniela Moreau, he had never understood the power of obsession, never understood what drove perfectly sane people to do remarkably stupid things. Until a week ago, he'd never fathomed becoming so obsessed with a woman that he would willingly compromise everything—his career, his integrity, his peace of mind—just to have a taste of her. There was no other word to describe his behavior where Daniela was concerned. He was obsessed with her. No other woman had ever made him feel this aware, this *alive,* as if her very presence heightened all his senses. She fascinated him. She challenged him. She made him laugh. And she drove him out of his mind with lust.

A memory of her hot, silken mouth wrapped around his throbbing erection made him harden at once, and shift uncomfortably in the driver's seat.

Caleb had never lacked for sexual partners, and he'd had more than his fair share of lovers whose appetites in the bedroom had ranged from tame to shockingly bold. None of those experiences, even the most pleasurable ones, came close to matching what he and Daniela had shared. The sexual chemistry between them was so explosive it took his breath away. Were it not for the fact that she was recovering from the flu and needed rest, Caleb would have kept her up all night, making love to her until neither of them could move a muscle.

The rational part of his brain told him he shouldn't—*couldn't*—have her again, to chalk up the forbidden experience to a lapse in judgment that would never be repeated. But his will had been all but severed from his intellect, leaving him open to anything, and everything.

Thorne men don't obsess over women. He heard his father's voice as clearly as if Crandall sat in the truck beside him, shaking his head in grim disapproval over his son's reckless behavior. From the time Caleb was old enough to comprehend the basic physical differences between males and females, his father had lectured him about the dangers of falling victim to lust. It got to the point where Caleb could hardly look at a girl without hearing Crandall's stern warnings about the "booty trap," and how no woman was worth throwing away his whole future for a few minutes of pleasure.

Once, when Caleb was seventeen, his father threw a lavish dinner party to celebrate the acquisition of a large corporate account that would launch the firm to a new level of success. The exclusive guest list included prominent businessmen, politicians, civic and community leaders, as well as some of Crandall's devoted employees, among them a beautiful twenty-two-year-old paralegal named Josephine. Caleb, who'd only spoken to Josephine a few times prior to that evening, was a little surprised when the girl sought him out on the moonlit terrace, where he'd retreated to escape the roomful of heavily perfumed strangers whose cool, calculated gazes appraised him as if he were champion Thoroughbred material—which, as Crandall Thorne's heir apparent, many perceived him to be. While the men openly speculated about whether Caleb would someday become as shrewd and formidable a businessman as his father, the women secretly wondered if his virility would surpass that of Crandall's, whose charm and magnetism were legendary. The fact that Crandall was a widower seemed to only heighten his appeal, as women on the prowl for wealthy husbands vied for the opportunity to become the next Mrs. Crandall Thorne.

Bearing an extra glass of chilled champagne and an engaging smile, Josephine had sidled up to Caleb that evening and struck up a conversation about… Hell, he couldn't remember what she'd been talking about. All he knew was that he was seventeen, bored out of his mind and more than a little eager to change his status as a virgin. When Josephine innocently asked for a tour of their palatial house, Caleb swore the Fates were smiling down on him. They'd wound up in his bedroom, kissing and groping each other like a pair of stags in heat. What followed were the most gratifying six minutes of Caleb's life, and afterward he'd fancied himself halfway in love with the beautiful older woman who'd brought about his sexual liberation.

A week later, Josephine called in tears to inform him that she'd been fired from the firm. When Caleb went to his father to demand an explanation, Crandall was already waiting for him with a look of amused long-suffering. As he calmly explained to his enraged son, on the night of the dinner party, he'd overheard Josephine remark to another woman how handsome Caleb looked in his tuxedo. He'd thought nothing of the girl seeking out Caleb's company, until he later learned that she had seduced his son. Afterward, she'd bragged about the experience to some of her colleagues at the firm, and word had gotten back to their boss.

"She was a gold-digger, Caleb," an unapologetic Crandall informed him. "She foolishly hoped that by ingratiating herself to my seventeen-year-old son, she'd secure a permanent place for herself at the firm. Heed my words, boy. Beautiful women are rarely, if ever, to be trusted. Enjoy them. Wine them, dine them, hell, make 'em your slave in the bedroom. But never, *ever,* trust them, or you'll curse the day you were born."

It was a hard lesson that followed Caleb into adulthood, enabling him to drift from one superficial relationship to the next, always keeping women at arm's length. Even Shara, whom he respected and cared deeply about, had not been able to breach the fortress he'd built around his emotions, or threaten his ironclad self-will.

No woman had. Until now.

Brooding, Caleb parked his truck in the underground garage and rode the elevator to the lobby to retrieve his mail. His boots rang out on the gleaming marble floor as he strode purposefully toward the steel bank of mailboxes.

"How's it going, Mr. Hammond?" he greeted the uniformed security guard posted at the reception station, an older black man with salt-and-pepper hair receding from a broad forehead.

Eugene Hammond glanced up from the San Antonio *Express-News* he'd been reading and beamed when he saw Caleb, one of the few tenants who actually spoke to him on a consistent basis. "Hey there, son!" As his dark gaze registered Caleb's rumpled appearance, and the fact that he'd been wearing the same clothes the day before, a knowing look crossed his face. "Long night, huh?"

"You could say that," Caleb muttered under his breath, slamming his mailbox shut. As he passed the reception desk, he said, "Take it easy, Mr. Hammond."

"You, too, son." As Caleb neared the elevators, Hammond added with a hint of sly insinuation in his voice, "Stay out of trouble."

Too late, Caleb thought darkly.

Chapter 13

Daniela underestimated how difficult it would be to sit in Caleb's class on Wednesday morning and pretend that nothing had changed between them. She couldn't look at him, pacing back and forth in front of the lecture hall, without remembering the way his body had felt under her, over her, thrusting in and out of her. And, unless she was imagining things, she wasn't the only one with a problem. Caleb's dark gaze seemed to land everywhere in the room but on her, though she sat directly in his line of vision in the second row. Every time she thought for certain he'd look her way, her mouth went dry and her heart lurched crazily, only to have his eyes skim over her as if she were invisible.

It was one of the most frustrating, nerve-racking experiences she'd ever endured.

And she was going to do something about it.

When class was over, she told April that she had to meet with one of their instructors, then she made her way over to Caleb's office in the law faculty building, hoping he wouldn't decide to have coffee with Shara first.

While she waited for him to arrive, she sipped her bottled water and studied his spacious office, committing every detail to memory, as if by doing so she could gain deeper insight into the man himself. Oak-paneled walls contained rows of law books, encyclopedias and every kind of dictionary imaginable. Books and papers covered nearly every available surface of his desk, and near the end of one wall, his Juris Doctorate degree was quietly displayed, as if he'd hung it there as an afterthought, or at someone's cajoling. No family photographs graced the walls or desk, nor did the office contain a single plant, poster or favorite engraving. The absence of personal effects intrigued Daniela, heightening her curiosity about a man who remained as elusive as the dark secrets she'd been sent into his life to unveil.

She heard the deep timbre of his voice in the hallway as he responded to a colleague's friendly greeting, and then he strode briskly through the door. At the sight of Daniela seated in one of the upholstered visitor chairs, his steps slowed a little, but his expression betrayed no emotion. Without a word, he closed the door behind him, and when Daniela heard the soft *click* of the lock, her pulse thundered.

Caleb rounded the corner of his desk and dropped his satchel to the floor before lowering his long body into the chair, his dark gaze holding hers in silent appraisal.

"How are you feeling?" he asked quietly.

Daniela smiled. "I'm almost back to one hundred percent," she replied, crossing one long leg over the other and watching, with a twinge of satisfaction, as his eyes followed the movement. She'd dressed with extra care that morning, donning a white halter top that ended just below midriff, and a khaki-brown ruffle skirt that featured an ultra low-rise waistband. The front of the tiered skirt curved upward to show off the smooth, shapely expanse of her bare legs—which, in her mind, had always been her greatest asset. Completing the gypsy look were a pair of wide hoop earrings, simple bands of gold that encircled her wrists and sexy platform sandals with crisscross straps that laced up the ankle.

Caleb's lazy gaze ran the length of her before returning slowly to her face. In silence he watched her raise the bottled water to her lips and take a long sip.

"What can I do for you this morning?" he asked softly.

"Nothing, really," she murmured, her tongue snaking out to chase a drop of water from her lower lip. Her belly quivered when she saw the way his pupils darkened. The air between them crackled with sexual tension.

"I missed being picked on in class today," she told him.

His gaze lingered on her mouth. "Did you?"

Daniela nodded slowly. "And I missed *you*."

Caleb closed his eyes and groaned softly, as if he were in pain. "Daniela—"

"I'm just being honest," she said. Suddenly restless, she set aside her water, rose from the chair and walked over to a floor globe mounted on a gleaming oak stand.

Idly she gave the globe a quick spin, saying, "My mother always taught me to speak the truth, so that's what I'm doing. I missed you, and I won't apologize for it."

"No one's asking you to apologize for anything, Daniela," Caleb said quietly. "If anything, I'm the one who should be apologizing for—"

Without turning around, Daniela held up a hand. "I already know what you're going to say. You're going to tell me that making love was a mistake, that you never meant for things to go that far. And you're going to apologize for taking advantage of me when, if anything, *I* probably took advantage of *you*. I wanted to be with you, Caleb, and I have no regrets about what happened between us. Whatever feelings you may have about the experience are entirely your own, but please don't let guilt be one of them."

After several long moments of silence, she heard the slight creak of his chair as he got up and came toward her. "Since you've become such an expert at reading my mind," he murmured, "can you tell me what I'm thinking right now?"

The husky timbre of his voice sent erotic images tumbling through her mind. Deep in her stomach, a knot of desire unfurled and spread sinuous fingers of heat through her limbs. As he drew nearer, her breasts grew heavy, her nipples hardening against the lace of her bra. She was vaguely aware of the room growing dimmer, as if Caleb had closed the blinds.

He stopped directly behind her, and her pulse accelerated as gentle, callused fingers swept the heavy mass of her hair over one shoulder, then cupped the back of her neck and began to stroke her skin in slow, tantalizing circles. She wanted to hear him say he'd missed her, too, but then he lowered his head and touched his lips to her nape, and she closed her eyes with an involuntary sigh and let her head fall forward.

"You always smell so incredible," he muttered thickly as his mouth trailed down the exposed column of her neck, nipping and raining hot, bone-melting kisses along her sensitive flesh. "What's the name of your perfume?"

Her mouth curved in a private smile he couldn't see. "It's a secret. If I tell you, you might run out and buy some for your girlfriend."

"I don't have a girlfriend," he murmured distractedly, nuzzling her throat.

"Don't you?" Much as she was enjoying the sexy interlude, some reckless part of her wanted to punish him, wanted to torment him as she was tormented by her overwhelming need for him.

She turned around slowly. Allowing herself only a glimpse of the smoldering heat in his gaze, she began to edge past him. "I should go," she announced, the firmness in her tone belied by the wobbliness of her legs.

She got as far as the desk before he caught her by the waist, pulling her tightly against him. "Stay," he whispered, his warm breath in her ear making her shiver. Resistance was futile.

Suddenly she found her bottom pressed against his straining arousal, her palms braced on the surface of the desk. She felt warm and dizzy as his hand glided possessively over her hips, inching the material of her skirt higher, while his other hand sought the smooth flesh of her exposed midriff. Her heart hammered in her chest as his mouth skimmed her ear, her neck and her jaw while he reached under her skirt, his fingers burning a path up the inside of her leg to the juncture of her parted thighs. She ached with a fierce need to have him inside her, and shamelessly rubbed her buttocks against his groin, drawing a rough sound of hunger from him.

His fingers eased beneath the elastic trim of her lace panties. A sharp moan of pleasure escaped from her mouth when he parted the soft, springy curls and slid one finger deep inside her.

"You're so wet," he groaned, the sound both tortured and approving.

As he teased and stroked her, his thumb simultaneously caressed the outer folds of her sex, circling the slick nub of her clitoris until she gripped the edge of the desk tightly, feeling as if she were about to be torn apart by an internal force she couldn't contain. Though she tried to be mindful of where they were, and how disastrous it would be if anyone overheard them, she felt a desperate cry welling up inside her. When Caleb pushed a second finger deep inside her, her back arched sharply. With skilled ease, he turned her in his arms and covered her mouth with his, capturing the helpless cries that tore from her throat as she came apart in an explosion of clenching pleasure.

Afterward, he cradled her protectively in his arms as she slumped against him, weak and spent, certain her mind and body would never be the same again. His own breathing was slightly erratic as he straightened her skirt, stroked her back and kissed her damp temple.

As he gazed down at her, tenderness shone in his dark, glittering eyes. "I missed you, too," he said huskily.

Her heart soared. "You don't have to say that just because I did."

He shook his head, his gaze intent on her face. "One thing you'll learn about me, Daniela, is that I never say things I don't mean." He leaned down, taking her lips in a hot, deeply possessive kiss that drugged her senses and left her feeling even weaker than before.

When he lifted his head, she could only gaze at him through heavy-lidded eyes. "Believe it or not," she murmured, her words sounding slurred to her own ears, "I didn't come here this morning to seduce you."

Caleb chuckled softly. "You don't hear me complaining, do you?"

"Mmm. But you should. I didn't return the favor."

Caleb groaned, nuzzling her throat. "Don't tempt me, woman."

"Oh, but it's so much fun," Daniela teased.

"Don't be cruel," he said, drawing away to tweak her nose playfully. He lifted her by the waist and deposited her gently on the corner of his desk before reclaiming his own chair.

As Daniela watched, he deliberately arranged his features into a sober expression. "I'm going to get serious on you now," he warned her, holding her gaze as if to channel "serious-mood" wavelengths into her. "Are you ready to go there with me?"

Smothering a grin, Daniela gave a dutiful nod. "I'm ready."

Caleb's mouth twitched. "I want to run a couple of things past you," he said, reaching for a pen and a small notepad tucked beneath a sheaf of paperwork. "I've been doing some thinking since our last conversation, when we spoke about what you hope to get out of law school. Have you heard of the National Black Law Students Association?"

When Daniela shook her head, he explained, "It's a national organization designed to improve the educational and social experiences of African-American law students. We have a chapter here at St. Mary's—the Black Law Students Association. As you already know, African-Americans are greatly underrepresented at the university, particularly in the law school, so an organization like NBLSA is really valuable in providing support and networking opportunities for black law students. NBLSA also sponsors various fund-raisers and community service projects, and hosts a minority law symposium in the spring." As he spoke, he scribbled in his notepad, then tore off the sheet and passed it to Daniela. "That's the name and phone number of the NBLSA president. She's a 3L—"

Daniela, still somewhat dazed from their steamy encounter, gave him a nonplussed look as she accepted the slip of paper. "3L?"

"Third-year law student," Caleb clarified, his mouth twitching. "Don't worry. Before long, the abbreviations will be rolling off your tongue. Anyway, if you're interested in attending an NBLSA meeting or just want to learn more about them, give Sonja a call. She's always looking to recruit new members, so I know she'd be happy to hear from you. I also think she could serve as a great mentor."

Daniela gave him a look of tender gratitude. "Thank you for thinking of me, Caleb," she said sincerely. "Maybe I *will* give Sonja a call. The NBLSA sounds like a wonderful organization."

"It is," Caleb concurred. "The students are terrific,

and really committed to fulfilling the mission of the organization. I was the faculty advisor up until last year, when I decided to take a break to work on some other projects. But I left the NBLSA in the good hands of my friend and colleague, Bernard Holt."

"Does he teach first-year classes, too?" Daniela asked curiously, crossing her legs and propping her elbow on one knee.

"No, but you've probably seen him around campus before. There are only three of us here—meaning, three black law professors—so at some point or another you'll run into all of us." Leaning back in his chair, Caleb laced his fingers together and rested them on the hard surface of his stomach. "That brings me to the next thing I wanted to discuss with you."

Smiling, Daniela leaned forward on the desk, her chin resting in the curve of her palm as she made an exaggerated show of giving him her undivided attention. "I'm listening."

His mouth twitched at her playfulness. "Would you be interested in doing an internship at my father's law firm?"

Her smile faltered, and she stared at him in bewildered disbelief. "Of course, but…I thought internships were only available to second- and third-year students?"

"Most are," Caleb agreed. "For example, you can only qualify for a judicial internship after you've completed your first year. But we're talking about a private firm here, which means that the hiring of interns is at my father's discretion."

"Does he normally hire first-years?"

"Not normally," Caleb admitted. "But he would consider it, if a particular student came highly recommended."

Daniela's eyes widened. "You would recommend me?"

He inclined his head. "I would."

She felt a surge of excitement, even as her conscience pricked her. She glanced away from him for a moment. "I—I couldn't let you do that for me, Caleb," she murmured.

His lips quirked into an ironic half smile. "Believe it or not, Daniela, I'm not making this offer because we're involved. I think you're a very intelligent, mature young woman, and your strong work history can be substituted for your lack of legal experience. In light of the conversation we had on Monday, I believe you could really benefit from interning in a law firm. It would give you a terrific opportunity to learn how the criminal justice system works and to gain firsthand knowledge of the legal profession. If nothing else, at the end of your internship, you may decide a law career is absolutely the *last* thing you want."

Daniela grinned. "Or it could turn out to be my life's calling."

Caleb smiled faintly. "Could be. Now, I have to warn you up front that my father puts his interns to work, and there's nothing remotely glamorous about the work they do. You'll be doing everything from typing lengthy court documents and assisting the paralegals with their research, to serving coffee to clients and running personal errands for the senior associates. It won't be a cakewalk, but I can guarantee that you'll learn a great deal and come away from the experience with a tremendous addition to your résumé. So, are you interested?"

Daniela laughed. "Are you kidding? I'd have to be

crazy to pass up on the opportunity to intern at San Antonio's top criminal defense firm."

"Good," Caleb said with a brisk nod. "I'll let my father know. Now, there's just one other thing."

"What's that?"

"He'd like to meet you in person."

Daniela's heart knocked. "You mean your father personally interviews *interns?*"

Caleb gave her a look of wry amusement. "You obviously don't know Crandall Thorne. He monitors everything at the firm, right down to the price of bulk pens. For as long as I can remember, he's been involved in the hiring of each and every new employee, from attorneys to mail clerks."

"Wow," Daniela murmured.

"I know," Caleb said, his mouth twitching. "To say my father is a control freak would be a huge understatement. But the firm is very important to him, and, to his credit, he's always made the right hiring decisions, which has largely contributed to the success of the business."

Daniela nodded. "When would he like to set up the interview?"

"As soon as possible. Are you available tomorrow evening? I thought we could all have dinner together at his ranch."

Daniela's mouth went dry. She could hardly believe that she was soon to meet the powerful, notorious Crandall Thorne in his own domain. When she'd accepted the undercover assignment earlier that summer, never could she have imagined that such a golden opportunity would present itself, seeming to fall right into her lap. Kenneth and Noah would be extremely pleased, she thought, then suffered another pang of guilt, this one sharper than the first. Caleb, out of a genuine desire to help her with her career, had gone out of his way to speak to his father on her behalf, all but securing an internship for her that any of her classmates would kill for.

And she would repay his generosity by deceiving and betraying him.

"Daniela?" Caleb's deep voice broke into her grim musings. She blinked, and realized that he was watching her quietly as he awaited her answer.

She forced a relaxed smile. "Tomorrow evening sounds perfect, Caleb."

He nodded, his dark gaze lingering on her face another moment before he reached into his desk drawer and withdrew a small white business card. "I'll pick you up at five-thirty," he said, scrawling on the back of the card, then handing it to her. "In case you have any questions or need to cancel at the last minute, here are my home and cell phone numbers."

"Thank you," Daniela murmured, accepting the card. She glanced at her watch, and saw that it was already close to ten-thirty. If she didn't get moving, she'd be late for her next class. And yet, she wanted nothing more than to stay right where she was. She wanted to spend the rest of the day with Caleb, sequestered alone with him as if they were the only two souls in the world.

When she looked up again, she saw a softness in his eyes that made her wonder if he'd read her thoughts, or if he, too, felt the same way. Holding her gaze, he got slowly to his feet.

"Better not be late to class," he said quietly.

With a reluctant nod, she slid off the desk and

rounded the corner to retrieve her purse and half-empty bottled water from the floor. At the door to the office, she paused and turned around to face him. "Thanks again for looking out for me, Caleb. I can't tell you enough how much I appreciate it."

He inclined his head briefly. "I'll see you tomorrow evening, Daniela."

She mustered a winsome smile before opening the door and slipping out of the room. She was so preoccupied with thoughts of Caleb and the pending dinner date with his father that she scarcely noticed Shara Adler hovering in the doorway of an office across the hall, watching Daniela's departure with a look of cold calculation.

Daniela remained in a melancholy mood for the rest of the day, plagued by a guilty conscience that warned her what she was doing to Caleb Thorne was wrong, no matter what she told herself to the contrary. She'd entered his life under false pretenses, pretending to be someone she wasn't, pretending to have career aspirations she didn't possess. And although Caleb claimed his reasons for helping her had nothing to do with their personal involvement, Daniela knew better, which only compounded her guilt.

She wished Caleb were an ogre—a cold, ruthless monster she'd have no qualms about deceiving. She wished his eyes didn't glow with genuine pride when he spoke about his students and their commitment to a campus organization. She wished the sight of him didn't take her breath away, and the sound of his voice didn't do dangerous things to her heart rate. Heck, she even wished he was lousy in bed.

She wished for something, *anything,* that would make her duplicity more acceptable, less...reprehensible.

She was still brooding when she arrived at Roarke Investigations that evening. Since it was after hours, the reception area was empty, the venetian blinds were drawn closed and the phones were silent. As she started toward Kenneth's office, the sound of angry male voices caused her to frown and hurry to the doorway, where she discovered her brothers on their feet and squaring off across Kenneth's desk like two raging bulls.

"Leave it alone, Noah," Kenneth was saying tersely.

"I think she has a right to know," Noah growled.

Daniela crossed her arms and propped a shoulder against the doorjamb. "*Who* has a right to know *what?*" she calmly inquired.

Two pairs of dark eyes set in strikingly similar faces swung toward her. For a moment both men looked surprised to see her, and then Noah scowled and glanced away.

"Hey, sis." Kenneth greeted her in a strained voice. "What brings you to this neck of the woods tonight? Don't you have a lot of studying to do?"

Daniela pointedly ignored the diversionary tactic. "Am I interrupting something, fellas?" she asked, dividing a speculative look between the two men. "What were you arguing about?"

Noah remained silent, a muscle working at the edge of his jaw as he glared stonily at his older brother.

"Noah and I were having a little disagreement about the best way to handle one of our clients," Kenneth explained through clenched teeth. "It's nothing for you to worry about. Isn't that right, Noah?"

Instead of answering, Noah shook his head in disgust and started for the door, muttering under his breath, "I'm outta here."

"Noah, wait," Daniela said, reaching out to detain him with a gentle hand on his arm. She lifted her gaze to search his taut features, wondering what had angered him so much. "What is it, Noah? You can tell me."

"I already did," Kenneth said irately from behind his desk. "It doesn't concern you, El. Now let it go."

Daniela looked askance at Noah, and after another tense moment he inclined his head in the briefest of nods. "It's all right," he said in a low voice, but Daniela wasn't convinced. Worse still, she couldn't shake the feeling that the two brothers had been arguing about her, though she couldn't begin to fathom what may have led to the volatile confrontation she'd stumbled upon.

Kenneth and Noah Roarke had long ago outgrown their rumbling days, when they hadn't seen eye-to-eye on anything and had settled their disagreements by throwing punches at each other. As they grew older and matured, they'd reached a peaceful accord in their relationship, a bond that was solidified when Noah decided to follow his big brother into law enforcement. Although they had worked in different areas—areas that frequently clashed over bureaucratic matters—the Roarke brothers had remained fiercely loyal to each other, defying anyone who dared to criticize the other. When Kenneth decided to leave the police department in order to start his own private detective agency, Noah's loyalty to his brother had transcended his love for being a cop; within a few months he'd resigned from the force and partnered with Kenneth on the risky business venture.

Although the two men didn't always agree on everything—after all, their personalities were as opposite as night and day—they rarely ever argued, resolving their differences by diplomatically agreeing to disagree.

Which was why the scene she'd witnessed tonight set off a warning alarm in her brain. But, fortunately for Kenneth—who seemed especially determined to keep her in the dark—Daniela had bigger fish to fry at the moment.

"Could you hang out for a minute?" she gently appealed to Noah, who still had one foot out the door. "I need to run a couple of things past you and Kenny."

His expression softened, and this time it was he who ran a critical eye over her face. "Is everything okay?" he asked gruffly. Without waiting for an answer, he laid the back of his hand against her forehead. "Are you feeling all right?"

Daniela nodded, gesturing him into one of the chairs opposite the large mahogany desk. "I'm fine. I just need to call an impromptu staff meeting. Please, have a seat," she half ordered Kenneth, who was watching her with mounting curiosity.

By the time she sat down next to Noah, she had both of her brothers' undivided attention. She drew a deep breath, then blurted, "Caleb Thorne has offered me an opportunity to intern at his father's law firm."

Her announcement was met by stunned silence. The two men stared at her, then at each other, before Kenneth broke into a wide, satisfied grin.

"I'll be damned," he exclaimed, shooting his brother a triumphant look. "She works fast, doesn't she?"

"Apparently so," Noah murmured, quietly scrutinizing his sister's face. Daniela knew he was wondering how she'd pulled off such a feat, and in such a short amount of time. She had no intention whatsoever of telling him.

"Congratulations, El," Kenneth said, leaning back in his chair and clasping his hands behind his head. He looked almost as pleased as he had the day the twins were born; at any moment Daniela expected him to whip out a chilled bottle of champagne and begin making toasts.

"It's not a done deal yet," she said wryly. "I still have to be interviewed. By Crandall Thorne himself, if you can believe it."

"I can," Kenneth said briskly. "I've heard that he's involved in the hiring—and firing—of anyone who's ever worked for him. He's very protective of the firm, and he doesn't trust many people."

"Great," muttered Daniela. "He'll take one look at me and know I'm a fraud."

"I don't think so," Kenneth said. "You've got Caleb fooled, and I've heard *he's* even less trusting than his father."

Instead of reassuring her, this news only made Daniela feel even worse about her treachery. Because Caleb trusted so few people, he probably had greater expectations of those he permitted into his inner sanctum. If he ever learned the truth about Daniela, he would be furious. Although she hadn't witnessed the full magnitude of his temper, somehow she knew she didn't want to be on the receiving end of it.

"Don't worry about the interview with Thorne," Kenneth assured her. "Just be yourself, and you'll have him eating out of the palm of your hand."

Daniela's eyes narrowed suspiciously on her brother's

handsome face. "Was that a compliment you just gave me?"

Kenneth looked affronted. "You don't have to sound so surprised. I've been saying from the very beginning that you'd have no problem pulling off this assignment, and I was right. Here we are at week *two,* and you've already got Caleb Thorne pulling strings to get you a job at his old man's firm. It's like I said before. You're our secret weapon." He jabbed an accusing finger at Noah. "*He's* the one who didn't think you could handle going undercover."

"I never doubted Daniela's ability to pull off the assignment," Noah corrected, speaking for only the second time since Daniela's big announcement. "What I was concerned about was what she'd have to do in order to pull it off." He gave his sister a meaningful look.

She glanced away from his discerning gaze, afraid he'd read the truth in her eyes, as he so often did. With the exception of their mother, no one knew Daniela better than Noah Roarke.

"When is your interview with Thorne?" Kenneth asked, reaching for his Palm Pilot.

"Tomorrow evening," Daniela answered. "We're having dinner at his ranch."

Kenneth's head jerked up from the electronic device, where he'd been accessing the calendar. Mouth half-open, he stared at Daniela across the width of the desk. "You're meeting at Thorne's *home?* Whose idea was that?"

"Caleb's."

Kenneth grinned. "This keeps getting better and better."

"Not necessarily," Daniela countered. "Even if I *do* land the internship, it's not like I'll have access to confidential records or financial ledgers. I seriously doubt that I'll uncover anything incriminating about Crandall Thorne while working as a lowly intern at his firm."

"That's because you're not thinking like a P.I.," Kenneth chided. "You have to be resourceful, Daniela. As an intern, you can be as obscure as a fly on the wall, which means you might see or overhear things others wouldn't, or be given assignments that would make you privy to sensitive information. You have to make the most of each and every opportunity that comes your way. At the same time, be prepared to create opportunities out of nothing. Think like a P.I."

"Yes, sir," Daniela said with a mock salute, though she knew everything her brother said was right. Any private investigator worth her salt would know how to capitalize on the prime opportunity she'd been given to infiltrate the enemy's camp and scout his artillery. For three years, Daniela had been imploring her brothers to take her more seriously by entrusting her with big cases. Now was her chance to prove herself, to show once and for all that she *did* have what it took to be an equal partner in the detective agency.

So why wasn't she excited?

You know why, her embattled conscience reminded her.

"Anyway, the most important thing is that you have a foot in the door," Kenneth said. "My guess is that it won't be long now before Caleb pours out his heart to you, giving you the information we need to nail his old man and collect the rest of our payment from Philbin."

Daniela bristled a little at her brother's cocksure

tone. "What if I don't learn anything incriminating from Caleb?" she challenged. "For that matter, what if there's nothing incriminating to learn? What if this is all one big wild-goose chase?"

Kenneth gave her a look that told her she should know better. "Hoyt Philbin is not the kind of man who forks over large sums of money for wild-goose chases. And we're all aware of how Crandall Thorne earned *his* fortune—by defending mobsters and corrupt labor union bosses who'd stop at nothing to keep from getting caught. We all know Thorne is guilty of *something*. It's our job to find out what." His deep voice softened to an urgent plea. "We're counting on you, Daniela. Don't lose sight of the goal—it's within your reach."

Daniela held up a hand. "All right, Kenneth. Enough with the lecturing. A lot's riding on my shoulders. I get it, okay?"

He chuckled, unfazed by her ire. "Just making sure we have an understanding. I'm trying to run a business here."

"Which reminds me," Daniela interjected dryly. "When are you guys planning to hire another secretary?"

Kenneth and Noah exchanged bemused glances. "I had to fire Carole this afternoon," Noah sullenly informed his sister. "The temp agency is sending someone over tomorrow."

"I have a better idea," said Daniela. "Why don't we hire Janie as our secretary?"

Kenneth frowned. "Janie who?"

"Janie Roarke. Your wife."

"What?"

"I think Janie could help us out tremendously,"

Daniela quickly forged ahead. "She's smart as a whip, efficient, superorganized. We all know she's more than qualified for the position—"

"Janie's not in the market for a job," Kenneth said through gritted teeth.

"Why not?" Daniela demanded.

"Because she already has a job—staying home and taking care of our children."

"Oh, come on, Kenny. We both know that the twins don't need Janie around half as much as they used to."

Kenneth scowled blackly. "Since when are *you* an expert on what my kids need? Last I checked, you were a single woman with zero children."

Daniela ignored the little dig. "Whether or not you're aware of it, Kenneth," she said with forced calm, "your wife desperately needs an outlet. If you don't believe me, just ask her how excited she was to take care of Mom when she was sick, simply because it gave her something productive to do with herself while the kids were in school."

A muscle ticked in Kenneth's tightly clenched jaw. "Did Janie put you up to this?"

"No," Daniela lied without batting an eye. Beside her, Noah fought to keep a grin off his face. "I've given this a lot of thought, and I think Janie could be the perfect solution to our secretarial problems. If you're worried about having to put KJ and Lourdes in after-care, I'm sure Janie's parents could pick them up from school and keep them until Janie gets off from work. They'd probably jump at the chance to spend more time with their grandchildren, since they're always complaining that they don't see the twins often enough. It's a win-win situation for everyone."

"Not necessarily," Kenneth said darkly. "My wife didn't earn an MBA from the Wharton School of Business to become a secretary—family business or not."

"With all due respect," Daniela murmured, "she's not exactly putting her MBA to good use now, is she?"

Kenneth's dark eyes flashed with anger, but he didn't disagree with her.

"I'm sure Janie doesn't care," Daniela pressed on, sensing victory, "but if it'll make you feel any better, we can change the job title from secretary to office manager, or executive assistant, or whatever you prefer." She looked to Noah for support. "Don't you think Janie would be perfect for us?"

Noah chuckled dryly. "Put it this way. I don't think Janie could do any worse than the secretaries we've had up until now."

Kenneth glared at him. "Are you crazy? My wife could run circles around those incompetent half-wits."

"Wonderful! Then it's all settled," Daniela declared, slapping the arm of her chair for emphasis and rising to her feet, deciding it was best to leave before her brother changed his mind about cooperating. "You can offer Janie the job tonight when you go home. And, by all means, please feel free to take credit for the idea when you speak to her."

Kenneth scowled. "I'm not taking credit for an idea I think is stupid."

Daniela paused in the doorway, her lips pursed thoughtfully. "Try to keep that opinion to yourself when you present the offer to Janie tonight," she suggested, her tone mild.

Subtle challenge flashed in the dark eyes that stared

back at her. "Are you giving me instructions on how to speak to my wife, Daniela?" Kenneth tersely inquired.

"Not quite," Daniela answered, choosing her words carefully. "But let me give you some food for thought, dear brother. If you try to talk Janie out of accepting the position, I might find a way—accidentally, of course—to tank the interview with Crandall Thorne tomorrow night. Oh, I'd try my best to make a good impression on the man, but you just never know what one might do in a pressure-cooker situation like that. I might chew with my mouth wide open, or give unintelligible answers to his questions, or make bad lawyer jokes, or—oh, I don't know—call him an unscrupulous pig to his face. *Accidentally,* of course."

Kenneth's expression darkened. "You wouldn't."

Daniela sighed dramatically. "Like I said, you just never know." She smiled sweetly at her eldest brother, who appeared more than ready to strangle her. "Be sure to tell Janie I said congratulations on the new job. Hopefully she can start as early as tomorrow. I'll let you two work out the logistics." She glanced down at her wristwatch, then tapped a manicured fingernail against the glass face. "If you fellas would kindly excuse me, I have a *ton* of reading to do."

With that she turned on her heel and walked out of the office. As she reached the empty reception area, she heard Noah's sudden bark of laughter. Daniela grinned, and strolled out of the building whistling cheerfully.

Chapter 14

For the remainder of the evening and throughout the following day, Daniela could think of little else but her pending dinner engagement with Crandall and Caleb Thorne. By 5:15 p.m., she had changed six times, going through one power suit after another, before finally settling on a straight black skirt and a plum-colored silk blouse with a scooped neckline that showed a modest amount of cleavage. After some deliberation, she piled her hair into a loose French twist and donned a pair of pearl teardrop earrings.

When she'd finished dressing, she surveyed her appearance in the mirror and nodded approvingly. She looked cool, sophisticated and professional, which was the effect she'd hoped to achieve. Although part of her had wanted to look sexy and alluring for Caleb, she also recognized the importance of making a positive first impression on his father and being taken seriously as a job applicant.

When her doorbell rang at five-thirty sharp, her heart leaped to her throat, and perspiration instantly dampened her palms. *Calm down,* she told herself, sliding her feet into a pair of tall, strappy heels that accentuated the sleek curve of her calves. *You're not going on a date. This is strictly a business meeting. A business meeting that happens to be at the home of one of the most powerful men in San Antonio, but a business meeting nonetheless.*

When she opened the door and saw Caleb standing there, her mouth went dry. He wore pleated black slacks with a stark white shirt opened at the strong column of his throat. In deference to the warm summer weather, he'd eschewed a jacket. With his hands tucked comfortably into his pockets, he looked incredibly handsome, virile and totally in control.

As his lazy gaze traveled the length of her, Daniela felt a surge of pleasure at the glint of male approval that lit his dark eyes.

"Good evening," he said huskily. "You look beautiful."

"Thank you," Daniela murmured, smiling. "You don't look too bad yourself, Professor Thorne."

He inclined his head in simple acknowledgment of the compliment. "Are you ready?"

She nodded, stepping onto the porch and locking the door behind her.

With a hand resting lightly at the small of her back, Caleb escorted her to the driveway, unlocking the doors to a gleaming black Jaguar as sleek and powerful as its owner.

Daniela ran an appreciative gaze over the luxury

vehicle and grinned. "Awesome ride, but where's the Harley?"

Caleb chuckled, glancing down at her slim-fitting skirt and the sheer black stockings that sheathed her long legs. "You're not exactly dressed for it," he said, repeating the same words he'd told her the day of their coffeehouse excursion.

Daniela laughed as he helped her inside the car, then rounded the gleaming fender to slide into the elegant, scooped leather seat beside her. She caught the clean scent of him, soap and the subtle spice of an expensive cologne that was undeniably male, and uniquely him.

She slanted him a teasing look as the V-6 engine purred to life. "I'm beginning to have my doubts about the existence of your motorcycle."

His mouth curved in a lazy white grin. "Yeah?"

Daniela nodded. "I think you carry the helmet to class to intimidate your students into believing you're a real bad-ass who'll fail them in a heartbeat if they step out of line."

Caleb threw back his head and laughed, a deep, rich sound that settled like a caress over her skin. As he pulled away from her house, he shook his head in mock chagrin. "When did I become so obvious?"

"You're not," Daniela assured him, enjoying the lighthearted banter so much that she nearly forgot to be nervous about meeting Crandall Thorne. "I'm just *that* good at reading people."

"Is that right?"

"Yep. It's a special gift."

"Mmm. Well," Caleb huskily intoned, sliding her a heavy-lidded look that made her pulse quicken, "you're a woman of many talents, Daniela Moreau."

Daniela didn't miss the veiled reference to their love-making, specifically in relation to the brazen ways in which she'd teased and pleasured him that night. She turned her face toward the window to hide the wanton smile that curved her lips.

"Are you in the mood for Boney?"

With a choked laugh, Daniela whipped her head around to stare at him. "Excuse me?" She couldn't have heard right. Had he just asked her if she was in the mood for *boning?*

"Jazz music," Caleb explained, poised to slide a compact disc into the elaborate player. "Do you like Boney James?"

"Oh! Yes, of course."

Caleb inserted the disc, then slanted her an amused sidelong glance. "What did you think I said?"

Daniela shook her head, covering her mouth with one hand to smother an embarrassed giggle. "Nothing. Nothing at all."

His mouth twitched, but he let her off the hook. Soon the first bluesy notes of a saxophone poured into the luxurious interior of the Jaguar, washing over them. Daniela crossed her legs and settled more comfortably into the butter-soft leather seat, feeling utterly relaxed and content.

"So you own a Jaguar, a Durango and a Harley?" she asked.

He grinned ruefully. "When I worked at my father's law firm, I needed ways to spend all the money I was earning—and the faster, the better. Buying vehicles seemed to do the trick."

"I'll bet," Daniela agreed.

As they passed block after block of elegant Victorians cradled by columned wraparound porches and neat manicured lawns, Caleb asked, "How long have you lived in the King William District?"

"A little over three years," Daniela answered.

"Do you like it?"

"I *love* it. The rich history, the quaint charm of the little shops and restaurants. And everything is within easy walking distance." A soft, reminiscent smile touched her lips. "I've wanted to live here ever since I was a teenager, and my mother took us to our very first art exhibit at the Blue Star. I remember having to park a few blocks away from the gallery because the lot was full, and as we walked past these amazing Victorian houses, I remember wishing I lived in one of them. I think that's when my affinity for all-things-antique was born." She sighed deeply. "Perhaps someday, after I've retired from...*whatever,* I'll open my own antiques store. I think I'd like that very much."

Caleb watched her as she spoke, his gaze almost tender. "Sounds like a great way to enjoy your retirement," he agreed. "If you're in the area, I'll be sure to drop in and buy a few things from you."

Daniela laughed. "You'd better!" Sobering after a moment, she studied his handsome profile with keen interest. "So what about you, Caleb? What are your retirement plans?"

He sent her a lopsided grin. "Who says I ever plan to retire? I may decide to teach until I've got one foot in the grave."

Grinning wryly, Daniela shook her head at him. "Even then, your female students would *still* swoon whenever you walked into the classroom."

He chuckled, the sound so warm her stomach began to melt. "I wouldn't go that far."

"*I* would."

Smiling, he glanced over at her. "All joking aside, to answer your question, I have been giving serious thought to life on a ranch after retirement."

"Really? You mean as a cattle rancher?"

"Sure. I enjoy working on my father's land, more than I ever thought I would, in fact. I could easily see myself settling into the quiet, simple life of a rancher, getting away from the hurried pace of the city and waking up to golden sunrises every morning."

"Mmm," Daniela murmured, closing her eyes on a deep, languid sigh at the vivid image his words painted. "That sounds heavenly, Caleb."

"I'm glad you think so," he said, and something in the deep rumble of his voice told her he really meant it.

She opened her eyes to look at him. "Speaking of your father's ranch, how far is it from here?"

"We've got another forty-five minutes," he replied, meeting her inquisitive gaze. A half smile quirked the corners of his mouth. "Are you in a hurry to get there?"

She chuckled dryly. "If you knew how nervous I am about meeting your father tonight, you'd know better."

"Don't be nervous," Caleb told her. "My father's bark is much worse than his bite."

Daniela eyed him suspiciously. "Do you really mean that, or are you just saying that to make me feel better?"

He cut her a sideways glance. "What did I tell you in my office yesterday?"

She gave a low, sultry laugh. "You said quite a few things yesterday," she drawled. "Shall I repeat them all?"

Caleb cleared his throat, his lips twitching. "What I told you is that I never say things I don't mean. If I tell you not to be nervous about meeting my father, then take my word for it."

"All right," Daniela conceded with exaggerated reluctance, "but if you're wrong, it's going to be a *long* ride back for you, buddy."

He merely grinned at the threat.

Soon the Jag was cruising out of the city and through rolling pasture land surrounded by steep, looming hills blanketed in the deep green of pine forests. With at least two more hours of daylight left, the sun remained high on the horizon—a vibrant, glowing orb.

For the next forty-five minutes, Caleb and Daniela talked, about anything and everything. They swapped tales about growing up in San Antonio, and discovered commonalities ranging from favorite foods to places they'd frequented as teenagers. As they laughed and conversed, their roles as teacher and student ceased to exist, nor did their eight-year age difference matter. They were simply two people enjoying each other's company as they became better acquainted. If there was any way Daniela could have extended the length of their trip to the ranch, buying herself more time alone with Caleb, she would have—in a heartbeat.

And that should have scared her.

Eventually the road narrowed into two twisting lanes that wound through the foothills of the mountain range. Caleb negotiated the steep curves with the skilled ease of someone who could drive the route in his sleep.

"We're almost there," he told Daniela.

She nodded, anxiety knotting in her stomach. But as she turned her head and stared out the window, nerves were all but forgotten as her attention was captured by the natural beauty of their surroundings. Perched high on a bluff before them was a rambling hacienda-style ranch house and several smaller outbuildings, and below that lay the valley, lush and green like a rumpled velvet blanket against the backdrop of rugged mountains that rose from the earth like proud, silent sentinels.

"Oh, Caleb..." Daniela breathed, soaking in the wondrous sight before her. "Your retirement plan just received my ringing endorsement."

He chuckled softly. "It has that effect, doesn't it?"

She nodded vigorously. "How long has your father lived here?"

"He bought the ranch as an investment property twenty years ago. He only began using it as his primary residence earlier this year, after he got sick." As Caleb spoke, he steered the car uphill, past several barns and outbuildings and a large roping arena, where a few ranch hands lingered, herding cattle into a holding pen and tending to other tasks that required completion before the day's end. The men, their faces covered in sweat and grime beneath the brim of dusty Stetsons, grinned and called greetings to Caleb when they spied the Jaguar. Caleb waved in response and continued up the road until they reached the main house, where he parked in one of the three detached garages.

As he cut off the ignition, the butterflies in Daniela's stomach returned. She was seized with the terrible fear that Crandall Thorne would take one look at her, see her for the fraud that she was and have her unceremoniously escorted from his property. But that wasn't even the worst part of it. The worst part was that Caleb would never speak to her again—except, maybe, to tell her what an indescribably horrible human being she was.

As if sensing her apprehension, Caleb reached over and gently cupped her cheek in his big, warm hand. "It's going to be okay," he said quietly. "Just be yourself."

Daniela felt a fresh stab of guilt. *Just be yourself.* Hadn't Kenneth told her the very same thing yesterday? What a cruel joke.

Swallowing hard, she forced a nod. "I'll be fine."

Caleb smiled, then climbed out of the car and walked around to open her door and help her out. He put his hand on her back, a warm, light pressure that guided her toward the sprawling two-story ranch house with a red-tiled Spanish roof and a wide, curving porch. They had barely reached the front door before it was swung open by a tall, handsome woman wearing a red cotton sundress with a matching belt cinched around her broad waist.

She beamed a welcoming smile at them. "It's about time you two made it!" she exclaimed in warm, lilting tones that hinted at a Southern accent.

With a lazy grin, Caleb leaned down slightly to plant a kiss upon the woman's upturned cheek, which was the color of dark caramel and looked just as smooth. "Evening, Ms. Rita," Caleb drawled with unmistakable affection in his voice. "You're looking pretty as a picture. Is that a new dress?"

The woman's smile widened with pleasure as she glanced down at herself. "What, this old thing? Shoot, no. It's just something I pulled out from the back of the closet for the special occasion."

Before Daniela could wonder what special occasion she referred to, the woman's dark gaze, alight with avid curiosity, landed on her. "This must be the young lady your father has been expecting."

"Yes, ma'am." Caleb turned to Daniela at his side, his hand returning to the small of her back in a gentle, subtly possessive manner she found rather pleasing. "Ms. Rita, I'd like for you to meet Daniela Moreau. Daniela, this is Rita Owens—the only woman on earth patient enough to have put up with my father for thirty years and counting."

Grinning and wagging her head at Caleb's introduction, the woman clasped Daniela's hand in the solid warmth of her own. "It's wonderful to meet you, Daniela. Welcome to our home."

Daniela smiled. "Thank you, Ms. Owens. I'm glad to be here."

"Come in, come in," Rita urged, opening the door wider to usher them inside the cool interior of the house. The wide foyer spilled into a large living area that boasted the finest in contemporary furnishings, and tall glass windows that soared to cathedral ceilings. Custom ceramic-tile floors gleamed beneath their feet as they followed Rita Owens down a wide hallway with archways on both sides that opened into several spacious rooms, each showcasing the handiwork of a very talented, and doubtless expensive, interior designer.

"Your father asked me to show you to the study when you arrive," Rita told Caleb, and he gave a brief nod, his hand never leaving Daniela's back. She felt the warmth of his touch through her silk blouse, infusing her with the strength and courage she needed to get through the evening.

At the end of the hallway, Rita stopped at a door that had been left slightly ajar. Without bothering to knock, she ushered Caleb and Daniela into the room. It was a large, richly appointed library that featured a twenty-foot ceiling and mahogany-paneled walls that contained rows and rows of books, the upper tiers accessible by a pair of tall ladders on wheels. The mingled odors of leather, ink and freshly polished wood scented the air.

Behind the carved mahogany island of a desk sat Crandall Thorne, a man who'd graced countless magazine covers and been at the center of more controversial court cases than Daniela could recall. His leather chair was angled away from the desk, one elbow propped on the gleaming surface as he pored through a sheaf of documents on his lap. Upon their entrance, he glanced over, then slowly set aside his paperwork.

"Your guests have arrived," Rita told him, unnecessarily.

"Yes, I can see that," Crandall Thorne said in a deep, gravelly voice that resonated with authority. Behind a pair of wireless reading glasses perched on the bridge of his strong nose, eyes the color of bittersweet chocolate unerringly homed in on Daniela's face. "You must be the young woman my son's been raving about."

Taken aback, Daniela threw Caleb a surprised look. "You have?"

His mouth twitched with faint humor. "I may have mentioned one or two complimentary things."

She felt an impish grin tugging at the corners of her lips. "Such as?"

His gaze roamed across her face. "If I wanted you to know," he drawled, an amused glint in his dark eyes, "obviously I would have told you already."

"Of course," she teased. *"Obviously."*

Crandall Thorne discreetly cleared his throat, and Daniela swung her gaze around, embarrassed at how easily she'd forgotten that she and Caleb were not alone in the room. She stepped forward, her hand outstretched. "Daniela Moreau," she introduced herself with a courteous smile. "It's a pleasure to meet you, Mr. Thorne."

As Crandall rose smoothly to his feet, Daniela realized that Caleb had inherited more than his father's dark good looks. Wearing a crisp white shirt over impeccably tailored gabardine trousers, Crandall Thorne exuded the confidence and charisma of a man who knew who he was, and knew how to get what he wanted—an innate quality his son also possessed, which made him impossible to resist.

Crandall's large, elegant hand swallowed Daniela's in a firm handshake. "The pleasure is all mine, Miss Moreau. Please have a seat," he said, indicating one of the oxblood leather chairs opposite his desk.

Daniela murmured her gratitude as Caleb pulled out the chair for her. But instead of claiming the other seat, he wandered over to a pair of French doors that overlooked a small courtyard, the stucco walls covered with a network of vines that were lush and green this time of year. As Daniela watched him, he leaned a negligent shoulder against the wall and stuffed his hands deep into his pants pockets, looking as if he had not a care in the world.

"I'm going to check on dinner," Rita announced before slipping out of the room and closing the door quietly behind her.

Crandall's dark, assessing gaze settled on Daniela. "My son tells me you're interested in doing an internship at my law firm."

"That's correct," said Daniela, pleased by how steady

her voice sounded. "I think it would give me a wonderful opportunity to explore how the legal system works, not to mention the tremendous opportunity to learn from some of the finest criminal defense attorneys in San Antonio."

Crandall inclined his head toward Caleb, whose back remained to them. "You're already learning from *the* best criminal defense attorney in San Antonio. Did you know that?"

Daniela smiled a little. "Yes, I did. He's pretty amazing in the classroom, as well."

"That doesn't surprise me," Crandall said gruffly. "My son excels at everything he does. Always has."

Caleb sent a bemused glance at them over his shoulder. "I thought we were here to discuss Miss Moreau," he said dryly.

Daniela and his father exchanged amused looks. "Speaking of the classroom," Crandall said, leaning back in his chair as he removed his eyeglasses, "I understand this is only your first semester of law school. What makes you think you're ready for an internship so soon?"

"I'm *not* sure," Daniela admitted, and saw a flicker of surprise in his eyes at her candid response. "My background was in accounting, so the field of law is pretty new to me. The truth is that if I were to intern at your firm, I would definitely get more out of the deal than you would. But what I may lack in experience, I more than make up for in a strong work ethic, proven initiative and a willingness to learn and be challenged. I guarantee you that being a first-year law student will not hinder me from successfully accomplishing whatever's required of me."

Crandall passed a slow, appraising gaze over her face. "I'm impressed by your tenacity, Miss Moreau, and I'm not easily impressed." His eyes narrowed thoughtfully on hers. "What do you think about the indictment of Carlito Olivares?"

Daniela paused, remembering Caleb's reaction to the news, and the speculation that Crandall Thorne would represent the corrupt labor union boss who'd been charged with embezzling funds from his union. Realizing that Olivares might already be a client of the man who now sat across from her, Daniela still opted for honesty. "I think Olivares's actions are deplorable," she said with unflinching conviction. "However, I realize, and appreciate, that the burden of proof rests with the state. If I were Olivares's attorney, it would be my duty to ensure that he receives the best legal representation possible."

Crandall arched a dubious brow. "You think it's that cut-and-dried?"

"Probably not. Few things in life are. But if I had to represent Olivares, my main priority *would* be to give him fair legal counsel."

"Ah, but how would you manage that, when your conscience is telling you that your client's actions are, as you put it, deplorable? How would you set aside your personal bias in order to best serve him?"

Daniela gave him her most charming smile. "I guess I'll have to cross that bridge when I'm an attorney working for Crandall Thorne & Associates," she said affably.

Unable to resist the audacity of her remark, Crandall threw back his head and roared with laughter. Caleb glanced over his shoulder and met Daniela's eyes, his own expression vaguely amused.

The door opened, and Rita stepped into the room.

"Gloria sent me to tell you all that dinner..." Trailing off at the sight of Crandall's broadly grinning face, she looked askance at Caleb, who merely shrugged.

"Dinner is ready," Rita informed them. "And Gloria says you all had better come now, before the food gets cold."

They dined outdoors on a balconied terrace that boasted a stunning view of the endless stretch of valley beneath them. Everything was perfect—from the pressed white linen that covered the table, to the fresh-cut flowers in crystal vases that perfumed the air with their sweet fragrance. Soon after the foursome was seated, they were joined by Crandall Thorne's private nurse, Ruth Gaylord, a beautiful woman in her late fifties whose gentle brown eyes and warm, engaging smile immediately put Daniela at ease.

Dinner, courtesy of Crandall's longtime personal chef, was a sumptuous culinary affair that opened with steaming crab bisque, and was followed by roast duck in a rich wine sauce and succulent Alaskan salmon that melted in Daniela's mouth from the first bite.

"So, Daniela, are you originally from San Antonio?" Ruth Gaylord inquired when the meal was underway.

Daniela nodded, taking a slow, appreciative sip of vintage Bordeaux. "I was born and raised here," she answered.

"You went to school here, as well?"

Again Daniela nodded. "I attended Trinity University."

"Trinity's a good private school," Crandall pronounced from his position at the head of the table, "but you probably would have fared better at UT-Austin, which is where Caleb went as an undergrad and for law school. Can't beat a UT education."

Seated directly across the table from her, Caleb sent Daniela a rueful smile that apologized for his father's high-handedness. She smiled back to let him know it was okay.

"Seems to me that Daniela fared just fine at Trinity," Rita spoke up on her behalf. She reached over and gave Daniela a gentle, comforting pat on the hand. "By the way, you have the most beautiful name. I thought so the moment I heard it. Quite honestly, though, I've never met an African-American woman named Daniela. It's a Hispanic name, isn't it?"

"For the most part," Daniela concurred. "But I was christened after my maternal great-great-grandmother."

"Was she Hispanic?" Rita prodded curiously.

Daniela shook her head. "Cherokee Indian."

"How interesting," said Rita, sounding genuinely fascinated. "Does your family still live in San Antonio?"

"Yes, they do."

"That's good. I think it's important for young women to stay near their kinfolk—helps keep you grounded. Nowadays, you see so many girls graduating from college and running off to big, noisy cities to pursue these stressful, high-powered careers. Nobody thinks about raising families anymore—until it's too late. And then they have to spend thousands of dollars on expensive fertility treatments because their biological clocks have stopped ticking." She clucked her tongue in patent disapproval. "It's a crying shame, I tell you."

"With all due respect, Rita," Ruth chimed in gently, "I think it's a bit unfair to place all the blame on the young women. I know there are plenty of women—my youngest daughter included—who *are* family-oriented and would love nothing more than to settle down and start having children. But the men they're dating aren't remotely interested in making such a commitment."

"Humph," Rita snorted. "That's because they're dating the wrong men."

Mildly exasperated, Ruth looked to Daniela for help. "Daniela, I'm sure you can attest to what I'm talking about."

Heat suffused Daniela's cheeks. "Um…well…"

"You two never know when to quit," Crandall objected from the end of the table. "Now you've gone and embarrassed the poor girl."

"It's all right," Daniela said quickly, all too aware of Caleb's quiet, watchful gaze. "I'm afraid Ruth is right, to a large extent. It *does* seem that many men go out of their way to avoid any sort of permanence in relationships."

"You're a smart, beautiful girl," Rita admonished, as if Daniela were speaking nonsense. "There's no reason you should have any problems finding Mr. Right."

"You'd be surprised," Daniela murmured, wondering if her face could possibly get any hotter than it already was.

Ruth slid a teasing look at Caleb, who had remained inconspicuously silent throughout the entire discussion thread. "Are we not sitting at a table with a confirmed bachelor?" she pointed out to Rita.

Rita guffawed. "Caleb's not a confirmed bachelor," she argued. "He's just waiting for the right woman to come along, and then you watch and see how long he stays single. Ain't that right, Caleb?"

The hushed silence that fell over the table was deafening. Silverware stilled, glasses stopped tinkling, even the eagles soaring above the surrounding treetops seemed to grow silent as all awaited Caleb's response. It was then that Daniela chanced a look at him.

With calm deliberation, he raised his wineglass and took a leisurely sip of Bordeaux before setting the glass down again. His deep voice was laced with lazy humor as he said to Rita, "Far be it from me to argue with the woman who used to nurse me through illnesses and covered for me whenever I got in trouble at school."

As laughter erupted around the table, Caleb's eyes met and held Daniela's for one heart-stopping moment. Crazy as it was, she felt as if he were silently communicating a message to her, though she couldn't begin to fathom what that message might be.

Only when his heated gaze slid away from hers did she dare breathe again.

"Wait a minute. What's this about you getting into trouble at school, boy?" Crandall gruffly demanded, and the conversation soon evolved into humorous anecdotes about Caleb's childhood exploits as a prankster who frequently got away with murder because his teachers, who were so enamored of him, seldom suspected him of any wrongdoing.

Daniela laughed, drank good wine and couldn't remember the last time she'd so thoroughly enjoyed herself. As the evening progressed, she found herself revisiting her previous opinion of Crandall Thorne. Observing the way he interacted with Caleb, he seemed less daunting, less austere, than she would have expected. He struck her as a man who was deeply devoted to his son, a proud, loving father who would do anything to protect him, just as Pamela Roarke would do for her own children. As Daniela watched Crandall tease Caleb, and get teased in return, she knew she was seeing a side of the shrewd, formidable businessman few people ever witnessed.

Was it possible Crandall Thorne wasn't as bad as she—and her brothers—had thought?

It was an unsettling prospect.

As the sun slid toward the mountain range, ushering in nightfall, candles were discreetly produced and lit along the table. After lingering over coffee and sinfully rich hazelnut cheesecake, the party began to break up. Crandall announced that he was tired; the four-hour dialysis treatment he'd undergone that day had taken its usual toll on him, he grudgingly admitted.

Bowing gallantly over Daniela's hand, he smiled at her. "It was a pleasure spending time with you this evening, Miss Moreau. I'll be in touch soon."

Daniela felt an immediate kick of guilt. "Thank you for inviting me into your beautiful home, Mr. Thorne," she said warmly. "I had a wonderful time, and I look forward to hearing from you again."

Shortly after Crandall departed, Ruth and Rita, offering vague excuses about needing to finish certain tasks before bedtime, wished Caleb and Daniela a good night and quickly retreated inside the house.

Before Daniela realized what had happened, she and Caleb were all alone.

Chapter 15

Gazing across the candlelit table at Caleb's darkly sensual face, Daniela was struck by a sudden attack of shyness. "I guess you can take me home now," she said, hearing the reluctance in her own voice.

She hadn't fooled Caleb, either. One corner of his mouth curved upward. "You don't want to go home yet," he told her, his voice like the stroke of velvet on her skin.

Her belly quivered. "I don't?"

He shook his head, keeping her gaze trapped in the banked heat of his own. "At least not until you've watched the sunset. It's an amazing sight from here, one of those simple pleasures everyone should experience at some point in their lives."

Daniela chuckled softly, recognizing her own words to him. "Like coffee and ice cream?"

He smiled, slow and sexy. "Exactly."

As she watched, breath trapped in her throat, Caleb glided to his feet with an effortless flexing of his muscles and came around the table to claim the chair beside her. As he scooted closer to her, the sides of their shoulders and thighs brushed. Daniela trembled, sensation passing from one nerve to another like a flow of warm honey.

"I really had a great time tonight," she told him somewhat breathlessly. She felt like a shy virgin on her first date with the handsome star quarterback of the high school football team. Which was ridiculous, considering how intimate she and Caleb had already been with each other.

"Glad to hear it," Caleb murmured, his gaze searching hers in the approaching dusk. "Did you mean what you said earlier, about men going out of their way to avoid commitment? Has that been your personal experience?"

Daniela laughed. "To be fair to your gender," she drawled, "it's not like I've ever met anyone I've seriously contemplated settling down with."

Until now, an inner voice whispered.

Shaken, she promptly shoved aside the dangerous thought.

"Are you seeing anyone right now, Daniela?" Caleb asked huskily.

She turned her head, and this time it was she who searched his face. "Does it matter?" she countered softly.

Something stirred in the fathomless depths of his eyes, an unnamed emotion that made her heart beat a wild tattoo in her chest. For several charged moments they stared at each other, and then Caleb glanced away, breaking the intimacy of their heated gaze.

"I tell myself it shouldn't matter," he quietly admitted, gazing out into the distance. "You're one of my students—"

"I'm twenty-seven years old, Caleb," Daniela reminded him. "Hardly a child."

A muscle bunched in his jaw. "That's not the point. The point is that there are certain standards, a code of ethics established to govern our conduct with students, and I've broken each and every rule. That's not easy for me to swallow."

As Daniela studied his brooding profile in the lengthening shadows, she felt a twinge of sympathy. For the first time, it dawned on her that Shara Adler had lied to her about Caleb's past indiscretions with other students, in order to make Daniela jealous enough to back off. The man seated next to her was genuinely conflicted about crossing the line with her. He was *not* a womanizer, as she'd been led to think, but an honest, upstanding man made of flesh and blood who'd succumbed to temptation. The truth of that was so obvious Daniela wondered how on earth she'd ever believed otherwise.

Because you wanted to believe it. You wanted to latch on to something negative about him that would make you feel better about your own deceitfulness.

Shame flooded her at once, and the mellow mood she'd been in all evening began to dissipate.

Seeing her downcast expression, and mistaking the cause, Caleb reached over and gently took her chin between his thumb and forefinger, forcing her to meet his dark, piercing gaze. "That said," he intoned in a low, husky voice, "I enjoyed every last second of making love to you, Daniela. And if I had to do it all over again, I wouldn't change a thing, except to prolong our time together."

Daniela's heart soared, tears biting beneath her eyelids. "Oh, Caleb—"

He slanted his head over her mouth, capturing the rest of her words. He parted her lips with his and kissed her with a melting hunger, slowly exploring her mouth with his tongue in deep, sensuous strokes that sent a hard shiver through her.

"Caleb," she half moaned against his lips, "what about your family? Do they know...? Do you think they suspect that we're...?"

She felt the vibration of his low chuckle all the way down to her toes. He dragged his mouth from hers to kiss her lowered eyelids, then her temple, before drawing back slightly to smile into her eyes. "What do you think the mass exodus was about? They wanted to give us time alone."

Daniela grinned. "I figured as much. Oh, look!" she cried in sudden delight.

Caleb turned his head, and together they watched the sun sink behind the vast mountaintops, spreading vivid flames across the sky in a display that was nothing short of breathtaking.

Daniela sighed deeply. "I think I've died and gone to heaven."

Caleb smiled a little, gazing down at her. "Kinda feels that way, doesn't it?" he said in a soft tone that made Daniela wonder if he was talking about the sunset, or something else entirely. She looked at him, and as she watched the play of candlelight across his strong, beautifully sculpted features, her heart swelled painfully in her chest.

Dear God. She was falling in love with him.

Even as her mind offered a swift, vehement denial, she knew it was true. She was falling in love with Caleb, and there was not a single thing she could do about it. She couldn't tell him how she felt, nor could she stop herself from falling harder. Which was exactly what she was doing with each passing minute, hour and day that she spent with him—falling harder.

"Dance with me, Daniela."

The low, seductive timbre of Caleb's voice broke into her tortured musings. She blinked, and realized that he had risen from the chair and now stood over her, his hand outstretched to her.

She swallowed, staring up at him uncomprehendingly. "Dance? But...there's no music."

"A minor detail." His midnight-black eyes glinted with mirth and something else, something so profoundly intimate that Daniela's pulse accelerated, doing double time.

Drawing in an unsteady breath, she placed her trembling fingers in his hand, rose to her feet and allowed herself to be led away from the table, to a clearing on the flagstoned terrace. Holding her gaze, Caleb drew her slowly into the solid warmth of his arms.

As they began to sway together, falling into an easy rhythm that seemed instinctive, Daniela inquired dazedly, "What're we dancing to, Caleb?"

"Whatever you want, sweetheart," he murmured huskily, the tender endearment sending a wave of indescribable pleasure coursing through her. "How about 'One Heartbeat' by Smokey?"

"Smokey Robinson?"

"Yeah." Caleb hummed a bar from the familiar song

in her ear, his voice a deep, velvety caress along her nerve endings.

"Mmm, that works," Daniela all but purred. With a sigh of dreamy pleasure, she closed her eyes, curved her arms around his neck and rested her head on his shoulder. What could be more romantic, she thought, than slow dancing on a secluded hillside summit against the backdrop of a breathtakingly glorious sunset? It was perfect as nothing else in her life had ever been, their bodies moving in perfect harmony as if they had danced together a million times before. She was intensely aware of his body against hers as they swayed together, keeping to the beat of a romantic ballad heard only in their own minds. Every sinewy muscle that defined the hard wall of his chest, the length of his muscular thighs against hers, the gentle brush of his fingers across her cheek. Her breasts felt incredibly heavy against him, aching for his touch. She wanted to curl into him, press herself fully against him—so she did.

Caleb groaned softly into her hair. One strong hand slid up her back to close lightly over the nape of her neck, and the other moved down to gently grasp her bottom through the snug fabric of her skirt. She gasped a little.

He tilted her head back, his hand firm on her neck. She breathed deeply, her eyes half-closed, watching him through the thick fringe of her eyelashes. She saw the sensuous curve of his mouth, and then he was kissing her, a slow, drugging kiss that made her feel deliciously boneless. His hand gently kneaded her bottom, dragging her closer until she felt the undeniable proof of his arousal. An answering need swept through her like wildfire.

He shoved his fingers through the sides of her hair, working at the French twist until the pins loosened and popped free, scattering across the ground. Caleb emitted a low, satisfied groan as her hair tumbled freely to her shoulders.

"I've wanted to do this all night," he uttered raggedly. He sank his hands deep into the curly, silken mass and seized her lips in another hot, soul-stealing kiss. Daniela kissed him back just as greedily, absorbing the heat and flavor of his mouth, running her hands up and down the corded muscles of his back, wanting him more than anything she'd ever wanted in her life. It scared her senseless.

"It's getting late," she whispered shakily when Caleb finally lifted his head from hers. "We should probably start heading back."

Before I lose my mind completely and beg you to take me right here and right now, and God help us if your family is watching!

Caleb must have had the same thought, for she could have sworn she saw his pupils dilate in the candlelit gloom. His mouth curved upward in a slow, wolfish grin that made her breath catch, it was so darned potent.

"You're right," he murmured silkily. "I'd better take you home now...while I still can."

"How'd the interview go with Crandall Thorne?" Janie Roarke inquired the next afternoon when she met Daniela for lunch at the Espuma Coffee and Tea Emporium located in the King William District, less than a ten-minute walk from Daniela's house. The quaint little café had been converted from an old house and featured cozy, well-lit rooms decorated with the works of local artists.

Daniela took a sip of her iced Vietnamese coffee, a signature menu item at the Espuma. "The interview, if you can call it that, went well."

Janie eyed her curiously. "What do you mean, 'if you can call it that'?"

"Well, the actual interview itself lasted about five minutes. He asked me a few questions, and then it was time for dinner. For dinner we were joined by Crandall Thorne's housekeeper, private nurse and, of course, Caleb, so there was really no opportunity for Crandall to continue the interview."

"Hmm," Janie murmured, nodding slowly. "Interesting."

Daniela could see the wheels spinning in her sister-in-law's mind. "What are you thinking?"

"Really want to know?" At Daniela's exasperated look, Janie grinned. "Okay, here's what I think. I think the interview was less about ascertaining your qualifications as an intern, and more about determining your potential as a future daughter-in-law."

"What?" At the loud exclamation, curious heads swung in her direction. Daniela gave the other diners a sheepish look, then returned her attention to Janie. "What are you talking about?" she demanded, keeping her voice low.

Janie's grin widened. "Think about it, El. How often would you guess Caleb Thorne takes his first-year law students home to meet his father?"

Daniela frowned, remembering the conclusion she'd reached about Caleb's nonexistent affairs with his students. "Probably not very often," she admitted.

"I'd venture to say he's *never* brought home a student. So you can imagine Crandall Thorne's surprise when, barely two weeks into the semester, Caleb comes to him with information about a student who should be considered for an internship at the firm. A *first-year* student, mind you, without a law background and no legal experience whatsoever. Now tell me. What do *you* think went through Crandall Thorne's mind?"

"That his son believes I'm exceptionally brilliant?" Daniela suggested, but without much conviction.

Janie chuckled. "While that may be true," she said wryly, "somehow I don't believe that's the case here. I think by the time Caleb finished telling his father all about you, Crandall realized that you must be pretty special to his son, special enough to bring home for an introduction."

Daniela grew silent, recalling the first words out of Crandall Thorne's mouth when he met her. *You must be the young woman my son's been raving about.*

Had Caleb really raved about her? She felt a thrill of pleasure at the thought.

Janie was watching her, a speculative gleam in her dark eyes. "Which makes me wonder... Exactly *how* close have you and Caleb gotten?"

Heat crawled up Daniela's neck. In the time it took her to drop her gaze and become absorbed in an examination of her half-eaten vegetable pita, Janie's eyes widened in shock. "*¡Ay dios!* Have you slept with him?"

"Must you be so loud?" Daniela hissed, throwing a self-conscious glance around the busy restaurant. Thankfully, no curious gazes met hers this time—although she did notice more than a few averted grins.

She scowled at her amused lunch companion. "Thanks for broadcasting my personal business to a roomful of complete strangers."

Mischief glimmered in Janie's dark eyes. "When were you going to tell me about you and Mr. Sexy Law Professor?"

"I don't know... Never, maybe?"

Janie laughed. "Oh, come on, El. I'm an old married woman. You know I have to live vicariously through you. Not that Kenny and I aren't—"

Grimacing, Daniela held up a hand. "Please. I don't even *want* to think about what you and my brother are, or *aren't*, doing behind closed doors." She shuddered at the thought, drawing another laugh from Janie.

"All right, out with it, Daniela. When did you and Professor Thorne begin your private tutoring sessions?"

Daniela was no recently deflowered virgin, but she suddenly felt like one as she reluctantly met Janie's gaze across the table. "He showed up unexpectedly at my house on Monday evening," she began.

"Seriously?"

Daniela nodded. "He wanted to know why I'd missed class that day. I told him I had the flu, invited him inside and..."

"And?" Janie prompted, leaning forward in her chair with an expression of rapt absorption.

Knowing that her sister-in-law would settle for nothing less than a detailed account, Daniela found herself telling Janie everything about the night she and Caleb made love. By the time she'd finished, nearly an hour later, Janie was smiling from ear to ear.

"Wow," she murmured, staring at Daniela. "Sounds pretty amazing."

"It was," Daniela agreed, somewhat wistfully. "*He's* amazing."

Janie grinned. "Clearly."

Daniela flushed. "I don't just mean in the bedroom. He's amazing in the classroom, the way he effortlessly commands the attention of his students, even the slackers. The passion in his voice is there when he talks about the law, and civil procedure, in a way that lets you know teaching is not just a job to him. He can be stern and intimidating one moment, unbelievably sweet and funny the next. And he has this intense way of zeroing in on my face whenever I'm talking, and making me feel as if what I'm saying is ultra-important to him."

"That's probably because it is," Janie observed with a gentle smile. "Sounds to me like Caleb Thorne is pretty crazy about you, El."

Her words filled Daniela with a mixture of pleasure and despair, two emotions she'd been vacillating between since last night, when she'd made the difficult decision not to invite Caleb into her home. After their incredibly romantic slow dance under the stars, followed by a sexually charged ride back to her house in which they held hands and shared heated looks, Daniela had wanted nothing more than to finish what they'd started at the ranch. But she'd turned him away, telling him that they needed to slow things down. It was one of the hardest things she'd ever had to do in her life. But it had been necessary.

If she was to make things right between them, she had to begin the process of letting him go. Because once he learned the truth about her, there'd be no gradual weaning. She'd have to go cold turkey without him.

Caleb, hurt and enraged, would give her no other option.

"Something tells me," Janie said, watching Daniela carefully, "that Caleb's feelings aren't one-sided."

Daniela hesitated, then shook her head with a deep, heavy sigh. "No, they're not." She paused, swallowing past the lump in her throat before quietly confessing, "I'm in love with him, Janie."

"Oh, honey..." The gentle compassion in Janie's gaze nearly brought Daniela to tears. "What are you going to do?"

"What else *can* I do? I have to tell him the truth."

"What about the investigation?"

"I don't know," Daniela said miserably. "I'm not even so sure that Crandall Thorne is guilty of anything other than making really bad decisions in his choice of clientele. And even if he *is* shady, who says it's my place to prove it? Hoyt Philbin? For all we know, Philbin may have one or two skeletons in his own closet!"

"Don't say that too loudly," Janie said grimly. "In this town, Hoyt Philbin can do no wrong. There's a reason most people wanted him to run for another mayoral term, even though he wasn't eligible."

"I know, I know," Daniela mumbled. "Kenny thinks the man walks on water because of all the good things he did for the city, and for African-Americans, while he was in office."

"His record does speak for itself," Janie pointed out. "And the fact that he's married to an African-American woman scores big points with the black folks in this city."

"I know. But the point is, Philbin obviously has an ax to grind with Crandall Thorne, and none of us really know the whole story, or his true motivation for wanting to bring Thorne down." She shook her head wistfully. "I'm such a fool for getting myself into this, for not anticipating the possibility that...that..." She couldn't even bring herself to utter the heartrending words again. Janie knew.

"I can't keep deceiving Caleb like this," Daniela finished, her voice husky with emotion.

Janie nodded sympathetically. "Talk to Noah first," she suggested. "He'll understand, and he may be able to come up with some ideas that might help you. Don't forget your exit strategy."

Of course, Daniela thought bitterly. *How could I forget my exit strategy?* According to the original plan devised by her brothers, after getting the goods on Crandall Thorne, she was supposed to "conveniently" withdraw from law school and quietly disappear from Caleb's life. If anyone asked, she was to say that she'd had a change of heart about pursuing a law degree, and leave it at that.

It had all seemed so plausible in the beginning, so straightforward and easy.

Now the idea of walking out of Caleb's life sent unimaginable pain knifing through her heart.

Janie glanced at her watch and frowned. "I have to pick up the twins from school," she murmured regretfully to Daniela. She signaled the waiter for the check, and a moment later he bustled over to drop the bill onto their table.

As Daniela reached inside her purse for money, Janie said quickly, "Don't worry about it. Lunch is on me."

Daniela gave her a wan smile. "You don't have to buy me lunch because you feel sorry for me."

"Of course I do. But that's not the reason I'm buying." Her eyes glowed with warmth. "Kenny told me you talked him into offering me the secretary position. I owe you big time, El."

Daniela waved off the gratitude. "Don't mention it. Remember, you're doing *us* a favor, as well. You're rescuing us from the incompetence of people who have no business calling themselves administrative professionals."

Janie chuckled, settling the bill and rising from her chair. "And *you're* helping me save my marriage. If there's ever anything I can do for you, Daniela, just name it."

Unless Janie possessed the ability to turn back the hand of time, Daniela doubted there was much anyone could do to help her out of the mess she'd made of her life.

Chapter 16

Later that night, Daniela was awakened from a fitful sleep by the ringing of the doorbell. Groaning, she rolled over in bed and squinted at the clock on her nightstand, frowning when she saw that it was ten o'clock. She'd gone to bed early to escape the beginnings of a stress-induced migraine, and had only just drifted off to sleep.

As she flung back the covers and padded barefoot into the closet for her robe, she wondered if her mother had decided to return home a day early. But Pamela Roarke would have her own key, so it couldn't be her. The only other possibility was that Kenneth had taken it upon himself to pay Daniela a visit in order to find out how dinner had gone at Crandall Thorne's ranch. He'd been trying to reach Daniela on her cell phone all day, and she'd purposefully ignored his calls, not ready to share with him the momentous decision she'd made about her role in the undercover investigation. She knew he would go ballistic, and would do everything in his power to talk, or bully, her out of it.

That's not going to happen, she muttered under her breath as she neared the front door, angrily tugging her robe together. If Kenneth Roarke wanted a fight, she'd damned well give him one.

By the time she swung open the door, the hostile challenge was on the tip of her tongue. "I swear to God, Kenny—"

But it was not her older brother who stood on the doorstep, a bemused expression on his face. Daniela's heart slammed against her rib cage at the sight of Caleb, looking ruggedly appealing in low-rise blue jeans, a white T-shirt and well-worn brown leather cowboy boots. "Caleb?" she whispered in disbelief.

"This time I don't have to ask if you were expecting someone else," he said sardonically. "Who's Kenny?"

"My brother," she answered, too stunned to take umbrage at his possessive tone.

He frowned. "I thought your brother's name was Noah."

"I have two, remember?" She searched his handsome face in the warm, buttery glow of the porch light. "What are you doing here, Caleb?"

"I came to give you a ride."

Heat stung her cheeks at the low, silky timbre of his voice. "I thought I said—"

"Not *that* kind of ride." Mouth twitching, Caleb looked pointedly over his shoulder, and standing on tiptoe, Daniela followed the direction of his gaze. Her eyes widened at the sight of a black-and-silver Harley-Davidson parked at the curb in front of her house.

"Is that yours?" she asked in a voice tinged with awe.

He nodded, a half grin curving his mouth. "I couldn't have you doubting the existence of my Harley, now could I?"

Daniela couldn't suppress the delighted laughter that bubbled up from her throat.

Caleb gazed down at her. "Take a ride with me, Daniela," he coaxed huskily.

Her mouth went dry. *"Now?* It's after ten o'clock."

"Which means the night is still young."

He was right, of course, but she knew better than to accept his dangerous invitation. She'd be playing with fire, plunging herself into deeper trouble than she was already in. And yet, she wanted nothing more than to be with him, knowing tonight would probably be her last opportunity. After tonight, there would be no more Caleb, no more nerve-racking classroom debates, no more laughter and loving. As she contemplated the bleak days, weeks and months that lay ahead of her, she told herself she deserved this one night, this final taste of bliss.

She smiled up at Caleb. "Give me five minutes to throw on some clothes."

His gaze darkened as it traveled the length of her body, as if he had X-ray vision that enabled him to see through the chenille fabric of her robe. "By all means," he murmured, a wolfish gleam in his eyes that made her pulse quicken.

She gestured him inside the house, then pivoted on her heel and headed quickly for her bedroom. As she hurriedly dressed, she felt like a giddy teenager sneaking out after curfew with the irresistible bad boy from school.

She called out, "Where are we going, by the way?"

"Just for a ride. Dress comfortably."

Five minutes later, she emerged wearing a short-sleeved red shirt and her favorite pair of blue jeans over ankle-length leather boots. She liked the way the stretch denim molded her legs and rode low on her hips, leaving her navel exposed.

So, apparently, did Caleb. He turned at her reappearance and swore softly under his breath. Concealing a pleased grin, Daniela grabbed her keys and stuffed her driver's license into the back pocket of her jeans so that she wouldn't have to carry her purse.

As they left the house and started across the front yard, Daniela waved at her neighbor, Mrs. Flores, who was peeking at them from behind the lace curtains of her living room window across the street. Grinning, Caleb also waved to the old woman, then laughed in surprise when a pale, bony hand lifted slowly in greeting.

Daniela gaped at him. "I think she likes you!" she said accusingly.

Caleb chuckled. "Hey, what can I say?"

"No woman is immune," Daniela grumbled. "Not even paranoid, ninety-eight-year-old spinsters who live alone."

That drew another low laugh from Caleb. But as they reached the Harley parked at the curb, their attention was quickly diverted.

Hands braced on hips, Caleb eyed the shiny motorcycle with an appreciation that Daniela shared. "Ain't she a beauty? An XL 1200C Custom Sportster—from the one-hundredth anniversary series. Torque like you wouldn't believe." He ran one hand across the gleaming steel engine compartment. "Sweet."

Daniela had to agree, admiring the bike's sleek, classic lines and shiny two-tone finish. "*Very* sweet. I'm glad she really exists."

Caleb grinned, picking up one of the matching black-and-silver helmets and passing it to her. He watched as she donned the helmet before he put on the other one and nimbly straddled the motorcycle.

With mounting excitement, Daniela climbed onto the leather seat behind him and wrapped her arms around his broad torso. The powerful engine rumbled to life, grabbing her heart and making it pump hard and fast. She tightened her arms around Caleb until he laughed.

"Easy on the ribs, sweetheart. Don't worry, I won't let you fall."

She could barely hear him above the roar of the engine, but she knew she was in good hands. She trusted Caleb with her life—literally, it now seemed.

He pulled away from the curb and sped off down the quiet, tree-lined street, making it to the highway in record time. At that late hour there was very little traffic, and Caleb took full advantage, weaving easily between lanes. Daniela pressed her head against his back and reveled in the wind rushing through the uncovered ends of her hair, whipping it about their faces. The engine pounded relentlessly beneath them, a living being consisting of silver and chrome, pumping, throbbing, burning, until Daniela felt as if she were one with the bike. She nestled closer to Caleb, feeling as if they, too, were one.

The Harley boasted a four-speaker enhanced sound system, so that when Caleb cranked a Lenny Kravitz song, she felt every pulsing vibration of the electrical guitar and Lenny's raw rock lyrics in her bones. Caleb sang and bobbed his head in time with "Fly Away," and, laughing, Daniela joined him. She felt joyously weightless, as if she were made of nothing but air. Though she'd ridden a motorcycle before, she couldn't remember the ride being so utterly exhilarating, so liberating.

Caleb took them into the bright lights of downtown San Antonio, zipping past beautiful old Spanish colonial buildings, and billboards advertising various local restaurants and Spurs' season tickets. Before long, Daniela realized that their destination was either the Riverwalk—or Caleb's apartment. Her heart raced at the latter possibility.

He pulled into the parking garage connected to the Towers of the Majestic and parked in his assigned space. Killing the ignition, he pulled off his helmet and swung his long leg from the Harley with fluid ease.

Daniela waited as he turned and lifted her easily out of the seat, setting her gently on her feet. Grinning, she removed her helmet and shook her curly mane forward, then backward, like some model in a shampoo commercial.

Caleb stared at her. "Do that again."

"What? This?" She swung out her hair again, and he groaned softly.

"God, everything you do turns me on."

She felt a thrill of pleasure, thinking that the feeling was mutual.

He grasped her hand, and together they started across the parking garage until they came to the street exit, joining the flow of other people heading down to the Riverwalk in search of exciting nightlife. Daniela didn't know whether to be relieved or disappointed that they weren't going up to Caleb's apartment.

"We'll come back afterward," he said low in her ear, as if he'd read her mind. "I want you to see my place."

Daniela's belly flip-flopped. "I'd like that," she told him, meaning it.

They crossed the next intersection and descended a staircase leading down to the Riverwalk, a meandering stretch of water that shimmered under the starry sky. Lapsing into companionable silence, Caleb and Daniela strolled, hand in hand, past a promenade of riverside restaurants, clubs, bistros and boutiques that featured a charming array of Mexican-made products, imports, art and clothing. As the two followed the winding path of the river, the sounds changed. First an acoustic guitar and companion cello, serenading the warm night air and drifting from the open door of a restaurant. And then, just a few steps later, the dueling guitars of native Mariachis sprinkled the evening with the festive culture for which the city was best known.

As Daniela took it all in, she felt an indescribable sense of completion wash over her and settle deep into her soul. She'd lived in San Antonio all her life, had been downtown more times than she could recall. But never before had the Riverwalk seemed more magical to her. With Caleb by her side, it was a breathtaking wonderland of soft light and beauty, where romance was thick upon the warm night air, and nothing else mattered but this enchanting moment in time.

The line to board the river barges was always shorter at night than during the daytime, when tourists crowded onto the sidewalk with their cameras and bags filled with souvenirs. Caleb bought two tickets at the window, and in no time at all they were at the front of the line. As Daniela watched, he murmured a low greeting to the fresh-faced Hispanic youth taking tickets and slipped a large bill into the boy's eager palm. When the next water taxi pulled into port, only Caleb and Daniela boarded, moving to the very back of the barge for more privacy.

As they started off, she sent Caleb a teasing look. "So now we're resorting to bribery to get what we want?"

His grin flashed white in the moonlit darkness. "Only when absolutely necessary."

"Of course," Daniela said with mock sobriety.

Caleb leaned close, his breath a soft, sweet whisper against her face. "You don't like being alone with me?" he murmured huskily.

His words sent a melting warmth rushing through her. She swallowed, gazing into his onyx eyes. "I think you already know the answer to that."

He smiled, dark and seductive. Her belly quivered in response.

The tour guide took one look at them, and correctly guessed that they weren't interested in a narrated ride. With a quiet, conspiratorial smile, he put away his microphone and simply concentrated on steering, his back turned to them.

As the barge drifted lazily down the winding, moonlit river, Caleb and Daniela paid scant attention to the colorful sights and sounds around them, so absorbed in each other that everything else ceased to exist.

"It's such a beautiful night." Daniela sighed as Caleb draped an arm over the back of the seat behind her. "The weather is perfect, not too warm or muggy. Just perfect."

"Like everything else about this night," Caleb agreed. He shook his head slowly, his expression soft with wonder as he stared at her. "I've been to the Riverwalk a thousand times before, but I can't remember ever enjoying this place as much as I am now."

Daniela's heart clutched and she glanced down, murmuring, "I had the same thought a while ago."

Hearing the note of sorrow in her voice, Caleb tipped her chin up to meet his probing gaze. "That's not a bad thing, Daniela," he said softly. "There's a reason we both feel this way."

I already know the reason, she thought moodily. *My reason, anyway.*

"Should we be out in public together like this?" she asked, allowing a trace of apprehension to intrude upon what had to be one of the most romantic nights of her life, second only to the slow dance on the hilltop terrace of his father's ranch. "What if someone from St. Mary's sees us?"

"I can't worry about that," said Caleb, the piercing intensity of his dark gaze taking her breath away. "Ever since I saw you in class this morning, all I've been doing is thinking of ways to get you alone to myself. God, Daniela, I don't know how I'm going to make it through an entire semester with you sitting, front and center, in the second row. I'm so distracted I can't think straight."

She couldn't help but grin, her toes tingling inside her boots at the ragged frustration in his voice. "You seem to be managing very well. No one would ever guess how distracted you are, especially when they're in the hot seat."

Caleb laughed. "*You* handled the hot seat exceptionally well."

Her grin widened. "Considering how terrified I was, that's saying *a lot*."

He eyed her with amused curiosity. "Did I terrify you, Daniela?"

"Only half the time." She slanted him a naughty look beneath her lashes. "The other half of the time, I wanted to jump your bones. From the very first day of class, you caught me daydreaming about kissing you."

He chuckled softly, his warm lips finding her ear as he confessed, "Then that makes two of us."

A hot flush heated her skin as he nuzzled her throat, his fingers gently massaging the nape of her neck. She closed her eyes and rested her hand on his knee, resisting the temptation to let her fingers slide up his leg, to cup that oh-so-wonderful swell of manhood. As if reading her mind, Caleb shifted in the seat, moving closer to her, and without a second thought Daniela accepted the unspoken invitation, easing her hand farther up his denim-clad thigh until she heard his breath quicken in her ear. She drew back slightly, meeting the blatant desire in his smoldering gaze. Before she could even think about what she was doing, or be shocked by her own brazen behavior, she closed her fingers around the straining bulge of his erection.

He inhaled sharply.

Her heart pounded furiously, and a wanton thrill of desire shot through her. "Caleb..." His name was a low, hoarse moan on her lips.

His callused palm cupped her face, then slid into the silken mass of her hair, holding her captive as he swiftly bent his head. His mouth opened over hers with fiery demand, and desire cracked like a whip through Daniela's body. Her arms stole around his neck and she leaned into him, kissing him back with equal hunger. His tongue delved inside her mouth, hot and sweet, and the pleasure was sharp, splintering, making her moan aloud. His tongue moved deep and sure, taking, and hers danced around his, seductively teasing. Heat pooled in her tummy and her breasts throbbed, aching for his touch. Before she knew what was happening she was on his lap, her bottom pressed to the rigid length of his arousal.

In the space of a heartbeat they went from kissing to devouring each other, oblivious to their surroundings.

It was Caleb who finally broke the kiss, tearing his mouth from hers. His eyes met hers. Dark, intense. "I know you asked if we could slow things down, and I respect your wishes," he said, his voice like coarse velvet. "But if we keep this up a moment longer, Daniela, nothing will stop me from laying you down in this boat and making love to you, and I can't promise that I'll be gentle."

Her pulse hammered. "Who says I want you to be?" she challenged, in a husky voice she hardly recognized as her own.

His eyes glittered under a canopy of cypress trees strewn with tiny lights. "We need to get out of here," he uttered raggedly, "before we get arrested for indecent exposure and a helluva lot more."

Chapter 17

On their way back to Caleb's apartment, they stopped at one of the riverside restaurants and ordered dessert to go. Armed with two hefty servings of tiramisu, they headed up the street to the Towers of the Majestic. Caleb escorted Daniela into the marble-tiled lobby where a uniformed security guard was buried behind the sports section of the newspaper.

"How's it going, Mr. Hammond?" Caleb greeted the man.

Eugene Hammond glanced up from the *Express-News* he'd been reading and beamed when he saw Caleb. "Hey there, Counselor! You're home a little early tonight."

"I know," Caleb drawled, making Daniela wonder if he regularly stayed out late, and with whom. She quickly shoved aside the ugly suspicion, determined not to let anything spoil the perfection of the evening.

"Mr. Hammond, I'd like you to meet Daniela Moreau. Daniela, this is Eugene Hammond."

Daniela smiled at the older man. "Nice to meet you."

Lowering his newspaper, Eugene Hammond leaned forward with an engaging smile. "Pleased to meet *you,* Miss Moreau." He winked at Caleb. "No wonder you're home early, son."

Caleb chuckled, and Daniela feigned an affronted look as he led her toward the gleaming bank of elevators with a gentle hand at the small of her back. They rode the elevator to the sixteenth floor and exited onto a plush, carpeted corridor. Caleb's penthouse unit was located at the very end.

Unlocking the front door, he gestured Daniela inside ahead of him. With the flick of a switch, cool white lights washed over a gleaming expanse of hardwood floors and dark, contemporary furnishings arranged around a living room that boasted twenty-foot ceilings, a wood-burning fireplace and a pair of tall French doors that opened onto enclosed side porches. Fifteen-foot windows with wrought-iron bars commanded a panoramic view of the glittering downtown skyline.

Daniela heard a soft gasp escape her lips as she crossed the length of the room, lured by the stunning vista.

"Oh, Caleb," she breathed. "You mean you wake up to this view every morning?"

"Something like that," he answered, disappearing into the kitchen. He emerged a few minutes later carrying a bottle of Merlot and a pair of wineglasses in one hand, and balancing two dessert plates in the other. By the time Daniela hurried over to help him, he'd already set everything down on the round mahogany table that occupied the cozy dining nook.

"Bienvenue à la maison de Thorne," he announced with a flourish. "Dessert is now served, *mademoiselle*."

Daniela grinned as he gallantly pulled out a chair for her before seating himself. "*Merci, monsieur*. Your enunciation is flawless, Caleb. *Parlez-vous français?*"

He chuckled, uncorking the Merlot and filling their wineglasses. "*Oui*. But only when I'm trying to impress a pretty girl."

"Ahh," Daniela said with an understanding nod. "Well, then, I suppose I should consider myself privileged."

"You could," Caleb agreed, straight-faced.

Daniela laughed, picking up her spoon. "Don't get carried away." She sampled her tiramisu, then closed her eyes on a dreamy moan as several exquisite flavors exploded on her tongue—mocha-flavored whipped cream, espresso and a tantalizing hint of liquor. "Oh, my God. This is *soo* good."

She opened her eyes to find Caleb gazing at her in a way that made her feel slightly self-conscious. "What?"

"I love to watch you eat," he said simply. "I've never known another woman who enjoys the simple pleasures of food the way you do."

She grinned. "Which is your polite way of telling me what a pig I am."

"Not at all." His dark eyes glinted at her. "In fact, I think it's incredibly arousing."

Her belly flip-flopped. "Arousing?"

"Mmm-hmm," he murmured. "But as I've already told you, everything you do turns me on."

"Everything?"

He chuckled low in his throat. "Everything. Now stop repeating after me like a broken record, and eat your tiramisu."

"With pleasure," she said, spooning up more of the delectable dessert. "So, when did you learn French?"

Caleb took a sip of Merlot. "In college. I already knew Spanish fairly well, so French seemed like the next obvious choice."

"Naturally. What better language to impress pretty girls with than the language of love?"

"Of course." He smiled lazily at her. "What about you? When did you take French?"

"In high school. Guess that means I got the jump on you, huh?"

"Not quite," he drawled, picking up his spoon. "By the time you entered high school, I was already on my way out of college."

"Oh, yeah, I'd almost forgotten what an old man you are," Daniela teased.

He laughed. "Who're you calling an old man?"

"Poor baby. Your hearing is already failing you? I've heard that's one of the first things to— Hey!" she protested as, without warning, Caleb flicked a spoonful of tiramisu at her, hitting her squarely in the chest.

She gaped at him as if he'd lost his mind. "What'd you do that for? You're wasting perfectly good dessert!"

Caleb's expression was one of exaggerated innocence. "What's that you said?" he asked, cupping a hand to his ear and leaning toward her. "I'm having trouble *hearing* you."

"Yeah? Well, maybe this will help." Before he could react, Daniela spooned up a chunk of tiramisu, reached over and smashed it against his ear.

With a startled exclamation, Caleb jumped up from the table, staring at her in incredulous disbelief as he dug cake out of his ear. "I can't believe you did that."

Daniela howled with laughter. "You started it!"

"You're right," he said calmly—too calmly. Grinning, he scooped up a handful of tiramisu from his plate. "And I always finish what I start."

Sobering quickly, Daniela leaped from her chair. He advanced on her, slowly and purposefully, dark eyes twinkling with mischief.

She eyed him warily, backing away, step for step. "Don't even *think* about it," she said. "I'm warning you—"

He lunged, and with a startled squeal Daniela took off in the opposite direction. She didn't get very far before he tackled her around the waist with one arm, whirling her around and pinning her against the wall.

She could do nothing but laugh at how easily he'd captured her. "Caleb—"

"Too late for begging now," he said with the impenitent glee of a predator that has successfully cornered its prey. Grinning as she squirmed in his arms, Caleb pinned her wrists above her head with one hand. With the other, he brought the handful of smashed tiramisu toward her face, a wicked gleam in his eyes.

Daniela shook her head wildly from side to side. "Don't do it! I'll do anything you ask! Just don't—"

Her pleas fell on deaf ears; the next thing she knew, Caleb was smearing cake across her cheek and down her neck. Choking with laughter and indignation, Daniela bucked against him, struggling vainly to escape.

He grinned down at her. "I've just invented a new dessert," he declared. "It's called Daniela à la mode. Think I can sell it to one of the restaurants down at the Riverwalk?"

Daniela tried, unsuccessfully, to glare at him, but she was enjoying herself too much to summon any real antagonism. "If you do sell the recipe, I get the lion's share of the profit, seeing that *I'm* the main ingredient."

Caleb chuckled softly. "We'll negotiate the terms," he drawled, his amused gaze running across her face. "I wonder, though, if my new concoction is as temptingly sweet as it looks."

As if he'd lit a fuse, the air between them changed, crackling with the sexual tension that always ticked between them like a time bomb. Daniela licked her lips, and his darkened gaze followed the gesture, stirring the flames inside her that were never far from igniting whenever he was near.

"I guess I'll just have to take a taste test," he softly proposed, lowering his head.

Daniela's insides clenched as his warm mouth landed on the curve of her throat. She trembled hard as his tongue flicked out, licking the sweet confection from the throbbing pulse on her neck with slow, lazy strokes.

"Mmm," he murmured against her, the vibration of his deep, sensuous voice making desire uncoil in her belly. "Just as I thought. Delicious."

She shivered as his lips and tongue trailed a simmering path over her throat and collarbone, sending her pulse into overdrive. She was intoxicated by the feel of his hard, muscled body pressed against hers, the exquisite torture of his mouth upon her flesh.

"Who says taste tests are mutually exclusive?" she purred, licking cake from his earlobe and delighting in the shudder that convulsed him.

He lifted his head, his dark, smoldering gaze boring

into hers. Still keeping her wrists imprisoned above her head, he bent and seized her lips in a kiss of such fierce, searing possession that Daniela moaned into his mouth. Their tongues tangled in a feast of wet and heat, and she rocked her hips against his pelvis, feeling the undeniable proof of his erection against her belly, hard and heavy.

It made her breasts feel heavy, too, so she pressed them against his chest and let her lips roam from his mouth to his chin, then down to the hot skin of his neck. His breathing grew ragged in her ear as her mouth found the beating pulse of his Adam's apple and gently suckled, causing him to groan.

Still gripping her wrists in one hand, he used his free fingers to slide beneath her stretchy shirt and cover the aching swell of one breast. When his thumb grazed her nipple through the satin of her bra, she cried out and arched into him, demanding more. He deftly released the front catch, then cupped the weight of her breast in the palm of his hand. She sucked in a sharp breath, her eyes closing at the sublime pleasure of his touch. He rubbed his thumb back and forth against her nipple, teasing and stroking the taut peak until she thought she would lose her mind.

When he stepped back abruptly, releasing her wrists, she moaned softly in protest, her hips lifting off the wall to chase the heat of his body. He chuckled, a sexy, satisfied sound. Before she could rebuke him for teasing her, he reached for her again, pulling off her shirt and tossing it aside. And then he just stood there, gazing at her in a way that turned her knees to gelatin.

"Take off your bra," he commanded, low and husky.

Holding his gaze, Daniela did as he told her, sliding the straps of her bra from her shoulders and letting the scrap of material fall to the floor. She felt both powerful and defenseless as she stood before him, her body bared to the possessive heat of his gaze. Her legs quivered as he ran his eyes over her breasts, as if he were seeing them for the first time.

"Beautiful," he uttered softly, taking a deliberate step toward her. "Absolutely beautiful."

When his hot, wet mouth latched on to her breast, she couldn't suppress the breathless moan that escaped. He sucked first on one nipple, and then the other, until Daniela was on the brink of losing control. She grasped the back of his head and urged his mouth up to hers, kissing him as if her very life depended on it. Desperate for the feel of him, she tugged at his T-shirt, stopping short of ripping it from his body. And then she drank her fill of him, taking in the sculpted beauty of his wide, muscled chest and hard, flat abdomen while he watched her, his lids at half-mast. When she reached out and touched his stomach, he trembled beneath her hand, filling her with a heady sense of power. She wanted him, all of him, regardless of the consequences.

He pulled her roughly against him, the wet tips of her breasts meeting the smooth, hard skin of his chest in an excruciatingly charged embrace that made them both groan. Reaching down, Caleb palmed her bottom in both hands and held her tightly against his straining arousal as their mouths fused in a wild, voracious kiss.

The slow seduction was over, eclipsed by a fierce, consuming need that demanded immediate satisfaction.

Breaking the kiss, Caleb knelt down in front of Daniela and unsnapped the button of her jeans. She quickly stepped out of her boots, then allowed him to work the tight denim off her body. She shivered as his fingers grasped her panties and slowly, deliberately, dragged the black satin over her hips and down the length of her legs. As she stood before him, naked and trembling, he hungrily devoured the sight of her, his eyes glittering onyx.

"You're so damned beautiful," he whispered raggedly.

She felt a thrill of pleasure that quickly intensified when he cupped her buttocks and buried his face in her abdomen. His warm breath was an enticing summer breeze, trickling past her navel to touch the most feminine part of her. She bent her head and kissed his crown, then ran her hand over the smooth, close-cropped texture of his black hair. His palms tightened on her bottom, tilting her closer, urging her legs to part for him. And then his fingers were separating the springy curls at the juncture of her thighs, and his hot, silken mouth was on her.

Daniela cried out and arched into him, pleasure breaking over her body like a tidal wave. "Caleb," she breathed, closing her eyes. "*Oh...*"

Her head fell back as his wet, velvety tongue stroked the delicate folds of her flesh, teasing and suckling, making her moan in mindless ecstasy. He licked deeper into her mound, the tip of his tongue circling the slick peak of her clitoris in a slow, erotic dance that sent flames sweeping through her body. Her hands gripped the back of his head for support as her legs threatened to collapse beneath her. She didn't know how much more of the exquisite torture she could take.

When his tongue plunged deep inside her, she spilled over the edge, letting out a wild, hoarse cry as her body convulsed uncontrollably. Caleb caught her in his arms as her knees began to buckle, his mouth taking hot, primal possession of hers. He backed her against the wall and grasped her hips, lifting her from the floor. She clutched his shoulders and wrapped her still-trembling legs around his waist, dimly aware of the fact that he hadn't gotten around to undressing completely.

With impatient fingers, Caleb unzipped the fly of his jeans and reached inside to free himself. Daniela cried out sharply as he drove into her with one long, demanding thrust. Her back arched tautly and he thrust into her a second time, burying himself deeper.

Cupping the roundness of her buttocks, he seized her mouth in a hot, plundering kiss. Her fingers dug into the muscles of his shoulders, and she held on for the ride of her life. And what a ride it was, every stroke more powerful than the one before, coming harder and faster at a pace that robbed her of breath. Her chest rose and fell rapidly, matching the erratic beat of her heart. Their coupling was urgent, marked with the blind, mindless desperation of two lovers who felt they'd been deprived of each other for too long.

As Daniela felt the fire of their union burning within her, driving her toward another earth-shattering climax, Caleb rocked his hips one final time and stiffened against her, his grip tightening on her bottom. They erupted together, their loud, exultant moans soaring to the vaulted ceiling.

And Daniela knew, with a certainty that brought tears to her eyes, that there would never be another Caleb Thorne for her.

Caleb was awakened by the ringing of the telephone. Groggy and disoriented, he glanced around his bedroom, and seeing that daylight had barely cracked the sky outside, he frowned. His frown quickly disappeared, however, when his gaze landed on the beautiful woman fast asleep in his arms, her warm, curvaceous body outlined beneath the thick cream coverlet. She lay curled against him, her hair a tangle of silky black curls upon the pillow, her breathing deep and even. As his mind flashed on the erotic night of passion they'd spent together, remembering the number of times they'd made love, he grew instantly hard.

The phone rang again, rudely intruding on his steamy recollection. Biting back an oath, he carefully reached over Daniela and snatched up the phone before it wakened her.

"Hello?" he growled, keeping his voice low.

"'Mornin', son. Hope I didn't wake you."

Caleb pushed out a deep breath, lying back on his pillow. "You did, but don't worry about it." He felt a prickle of alarm. "Is everything all right, Dad?"

"Everything's just fine. The reason I'm calling—"

"—at the crack of dawn," Caleb interjected dryly.

Crandall chuckled. "The reason I'm calling is to let you know that I'm going out of town this weekend. I'm accompanying Ruth to San Diego to visit her daughter, the oldest one, who's expecting her first baby. She was admitted to the hospital overnight—"

"What happened?" Caleb demanded, with fresh alarm.

"Well, there's a possibility she might be going into labor. Given her age, and the fact that she's only five months along, the doctors don't want to take any chances. Ruth's been up half the night worrying. This morning she finally decided to fly out there, but the earliest flight she can get to San Diego won't be until this evening. So I offered her the private jet, and I'm going along with her to lend some moral support."

Caleb felt a quiet smile touch his lips. He'd always known that beneath Crandall Thorne's tough, crusty exterior lay a softie—though it would take nothing short of torture to pry such an admission from his father.

"Anyway," Crandall continued, "since the ranch will be virtually deserted this weekend—I gave everyone time off for Labor Day—I thought you might want to invite Miss Moreau up for some horseback riding and…whatever else you two decide to get into."

Caleb held the phone away from his ear and stared at it in amused disbelief. He could hardly believe his father, who'd always forbade Caleb from bringing girls to the house whenever Crandall wasn't home, was actually *encouraging* Caleb to use the ranch for a romantic getaway with Daniela—a woman who also happened to be one of his students. Granted, it had been years since Crandall imposed any sort of rules on him, and now that Caleb was a grown man, he could damn well do as he pleased. Still…it felt weird to be invited to use his father's home as a trysting spot.

Never mind that the idea had already occurred to him.

"You still there?"

Caleb smiled into the phone. "I'm still here, Dad. Thanks for the offer…I might take you up on it."

"You do that." Crandall paused, then added almost gruffly, "I like her, son. There's something special about her. She's not like the others."

By "others," Caleb knew his father meant the other women he'd dated in the past, many of whom turned out to be after his money and the legal empire he stood to someday inherit from his father. Since Caleb had never been seriously interested in any of those women, he'd suffered little more than a twinge of disgust when they showed their true colors.

He knew it would be different with Daniela. She, unlike the others, had the power to hurt him. It scared him to realize just how *much* power she had.

Keeping his gaze trained on her face, searching for any sign that she was faking sleep in order to eavesdrop on his conversation, Caleb said to his father, "I take it, then, that you approve."

A low, gravelly chuckle filled the phone line. "If you're asking whether I approve of your relationship with a student, the answer is no. I think it's mighty reckless and dangerous of you, son, and I hope to God you know what you're doing." He paused, pushing out a deep breath. "That said, you're a Thorne, and Thorne men have always marched to the beat of our own drum. I wouldn't be where I am today if I had adhered to the dictates of others, nor would you. Thankfully, to balance our willful natures, the Good Lord blessed us with an abundance of sound judgment. I think you've already decided that Miss Moreau is worth any risk you're taking in being with her, and based on what I observed of the young lady, I think you've made the right call."

Caleb closed his eyes briefly. "Thanks, Dad. I hope you're right."

"I usually am." A sly note crept into his father's voice as he said, "Well, I'll let you get back to sleep, though I don't suspect you'll be doing much resting. Give Miss Moreau my warm regards. I'll keep you posted on the status of Ruth's daughter and the baby."

"Thanks, you do that."

As Caleb disconnected the call and reached over Daniela to replace the receiver, she stirred awake. The thick, silky fringe of her lashes fluttered upward, those big, dark eyes opening and settling on his face.

When a soft, dreamy smile curved her lips, his heart slammed against his rib cage. "Good morning," she whispered, her voice a little husky from sleep. "You stayed this time."

His mouth twitched as he brushed a lock of hair from her face, his fingers skimming her cheek with the tender gesture. "I didn't have much of a choice. I live here."

"Oh, yeah, that's right." She smiled again, and as he gazed down at the unblemished beauty of her face, he wondered what kind of fool he'd been to skip out on the simple pleasure of having her wake up in his arms.

A running-scared fool.

"Who was on the phone?" Daniela asked, covering a yawn behind her hand.

"My father." Caleb told her about Ruth's daughter, marveling as her eyes softened in concern for a complete stranger.

"I hope she and the baby will be all right," she said, and Caleb could tell that she wasn't merely mouthing an empty sentiment for his benefit; she genuinely meant what she said.

"I hope so, too," he murmured. Dipping his head, he brushed a soft kiss to her temple, then drew back and smiled at her. "Monday is Labor Day. What are you doing this weekend?"

She chuckled softly. "You mean after I somehow manage to drag myself out of this bed and back to my own house?"

He grinned. "Or, you could just stay here with me."

Her expression clouded for a moment, her eyes dropping away from his. "I can't."

"Why not?"

Hearing the jealous edge to his voice, she gave him a teasing look, the sorrow he'd glimpsed in her eyes a moment ago disappearing. "Because I have other plans," she told him saucily.

"Oh, really?" As Caleb gazed down at her, he felt an indescribable wave of possessiveness wash over him. He'd never thought of any woman as his own, had never wanted to. How Daniela had so easily slipped beneath his radar, he still wasn't sure. But she had. And now he couldn't look at her without wanting her, couldn't have her without wanting more.

And he definitely couldn't stomach the idea of her being with another man, giving herself to him with the same passion and abandon with which she'd surrendered to Caleb.

Rolling her onto her back, he climbed on top of her and felt his blood heat instantly at the contact with her lush, silken body. Raising himself above her, he braced his weight on both arms and planted his hands on either side of her head. "I want you to spend the weekend with me at the ranch," he told her in a tone that made it clear the request was nonnegotiable. "We'll have the place all to ourselves."

She gazed up at him, the edge of her teeth digging into the soft flesh of her bottom lip. "It sounds terribly romantic—"

"It will be." Lowering his head, he captured that enticing plump lip, nibbling and tasting her. "Say yes," he whispered against her mouth.

"Caleb—"

He slid his body up along hers in one long, provocative caress, smiling devilishly at her sharp intake of breath. "Say yes, Daniela," he commanded huskily.

"No fair," she whimpered. "You're playing dirty."

Leaning down, he flicked his tongue over her lips, but pulled away before she could kiss him back. She groaned in frustration, making him chuckle softly.

"All you have to say is one simple word. *Yes.*"

Her dark eyes glinting with sudden challenge, Daniela made a move to touch him, but he caught her hand and shook his head slowly, knowing how easy it would be for her to turn the tables on him. All she had to do was slide one foot up his leg, press the silken heat of her mouth to his chest and flick her wet tongue over a flat, dark nipple….

With a tortured groan, Caleb realized that was *exactly* what she was doing. Torn between disbelief and awe, he stared down at her, this woman who should have been forbidden, this woman who had the power to find the most hidden corners of his heart and expose them.

Unable to resist the sweet temptation of her, he lifted her and turned her over onto her stomach. He kissed and licked his way down the silky length of her spine, his tongue discovering places on her back that made her arch in surprised pleasure. As he cupped the lush, curvy swell of her buttocks, he felt like he'd died and gone to heaven. He stroked and caressed her tempting rump, his fingertips probing the secret crevice between her thighs, where he could already feel the promise of wet heat.

He grabbed two large, overstuffed pillows and pushed them beneath her hips, giving himself a deeper angle of penetration as he entered her slowly from behind. Daniela moaned loudly and undulated against him, clutching handfuls of the bed linens in her fists. Grasping the sides of her waist, Caleb thrust high and deep inside her, and her moans became uncontrollable, the wild twisting of her hips nearly making him come. When he withdrew from her suddenly, she whimpered in protest.

"Caleb," she begged, "oh, don't stop. Please don't stop...."

Caleb shuddered convulsively as he reentered her, taking her with the same hot fervor of the night before, driving into her with a force that was sure to chase any remnant of doubt from his mind. He thrust hard and fast, hearing her breathless little cries, feeling her slick, velvet warmth envelop him as if she were his very own custom-made glove. He slid his arms around her body, groaning at the delicious fullness of her breasts, the silk of her skin, the moist heat of her mouth as she suckled his thumb. He was amazed at the sense of rightness, of belonging inside her. He wanted their lovemaking to last forever, but knew he couldn't hold on much longer.

She cried out his name as her body clenched around his penis in pulsing contractions, milking a climax from him that tore a savage growl from his throat.

Breathing hard, he kissed the sweat-dampened curls at the nape of her neck, then gathered her into his arms and drew them down onto the bed.

Daniela snuggled up against him. "You don't play fair," she protested sleepily.

He chuckled, low and soft. "Not when I want something badly enough." He angled his head to look down into her flushed face. "Does this mean you'll spend the weekend with me?"

She smiled lazily. "You didn't exactly give me a choice," she mumbled, her eyelids drifting closed. Within moments, she was fast asleep.

And as Caleb followed her into dreamland, three words he'd never spoken to another woman drifted through his mind.

I love you.

A few hours later, Daniela climbed off Caleb's Harley and removed her helmet. Tucking it beneath one arm, she gave him a demure smile. "Thanks for the ride."

"Anytime," Caleb said softly. He lifted his helmet enough to uncover his face, the shadowed growth on his jaw making him unbearably sexy. As memories of their erotic lovemaking marathon filled her mind, she felt her cheeks grow warm.

"I had a wonderful time," she murmured.

"Me, too," Caleb said. "I'll be back at six to pick you up."

She smiled, anticipation quickening her heartbeat. "I'll be ready."

Their gazes held for a heated moment. Daniela stepped forward, cradled his face between her hands and pressed a sweet, silky kiss to his mouth. When she drew away, the eyes that met hers were smoldering.

"Make that four o'clock," Caleb said huskily.

Daniela gave a low, sultry laugh. "I'll be ready."

With a darkly seductive smile, he resettled his helmet over his head, revved the motorcycle's engine, then roared off down the street.

Daniela stood watching until he'd disappeared

around the corner. Then, feeling like a lovesick schoolgirl returning home from her first date, she turned and skipped to the house.

Pamela Roarke awaited her in the living room, where she'd apparently witnessed the whole scene from the window. Daniela drew up short, her face heating with embarrassment at getting caught.

But then elation at seeing her mother took over, and she threw her arms around Pamela. "Mom, you're home! I missed you!"

Pamela chuckled dryly. "Could have fooled me." She drew back, looking vaguely amused as she searched her daughter's face. "Who was that young man on the motorcycle?"

Daniela shrugged. "Just someone I met at the university," she replied, trying to sound offhand—but not so offhand that her mother would think she was engaging in cheap, meaningless flings with random men.

Pamela looked skeptical. "Just someone, huh?"

"Yes, just someone." She dropped a kiss onto her mother's soft, fragrant cheek before heading toward her bedroom. "I want to hear all about your trip to Houston—"

"Then why are you walking in the opposite direction?" There was a trace of humor in her mother's tone.

Daniela glanced over her shoulder with a sheepish grin. "Because if I stand there a minute longer, Mom, you'll have me confessing to everything I've done over the past week. Give me time to get my story straight."

At that, her mother laughed.

Thanks to Deacon Hubbard, who arrived an hour later to take Pamela out to lunch before escorting her to a gospel choir concert at church that evening, Daniela was spared from having to answer her mother's questions about Caleb.

As she observed the warm, friendly interactions between Pamela and the quietly handsome church deacon, a pleasant suspicion took root in her mind, and she found herself wondering if her mother and Lionel Hubbard were falling in love with each other. And then her mind went a step further: If the two got married, Daniela wouldn't have to worry about her mother growing old alone.

And she wouldn't have to feel so guilty about not getting her mother the ranch.

After seeing the couple off, Daniela treated herself to a long, leisurely bubble bath. As she soaked in the hot, steaming water scented with her favorite bath crystals, her thoughts invariably turned to Caleb. She fantasized about him, reliving every sensuous detail of the past twenty-four hours, blushing when she found herself becoming aroused.

She had no business spending another hour with him, much less the entire weekend—a *three*-day weekend, at that. When she'd agreed to go for a ride with him the night before, she'd told herself it would be the very last time. And now here she was, preparing to be whisked away to his father's stunning, secluded ranch for what promised to be the most romantic weekend of her life.

It was an opportunity she couldn't refuse.

And though she knew she was being selfish, that it was wrong to prolong her relationship with Caleb when they could have no future together, she wasn't about to cancel her plans with him.

Daniela rose from the clawfoot tub, wrapped her body in a big fluffy towel and padded to her bedroom. After dressing in a pale linen skirt and a pink tube top, she packed her overnight bag, wishing she hadn't thrown away all of her sexy lingerie when she'd declared her no-dating moratorium a few years ago.

Not that she remained clothed for very long in Caleb's presence anyway, she thought, a wanton smile curving her lips.

Caleb arrived an hour and a half later, clean-shaven and incredibly handsome in a pair of khaki trousers and a hunter polo shirt that showed off his powerful physique.

As his gaze ran the length of her, his eyes glinted with frank male appreciation. "Are you ready?"

Daniela nodded. "First I want to give you something." As he raised a curious brow, she went into her bedroom and returned carrying the framed photograph of the Majestic Theatre that she'd bought from April.

Caleb looked surprised as she handed it to him. "You don't have to—"

"I know," she interrupted softly. "I want you to have it, Caleb."

"But you like this photo. That's the reason you bought it."

"True," Daniela admitted. "But *you* also liked it, and were it not for the fact that I beat you to it, you would have bought the photo first. So please take it, Caleb. I insist." When he continued to hesitate, she added quietly, "I think we both know that the Majestic Theatre has more sentimental value for you than me."

He gazed at her with an expression of such tender warmth that her throat closed. "Thank you, Daniela," he said huskily. "This is a wonderful gift."

Daniela felt the sting of tears behind her eyelids. She swallowed hard. "It'll give you something to remember me by," she joked, then wished she could take back the revealing words.

Hearing the note of finality in her voice, Caleb frowned a little. "Are you going somewhere?"

Instead of answering right away, Daniela reached up and touched his face, her fingers splaying across the hard line of his jaw, the sculpted softness of his mouth.

I love you, she thought. *I'll never forget you.*

Caleb had grown very still as he awaited her response. "Daniela?"

She mustered a wobbly grin. "Of course I'm going somewhere," she said lightly. "Unless I'm mistaken, we're *both* supposed to be going somewhere." She glanced at her watch. "And if we don't get out of here before my mother returns, we're going to find ourselves in the hot seat, the kind that makes what you put us through in class look like child's play."

Chuckling softly, Caleb picked up her overnight bag, then followed her from the house with his hand resting in its familiar place at the small of her back.

It was one of those simple pleasures that Daniela would remember, and ache for, long after he was out of her life.

Chapter 18

On Tuesday morning, Caleb was riding high on an emotion that could only be defined as euphoria. He'd spent the most incredible weekend with Daniela, a weekend in which they went horseback riding, dined by candlelight, slow danced under the stars, talked into the wee hours of the morning and made love so often, it became difficult to discern where one body ended, and the other began. He couldn't get enough of her, in bed or out of it, and that was an unprecedented experience for him.

All too soon Monday had rolled around, signaling the end of their time together in their own private paradise in the mountains. As Caleb drove Daniela home, he was already thinking of ways to get her alone again.

And when he awakened that Tuesday morning bereft of her warm, enticing body curled against him, he knew he had to get her into his life on a permanent basis.

When his father called and casually asked him to drop by the ranch after his last class of the day, Caleb thought nothing of it.

But the moment he crossed the threshold of his father's study and saw the grim expression on Crandall's face, he knew he wasn't going to like what he heard. And that was putting it mildly.

"Have a seat, son," Crandall offered, waving him into a chair. There were pronounced lines of strain around his mouth that hadn't been there the day before, when Caleb picked him up from the airport after taking Daniela home.

Caleb eyed his father warily as he sat down. "What's going on, Dad?"

"This morning I received a visit from the private investigator I hired to run surveillance on Hoyt Philbin."

Caleb automatically tensed at the mention of the former mayor, who'd been on a relentless campaign to ruin Crandall Thorne ever since learning that his wife and Crandall had once been in love.

When his father fell silent, Caleb prompted, "And?"

Crandall pinched the bridge of his nose tiredly, looking as if he'd rather scale Mount Vesuvius during a volcanic eruption than deliver the bad news weighing heavily on him. "He came to report information on the private detective agency that Philbin hired to dig up dirt on me. The name of the agency is Roarke Investigations, a local outfit run by two former law-enforcement officers and their younger sister." He paused, his lips thinning to a flat, hard line. "Her name is Daniela Roarke."

Caleb stared at his father as if unable to absorb what he had just heard. "What are you saying?" he inquired evenly. "Are you telling me that Daniela Moreau is actually Daniela Roarke, a *P.I.?*"

Crandall studied him in silence for a moment, then inclined his head in a grim nod. "She's not a law student, son. Apparently she's working undercover as part of an investigation to expose me for some wrong Philbin is convinced I'm guilty of." His tone hardened. "My guess is that she—they—were hoping to get to me by luring you into sharing confidences about my alleged criminal conduct. Daniela was the bait they used."

Caleb kept his expression carefully blank, because Thorne men weren't prone to fits of hysteria or extreme outbursts of emotion. But inside he was screaming, raging at the world as a secret hope slowly shriveled and died inside him.

He hid his wrath behind a flat, terse tone. "I want to see the photos."

Crandall frowned. "I really don't think—"

"It's too late to protect me now, Dad. The horse is already out of the stable. It can't get much worse. I want to see the photographs." Because a small, foolish part of him—the part that had allowed him to fall in love with Daniela—was still in denial. He needed indisputable proof of her betrayal.

Slowly Crandall slid a thick manila folder across the desk at Caleb.

Wordlessly Caleb took the folder and opened it. Inside were typed reports nestled between black-and-white photographs that consisted mainly of Hoyt Philbin entering a nondescript, single-story brick building on various dates and times. Jaw clenched in mounting fury, Caleb sifted quickly through the stack, then froze when he came to what he was looking for. There, right before his very eyes, was a close-up shot of Daniela emerging from the same building, wearing the brown gypsy skirt and sexy lace-up sandals that had sent his imagination into overdrive. The picture had been taken just last Wednesday, the day she visited his office after class and claimed she'd missed him.

The day he offered to introduce her to his father.

She'd probably left campus that afternoon and driven straight to the detective agency to share the good news with her partners in crime. What a coup that must have been for her, to land such a prime opportunity less than two weeks after going undercover. She must have realized, then, what a gullible fool Caleb was, to have played into her hands so easily. Judging by the triumphant smile on her face in the photograph, the joke was definitely on him.

He had been played for a fool, and he had no one to blame but himself. He—who'd always been taught not to trust beautiful women, who'd had more than his fair share of dealings with gold-diggers who were only after his father's wealth and prestige—should have known better. Instead he'd allowed himself to be tempted and seduced by a woman who should have remained off-limits to him.

He'd been so mesmerized by her that, as of that morning, he'd planned to ask her to marry him.

Oh, yeah. The joke was definitely on him.

With the manila folder still clamped in his fist, Caleb got abruptly to his feet and strode purposefully to the door.

"Don't do anything rash, son," his father called out in warning.

Caleb didn't break stride as he left the room. He was past hearing, past caring and—soon enough, if he was lucky—he'd be past feeling at all.

The house was silent when Daniela returned from campus that afternoon.

She'd attended all of her classes as if it were a normal day, then she'd calmly walked to the admissions office and withdrawn her status as a student. Mistaking the cause of the tears that blurred her eyes, the kind admissions clerk had attempted to console Daniela by telling her that there would always be a place for her at the university whenever she was ready to continue her studies.

Daniela cried all the way home.

When she stepped through the front door and was greeted by empty silence, it only punctuated the sense of loneliness and despair threatening to engulf her.

After checking her mother's bedroom and finding it empty, Daniela assumed that Pamela had stepped out to run errands or visit her friends at the senior center where she volunteered.

Returning to the living room, Daniela kicked off her shoes and sank down on the sofa with the remote control. As she wandered aimlessly through channels, she marveled at the pendulum of her emotions. After the glorious, magical weekend she'd spent with Caleb, she'd been walking on cloud nine. In the span of a day she'd gone from feeling the highest of highs, to the lowest of lows.

Because today was the day she'd decided to tell Caleb the truth about herself.

Withdrawing from the university had been the first

step, a way to bolster her courage for the difficult task that awaited her.

Difficult? Daniela thought sardonically. *Try excruciating.*

Her only consolation, if one could be found, was that once she came clean to Caleb, dealing with her brothers would be a veritable cakewalk. Because there was nothing Kenneth could say that would make her feel any worse than she already did, knowing she'd betrayed Caleb in the worst possible way, and knowing that her punishment was to face a future without the first and only man she'd ever truly loved.

When the doorbell rang, she got up and shuffled to the door on leaden legs. As if he'd been conjured by her thoughts, Caleb stood on her doorstep.

Her pulse raced at the sight of him. She loved him so much. And though she knew it was a long shot, deep in her heart lingered the hope that somehow, some way, she could tell him the truth about everything, and still not lose him.

She licked her lips nervously. "Hi, Caleb," she said with forced normalcy. "You must have read my mind. I was just going to call you and ask you to come by after your last class."

His mouth curved upward in a half smile, but there was something in that smile, something barely perceptible, that sent a whisper of foreboding through her. "In that case," he drawled softly, "I guess it's a good thing that I'm a mind reader, isn't it?"

Unsure how to respond to the strange undertones in his voice, Daniela merely smiled and stepped aside to let him enter. As he shouldered past her into the house, she noticed a manila folder tucked beneath his arm.

"Would you like something to drink?" she asked, closing the door and leaning against it for support, her knees feeling oddly weak—even weaker than they normally felt whenever Caleb was near.

"No, thanks. I'm fine, Daniela."

Was it just her imagination, or had there been a slight edge to his voice when he said her name?

Deciding it was just her guilty conscience getting to her, Daniela pushed away from the door, walked over to the sofa and sat down, automatically expecting Caleb to follow suit.

He didn't. Remaining by the window, he propped a shoulder against the wall and regarded her in calm, implacable silence. He seemed to be waiting for something, though she couldn't fathom what that might be.

Her hands twisted nervously in her lap. "Have you already eaten? I could fix you something, like a sandwich or—"

"I'm fine, Daniela." A shadow of cynicism curved his mouth. "Or would you prefer to be called Miss Roarke?"

For one stunned moment Daniela stared at him, his words not fully registering. But once they did, she felt a huge wave of sorrow, and a shame so intense she could scarcely hold her head up.

She got to her feet slowly. "Caleb—"

He pinned her with a look of such scathing contempt that tears burned her eyes. "How long were you planning to keep up the charade, Daniela?" He sneered. "Weeks? Months? *Years?*"

She shook her head quickly. "No, of course not. I—"

"*Of course not?*" he thundered furiously, advancing on her. "You say that as if I should know better, as if the idea of your going undercover for 'years' should be any more outrageous than your going undercover at all!"

Daniela strove for calm, though her insides were quaking violently. "Caleb, please let me explain—"

"Don't bother!" He slapped the manila folder down onto the coffee table, spilling some of the contents to the floor. Daniela stared, in abject horror, as a black-and-white photograph of herself leaving Roarke Investigations landed right at her feet.

"How apropos," Caleb jeered. "That's the very same photo I wanted you to see. They say a picture is worth a thousand words, Miss Roarke. What do you suppose that particular picture is saying?"

Daniela knelt down to pick it up, her heart sinking further when she saw her smiling image, and realized how Caleb must have interpreted it. She looked up at him. "It wasn't like that, Caleb," she said, imploring him to believe her.

"Oh, really?" he mocked bitingly. "So you *didn't* leave campus after we spoke that day and run straight to your brothers to brag about landing an interview with my father?"

"I didn't brag!" she cried, surging to her feet. "If anything, I was hoping they'd talk me out of going!"

Shaking his head slowly, Caleb raked her with a look of withering scorn. "You must really take me for a fool, Daniela. And why wouldn't you? I fell for your little scheme—hook, line and damn sinker. Oh, you were good, I'll give you that. Oscar-winning good. That whole help-me-find-my-calling act was inspired."

"It wasn't an act!"

His brow arched in cynical disbelief. "So you really

do have an interest in becoming a lawyer? Is that what you're telling me?" When she floundered, he nodded tersely. "That's what I thought."

Daniela took a beseeching step toward him. "Listen to me, Caleb. Almost everything I told you about myself is true. About my family, about where I attended college—"

"That's even more insulting," he bit out. "You were so confident in your ability to win my trust that you didn't even bother to invent a solid alias. It never once occurred to you that I might see through your lies, that I might grow suspicious enough to check into your background. My God, Daniela, you didn't even bother supplying the school with a fake address! All it would have taken was *one* phone call to ascertain the name of the homeowner at this address, and you would have been busted. But that never occurred to you, did it? You and your brothers knew I would be easy prey—"

"No!" Daniela cried, unable to bear the thought of him somehow blaming himself for letting down his guard with her. "That wasn't it at all! I never for one moment thought you'd be easy prey! We made the decision to stick as close as possible to the truth to make it easier for me to…to—" She couldn't even bring herself to complete the awful explanation, which sounded far worse than she could have ever imagined.

"To lie to me," Caleb finished for her, his mouth twisting contemptuously. "You stuck close to the truth to help you keep your lies together. Brilliant strategy."

Tears crowded in Daniela's eyes and rolled, unchecked, down her face. "If you believe nothing else I say, Caleb," she told him in an aching whisper, "believe me when I tell you that I never meant to hurt you."

His gaze hardened. "You'll forgive me if I have a hard time believing that," he mocked scornfully. His eyes narrowed on hers. "Tell me something," he said, understated menace in every inflection. "What did you really expect to learn about my father? What deep, dark secret did you hope to expose by befriending me?"

She shook her head helplessly, on the verge of hysteria. "I don't know, Caleb!" she choked out miserably. "Hoyt Philbin thinks your father has ties to the Mexican mafia, that he tampers with juries and engages in economic espionage, that he accepts bribes from corrupt labor union bosses and extorts money from his clients."

When she'd finished rattling off the litany of alleged offenses, Caleb said in a low, quelling voice, "Hoyt Philbin doesn't believe a single one of those things. And you know why? Because they're not true."

"I'm just letting you know what I was told!"

"Yeah? Did Philbin also tell you that he's hated my father for over forty years, long before Crandall built his empire and became a target of random government audits and secret investigations?" At Daniela's surprised look, his mouth twisted sardonically. "Did you seriously think your 'undercover operation' was the first my father has ever endured? Did you think your little detective agency was the only one Philbin had ever approached to help him in his personal crusade to take down my father?"

He didn't raise his voice above a low growl, and yet each word snapped in the air like the crack of a whip, lashing at Daniela, breaking her down until she sank weakly onto the sofa and dropped her head into her hands.

But he wasn't finished with her yet. "Did Philbin tell you the *real* reason behind his grudge against my father? No? You mean he didn't tell you that long before he met his wife, Tessa, she and my father were madly in love with each other? He didn't tell you how young, social-climbing Tessa deserted my father for Hoyt Philbin because he was white, and his political future looked more promising than Crandall's? And he didn't tell you that forty years ago, my father and Tessa saw each other again for the first time in ages, that one thing led to another and they wound up having an affair? And out of that affair came my half sister, Melanie, who was born a little too dark-skinned for Hoyt's liking, so he made Tessa give her up for adoption, telling her that they'd have other children later, when his political career was more established."

Aghast, Daniela could only stare up at him, unable to believe the incredible tale he was sharing with her.

Amused by her horrified expression, Caleb gave a soft, mirthless laugh. "This is the kind of dirt you were looking for, isn't it, Daniela?" he taunted bitterly. "This is what you hoped I would share with you during pillow talk. But wait, it only gets better."

Her heart constricted. "Caleb—"

"Let me finish!" His voice softened to a silky, dangerous caress as he added, "After all, it's the least I can do, since I never gave you the ammunition you came into my life seeking."

Swallowing hard, Daniela closed her eyes for a moment. It was impossible to reconcile this cold, ruthless version of Caleb with the tender, fiercely passionate lover who'd brought her to shuddering heights of ecstasy every time they made love.

But it was *she* who'd brought him to this dark moment, tension and fury radiating from his body as he stood a few feet away from her, no doubt wishing he'd never set eyes on her.

"When I was fourteen years old," Caleb began, his voice low and controlled, "I came home from school one day to find my parents kneeling over the dead body of a nineteen-year-old girl. They told me that the girl had broken into the house wielding a gun, and that she planned to rob and kill them. When I looked down at the body, all I saw were torn jeans, ratty sneakers and wild, dirty hair. I remember thinking that she *looked* like a homeless person capable of violence, so I believed them. I was so scared and shaken that it didn't even occur to me to wonder why the girl looked so much like me. And then the police arrived, and my father told them what had happened, that he'd accidentally shot the intruder during a struggle for the gun. The police filed a report and conducted an investigation that eventually cleared my parents of any suspicion of wrongdoing, and after a while the whole thing went away. Until sixteen years later, when Hoyt Philbin paid me a visit at work. *That's* how I found out that the girl my father accidentally killed that day was actually my half sister, Melanie, who'd been bounced around foster care homes all her life until she finally aged out of the system at eighteen.

"Before that day, I'd never even suspected that I had a sister out there somewhere. Philbin told me that she'd gone to the house to confront my father about abandoning her, just as she'd confronted Tessa the day before. He claimed that my father killed Melanie to keep her from going to the press, but he was never able to prove it—though he's never stopped trying. As you can imagine, I was devastated by this news, and to have to learn about Melanie from my father's long-time enemy sent me into a rage. I'd already been thinking about leaving the firm. As I told you before, I was burned-out, physically and emotionally. Learning about my half sister, knowing that my father had kept the truth from me all those years, hastened my decision to leave."

As Daniela gazed at him, tears welled in her eyes and her heart broke for him. She mourned the tragic loss of innocence he and his sister had suffered so senselessly. And she mourned the life of a desperate young woman who'd been cast aside like a rag doll because of the selfish, reckless actions of the three adults who'd failed her.

"I'm so sorry, Caleb," Daniela whispered brokenly. "I had no idea."

"Of course you didn't," he snarled, advancing on her. "Philbin didn't see fit to tell you and your brothers before you signed on the dotted line. But that's the kind of man you're dealing with, a man so hell-bent on revenge that he'd sacrifice his own wife in the process of exposing my father's dirty little secret. He was hoping you'd succeed where he'd failed to pry the 'truth' out of me. He was counting on the fact that somewhere along the way, my father had tearfully confessed his crime to me, admitting to me that he did, in fact, purposefully kill my sister to protect his own reputation. But what Philbin has always failed to realize is that I've never doubted my father's innocence. I think he was a conniving, heartless bastard for not telling me about my sister, and he was dead wrong for having an affair with another man's wife, old flame or not. But Crandall Thorne is not a cold-blooded murderer, and

Hoyt Philbin can damn well go to his grave trying to prove otherwise.

"So here's my question to you, Daniela." Caleb sneered, dropping to a crouch in front of her. Hard, angry fingers bit into her chin, forcing her to meet his contemptuous gaze. "How much money did it take to make you sell your soul to the devil?"

She closed her eyes, awash in shame and regret. "It's not important, Caleb," she said tremulously.

"The hell it isn't!" he growled. "I want to know how little it takes to make a woman like you sink so low."

Her eyes snapped open. "I'm not a whore, Caleb!" she exploded, wounded by his cruelty. "I didn't sleep with you because I was trying to pry information out of you. I slept with you because I *wanted* you. Because I love you!"

His eyes turned to shards of black ice, unthawed by her fervent admission. "That's just too damned bad, Daniela," he said, ominously soft. "Because if I never see you again, it'll be too soon."

Her heart ripped in half. "You don't mean that," she moaned tearfully, begging him to take the words back, even if he really meant them.

Without another word, Caleb got abruptly to his feet and stalked to the front door, slamming out of the house with shattering finality.

As her shoulders began to shake with silent sobs, Daniela covered her face with her hands and wept uncontrollably.

When she felt a gentle hand on her shoulder, she looked up in startled surprise to find her mother standing there, wearing overalls and her favorite wide-brimmed straw hat.

Daniela gulped in a breath. "I didn't know you were home, Mom," she mumbled.

"I was in the backyard, working in my garden," Pamela said quietly. "I heard shouting, so I came inside to see what all the commotion was about. Once I realized what was going on, I stayed in the kitchen."

"Y-You heard everything?"

"I heard enough." Pamela's expression was full of tender sympathy as she sat down beside her daughter and gently gathered her into her arms. "Oh, baby. I'm so sorry," she said soothingly as a fresh wave of heart-broken sobs racked Daniela's body.

Long after the emotional storm receded, Daniela remained in her mother's arms, comforted by the rocking motions of her body.

"I made a terrible mistake, Mom," she whispered hoarsely.

"Sounds like you did," Pamela murmured in agreement.

"He's never going to forgive me."

"You don't know that for sure. Sounds to me like Caleb really cares for you. He wouldn't have been so angry if he didn't." She ran soothing hands up and down Daniela's back. "It's going to be all right, baby. One way or another, it's going to be all right."

Daniela wished she could believe her mother. But as she remembered the cold, lethal fury in Caleb's eyes, she knew she had to accept reality.

Caleb was never going to forgive her.

In that moment, she wondered if she'd ever be able to forgive herself.

Chapter 19

In the days and weeks that followed, Daniela coped with her heartache in the only way she knew how: by throwing herself into work and a flurry of other activities that would keep her mind off what she'd had, and lost. She put in longer hours at the office and took on more cases; she even managed to drum up more business for the agency by hanging out at the courthouse and passing out business cards to attorneys, who often hired P.I.'s to track down the information they needed to prosecute or defend personal injury, civil liability and child custody cases. Although much of the work kept her chained to her desk as she pored through mountains of public documents and scoured the Internet for research, Daniela didn't mind the monotony. After the way her *last* undercover assignment had ended, she no longer craved the drama and excitement of a big case.

She'd had more than enough drama to last her a lifetime.

The day after her agonizing showdown with Caleb, Hoyt Philbin had stopped by Roarke Investigations to inform Daniela and her brothers that their services were no longer required. As he explained to them, he'd changed his mind about investigating Crandall Thorne, and didn't want them to waste another second on such a "futile endeavor." Although he spoke as if he'd reached the decision all by himself, Daniela and her brothers suspected he'd had a little help—namely in the form of Crandall Thorne's threat to go to the media about the former mayor's shady business dealings while in office. Apparently, two of Philbin's major campaign contributors during the last election had been high-ranking members of the Mexican mafia, a fact that had been concealed from the public and would remain as such, unless Crandall decided otherwise.

After what she'd learned about the former mayor, Daniela took a certain amount of pleasure in knowing that Crandall having the upper hand would keep Philbin in line, once and for all.

Had Caleb not left the manila folder at her house, which included the incriminating evidence about Philbin, Daniela may never have realized just how unscrupulous the man was.

After reading the private investigator's report on Philbin, she'd calmly packaged everything up and mailed the folder back to Crandall, not Caleb, because the mere thought of writing Caleb's name on an envelope had caused her too much pain.

Days merged into weeks that passed in a blur of long days at the office, and sleepless nights at home. Although

Daniela was often exhausted by the time she returned to her house late at night, once her head hit the pillow, she found it difficult, if not impossible, to fall asleep right away. Visions of Caleb haunted her, tormenting her with memories of their all-too-brief time together.

She remembered Caleb, dark eyes gleaming as they enjoyed a laugh over coffee and ice cream.

Caleb, dragging her into a supply closet and kissing her with such unrestrained passion her bones dissolved to liquid.

Caleb, holding her in his arms and humming a Smokey Robinson tune as they slow danced on the terrace after watching the sunset.

On most nights, she fell asleep thinking about the times she'd lain in his arms after they'd made love, her head nestled against his shoulder, his hand lazily caressing her as they whispered endearments to each other before sleep overcame them—or a fresh wave of desire.

No matter how hard Daniela tried, she couldn't stop thinking about him, couldn't stop dreaming about him. Couldn't stop missing him.

There was no cure for it. All she could do was hope that in time, her mind and body would learn to forget him.

She knew her heart never would.

At the office, Kenneth, Noah and Janie stole worried glances at her whenever they thought she wasn't looking. More than once, Daniela had walked into a room that grew suddenly quiet when she appeared; the guilt-ridden eyes that shifted away from hers betrayed the fact that she'd been the topic of discussion. Although they all knew what had happened between her and Caleb—thanks to Pamela Roarke, whose worried face greeted

Daniela every night when she came home—no one dared breathe a word of it to Daniela. In fact, they all went out of their way *not* to mention Caleb's name, or anything remotely related to him, in her presence. Which meant that any allusions to St. Mary's University, or law school, or the Majestic Theatre, or ranches, were strictly off-limits. Daniela would have found their precautions amusing—if she still had a sense of humor left.

One afternoon, she rapped on the door and walked into Kenneth's office to ask him a question about a case she was working on. She was totally unprepared for the sight of Janie propped on the desk with her legs wrapped around Kenneth's waist, locked in a passionate kiss.

At Daniela's startled gasp, they sprang apart guiltily. Janie jumped down from the desk, smoothing her skirt over her thighs while Kenneth hastily straightened his tie.

"I'm sorry," Daniela mumbled, embarrassed as she backed quickly toward the door. "I knocked, but I guess you guys didn't hear me."

"Uh, no, we didn't." Janie sent her husband an accusing look, hissing out of the corner of her mouth, "I thought you locked the door!"

Kenneth grinned sheepishly. "Guess I forgot."

"I'll come back," Daniela said, and ducked out of the room.

Janie appeared in the doorway of her office a minute later, her cheeks flushed with color. "I'm really sorry about that, Daniela," she muttered.

Daniela waved a dismissive hand. "Don't worry about it. I should have knocked louder...although I'm not sure it would have done any good, with all the heavy panting that was going on in there."

Speechless, Janie gaped at her, and then before Daniela knew it, they both burst out laughing. It was the first time Daniela had laughed in weeks, and it felt good. Healthy, normal.

When their mirth had subsided, she smiled across the cluttered desk at her sister-in-law. "Though my eyesight is permanently damaged from what I just saw," she teased, "it was worth it. Looks like things are working out for you and Kenny."

Janie nodded, grinning happily. "We've been having long, productive talks about our relationship and working through some issues neither of us wanted to face before. It's been wonderful."

"I'm so happy for you guys," Daniela said warmly.

"Thanks, Daniela. And thank you, once again, for helping me land the job here. I've really enjoyed working at the agency—and not just because I get to have sex with the boss during lunch breaks."

Daniela gave a mock shudder, holding up a hand. "Please. My eyesight, remember?"

Janie chuckled. "Seriously, though. I never thought I'd enjoy working as a secretary so much—not that there's anything wrong with being a secretary," she hastened to add.

"I know what you meant," Daniela assured her.

"I have so much freedom and autonomy here, the opportunity to implement new things and interact with your clients—some of whom are quite fascinating, I might add."

Daniela grinned. "No argument there. Anyway, we love having you here, Janie. You're doing a fantastic job. We're very lucky to have you."

"Thanks, El." Janie paused, her gaze softening on

Daniela's face. "It was good to hear you laugh. We've all missed the sound."

"I know," Daniela murmured, straightening a pile of paperwork on her desk. "Guess I haven't had much to laugh about recently."

"I know." Janie pushed out a deep, heavy breath. "I just wish there was something I could do, Daniela."

"Short of giving Caleb a bad case of amnesia," Daniela grimly joked, "I'm afraid there's not much you *can* do. Don't even think about it," she added wryly when she saw the thoughtful look that crossed Janie's face. "I think I've already caused Caleb enough harm. The last thing he needs is to be accosted in a dark alley and clobbered over the head by one of my family members trying to make him lose his memory."

Janie grinned. "Well, *I'm* not so sure he doesn't need to be clobbered over the head for being so stubborn. But if anyone's gonna take a crack at him, it won't be me. It'll be Noah. He's been chomping at the bit to go talk to Caleb and make him see reason."

Daniela frowned. "He has?"

"Yep. You know how overprotective Noah is when it comes to his baby sister. And I think he feels really guilty for forcing you to go undercover in the first place."

"No one 'forced' me to do anything," Daniela muttered.

"That's not the way Noah sees it. Haven't you noticed the way he's been avoiding you lately—even more so than the rest of us? He feels really bad for you, Daniela, and just between you and me, I think he's planning to do something about it very soon."

Daniela groaned. "God, I hope not. That would only make matters worse."

Janie's expression gentled. "How much worse can they get?"

Daniela glared at her. "You're not helping."

"Actually, I *am* helping. I made Noah promise me that he would give you and Caleb more time to work things out between you before he talks to him. And," she continued, holding up a hand when Daniela opened her mouth to protest the possibility of a reconciliation between her and Caleb, "he also promised not to resort to brute force when, and if, he does decide to talk to Caleb."

"Oh, God," Daniela groaned again.

"Don't worry," Janie said blithely. "As my mother always says, '*Cuando se significa para ser, se significa para ser.*' When it's meant to be, it's meant to be. If you and Caleb are truly meant for each other—which we all think you are—then you *will* be together."

Daniela wished she could share her family's certainty, but remembering the cold, awful finality of Caleb's parting words to her, she knew there would be no reconciliation between them, not in this lifetime or the next.

"Professor Thorne, wait up!"

Caleb stopped and turned to watch as April Kwan hurried to catch up with him, her long legs carrying her quickly across the courtyard. "Miss Kwan," he murmured when she reached his side.

"I'm glad I caught you," she said, panting lightly. "I called your name three times, but you didn't hear me. You must have been deep in thought."

"I was," Caleb admitted, though he wasn't about to tell April who, or what, had been occupying his mind. "What can I do for you, April?"

"Well, I wanted you to be the first to know that after this semester, I'm leaving St. Mary's."

Caleb looked down at her in surprise. "Really? Are you transferring to another law program?"

"Nope," she chirped. "I'm dropping out of law school in order to pursue a career in photography."

"Really?"

She nodded. "I've given the matter a lot of thought, and I think this is the best decision for me. It was never my dream to become a lawyer—no offense, Professor Thorne."

Caleb chuckled. "None taken," he assured her. "You're a very talented photographer, Miss Kwan. I've received a lot of compliments on the photographs I bought from you at First Friday."

She beamed. *"Seriously?"*

He smiled. "Seriously. I have the photos hanging in my office." Except the one of the Majestic Theatre, which still held a place of honor on the wall above his bed. He couldn't bring himself to take it down, though every time he looked at it, he was reminded of Daniela, and the aching tenderness he'd seen in her eyes when she'd given him the photo.

It'll give you something to remember me by, she'd told him. At the time he hadn't understood the strange note of farewell in her voice.

Afterward it had made sense.

"I've been selling a lot of my work," April was telling him excitedly, "and I've recently been invited back to exhibit at First Friday."

"Congratulations," Caleb said with a warm smile. "That's really great, April. But are you absolutely certain you want to drop out of law school now?" he gently probed. "Why not give the photography a little more time to take off?"

April grinned. "You sound like my parents."

Caleb grimaced. "Sorry."

"It's okay. I know that what I'm doing is very risky, but it's a risk I'm willing to take. Photography is my passion, Professor Thorne, and sometimes I think you have to follow your heart in order to be happy. Know what I mean?"

Caleb nodded slowly, her words hitting close to home. *Too close.*

Seeing his grim expression, and mistaking the cause, April grinned ruefully. "I guess that makes me the *second* of your first-year students to bite the dust this semester," she teased. "First Daniela, and now me. I hope you won't take it personally, Professor Thorne."

"I'll try not to," he murmured, thinking of just how personally he'd taken Daniela's desertion. Nearly two months later, he was still taking it personally.

"I'm having dinner with her this evening," April told him cheerfully. "I had been calling her for weeks to find out how she was doing, but she never returned any of my phone calls. I finally heard from her last night, and we agreed to meet for dinner. Before we got off the phone, she said she had something important to tell me—something about her 'real' reason for leaving the university." April frowned slightly. "Do you have any idea what she might be talking about, Professor Thorne?"

Caleb kept his expression carefully blank. "I haven't the faintest."

April shrugged, then glanced at her watch. "Guess I'd better be heading to class. Professor Adler doesn't take kindly to latecomers. Although, now that I think about it, she's been in a very good mood lately. I could probably show up halfway through class and still not get in trouble."

Caleb chuckled. "Don't push your luck, kiddo," he said, knowing that Shara's good mood was the result of Daniela's abrupt removal from the picture. He hadn't told Shara what happened, nor had she prodded him for information. It was enough for her that with her competition out of the way, she would have Caleb all to herself again. And though Caleb knew it was wrong to give Shara any false hopes about their future together, he hadn't refused her invitation to have dinner on Friday. The truth was that he was hurt and angry, and unbearably lonely without Daniela in his life, and in his bed. If he could find some relief from his torment, however temporary, then so be it. He'd worry about the repercussions later.

As he sent April off to class and started toward the faculty building, she called out, "Professor Thorne?"

He turned back, one brow arched expectantly.

"Is there anything you want me to tell Daniela when I see her tonight?"

His heart knocked against his rib cage. *Tell her I wish I'd never laid eyes on her. Tell her the sight of her empty seat in class is driving me insane. Tell her I'll never look at another bowl of vanilla ice cream, or tiramisu, the same way again. Tell her I can't close my eyes at night without seeing her face, without remembering the way she fit perfectly in my arms. Tell her that no matter how many times I wash the bedsheets, I still smell her in my dreams.*

Tell her I love her.

Of course, he said none of those things to April.

"Tell her I said hello," he murmured, because it seemed the only appropriate response he could give without arousing the girl's curiosity.

Grinning, April lifted her hand in mock salute. "Will do, Professor Thorne."

When Caleb reached his office, he was startled to find his father waiting for him, hands clasped loosely behind his back as he stood before the oak-paneled wall examining the titles on the bookshelves. "Dad?"

Crandall turned and smiled at him. "Hey there, son. Nice office you have here—nicer than I expected."

Caleb's mouth twitched as he stepped inside the room and closed the door. "And here all this time you thought they'd stuck me in a broom closet in the basement," he said drolly, sitting down behind his desk. "To what do I owe the pleasure of this visit?"

Crandall walked over and picked up the crystal paperweight he'd given Caleb years ago, idly turning it over in one hand before placing it back on the desk. "I had to come into town for a meeting," he explained, "so I thought I'd drop by and see you."

Caleb nodded, knowing there was more to his father's unannounced visit than he let on. "Have a seat," he offered, waving his father into a chair.

Crandall sat down, then got right to the point. "How long are you going to prolong this ridiculous feud with Daniela?"

Caleb frowned, leaning back in his chair with a relaxed calm that belied the sudden tightening of his nerves. "Did I miss something? Aren't you the one who brought me the information that Daniela Moreau—Roarke—was a fraud?"

"I did," Crandall agreed, a touch impatiently. "And

it was probably one of the worst decisions I've ever made in my life."

Caleb thought his ears were deceiving him. "Excuse me?"

"You heard me, boy. I wish I hadn't told you the truth about who she was."

Caleb's mouth curved cynically. "Yeah, well, the truth has never been very high on your list of priorities, has it?" The moment he saw his father wince, he regretted the caustic words. "I'm sorry," he said grimly. "That was uncalled for."

"It was, but I had it coming." A quiet, self-deprecating smile touched Crandall's mouth. "Sometimes I take for granted just how far we've come in our relationship, and I forget that the only reason you let me back into your life was that I was knocking on death's door, thanks to my failing kidney."

Caleb smiled a little. "That's not the only reason I wanted a reconciliation with you, Dad. I was tired of being enemies with you. It required more energy than I was willing to expend."

Crandall laughed. "Only a lawyer would put it that way." Sobering, he gazed across the desk at his son. "Seems to me that if you can forgive me for the unpardonable sin I committed, you can forgive Daniela."

Caleb's jaw hardened. "I don't want to talk about her, Dad. Contrary to how you may feel, I'm glad you told me the truth about her."

"Are you?" his father challenged. "Or are you just telling yourself that to help you cope with your regrets?"

"I don't have any regrets," Caleb said tersely, "and I can't believe you'd even suggest that it would have been better for me to remain in the dark about her true identity. She *lied* to me, Dad. She deceived me and betrayed my trust. How can I just overlook that? *Why* would I want to?"

Crandall looked him squarely in the eye. "Because you're in love with her, son. And if you don't go to her and make things right between you, you're going to spend the rest of your life alone and bitter. Or worse yet, you'll end up married to some woman you don't even love, and you'll spend your days and nights wondering about the one that got away." He paused, then added quietly, "Like I did with your mother."

Caleb grew very still. Outside the closed door he could hear the familiar sounds of phones ringing and keyboards clicking, could hear the low drone of conversations between his colleagues.

Inside his office, it was deathly silent.

Crandall was watching him intently. "You've always known that your mother and I didn't have the ideal marriage."

Caleb nodded slowly. "But this is the first time you've ever admitted it to me. Why now?"

"Because I don't want to see history repeat itself. I loved your mother, Caleb. God rest her soul, she was a sweet, kind, wonderful woman. But I wasn't *in* love with her. Not the way you are with Daniela. The minute you two walked into my office, I knew she was the one. No, take that back. I knew she was the one the day you came to me with the idea of offering her an internship at the firm. Aside from the fact that you'd never done that before, there was something in your eyes when you talked about Daniela—something I'd never seen there before. And I'm not the only one who noticed the way you were with her that night. Ruth and Rita did, too. We all spoke about it afterward."

Caleb scowled. "I'll try not to be so transparent next time," he muttered darkly.

"There won't be a next time," Crandall said softly. "Daniela Roarke is the only woman you're ever going to love that way. Take my word for it, son."

"Your word, huh? Aren't you the one who told me you had a good feeling about her, that she wasn't like all the others?"

"She's not," Crandall said, undaunted by the biting sarcasm in Caleb's voice. Pushing out a deep breath, he leaned forward in his chair. "Listen, I'm not condoning Daniela's behavior. She made a terrible mistake. We all do at some point in our lives." He smiled wryly. "Except maybe you."

Caleb frowned. "I've never suggested that I don't make mistakes, but I'd like to think that if given the same opportunity, I wouldn't have made the same choice Daniela did."

Crandall gave a diffident shrug. "Maybe, maybe not. We'll never know. But I'm sure Daniela had her reasons for accepting the assignment, and the moment she met you, she probably regretted those reasons." He paused. "Think of it this way. If she'd made a different decision, the two of you would never have met. Can you imagine that alternative?"

No, Caleb couldn't.

He rose slowly from his chair and paced to the window, his hands thrust into his pockets. "There's a reason you always taught me not to trust beautiful women," he reminded his father.

"That was cynicism talking, baggage from the past

that I never should have burdened you with. You have a chance to make a future with the woman you love, Caleb. Tessa took that option away from me." He paused, then added somberly, "Don't rob yourself, or Daniela, of the opportunity to be happy."

Chapter 20

When Daniela arrived at the office bright and early the following morning, Noah stood at the reception desk going over paperwork with Janie. He broke off when he saw Daniela, his expression softening at once.

"Hey, kiddo," he murmured as she approached. Dark, assessing eyes roamed across her face. "You look a little better today. Did you sleep well?"

"No worse than usual." Daniela smiled wanly at him, remembering what Janie had told her about Noah's intention to speak to Caleb on her behalf. It shouldn't have surprised her. Noah had always been her protector, so she knew how difficult it must be for him to sit helplessly on the sidelines and watch her suffer through a broken heart.

Lifting her hand, she touched his face gently. "It's okay, Noah. You're going to have to let me grow up eventually."

He scowled. "*I'll* be the judge of that."

Daniela grinned, knowing he would never change, loving him for it anyway.

She murmured a greeting to Janie, then left the reception area and walked down the hall to her office, where she immersed herself in a mountain of paperwork.

Two hours later, she was so absorbed in her work that she scarcely looked up when Janie appeared in her doorway.

Janie had to clear her throat to get Daniela's attention, and there was an odd note of excitement in her voice when she announced, "You have a visitor, Daniela."

Daniela glanced up—and froze. There, standing behind Janie in the hallway and wearing an impeccably tailored dark suit, was Caleb.

Heart pounding wildly, Daniela just sat there, afraid to speak, afraid to move, gazing at the unbearably handsome face that had haunted her dreams and tormented her every waking thought for the past sixty-three days, and counting.

She wondered if he were a figment of her imagination. Had her grief over losing him finally sent her over the edge, where she was now hallucinating and conjuring visions of him?

Janie cleared her throat again, louder this time, and the sound was as jarring as if she'd snapped her fingers under Daniela's nose. "Daniela," she said in the same pleasant, courteous tone she used to announce the arrival of their clients, "I believe you already know Mr. Thorne."

"Of course," Daniela murmured, getting slowly to

her feet on legs that felt like overcooked pasta. "Thank you for showing him back," she said to Janie, signaling that she could now leave.

But Janie lingered. "Would you care for some coffee, Mr. Thorne?"

Caleb's dark gaze stayed on Daniela's face as he stepped into the cramped office. "No, thank you."

As Janie departed, she gave Daniela a huge grin and a thumbs-up sign, both of which were lost on Daniela, who couldn't take her eyes off Caleb.

Once they were alone, she didn't know what to say, or how to even start. Whenever she'd imagined this moment, she'd always said…nothing. Because she'd never imagined that this moment could ever come true.

She opened her mouth. "Caleb—"

One dark brow sketched upward. "Do you always greet your clients by first name?" he inquired in the deep, compelling voice she'd missed so much.

Her nervousness turned to puzzlement. "No, but…you're not a client, Caleb."

"Don't be too sure about that."

Her heart sank. "You—you're here to use our services?" Of course he wasn't here seeking a reconciliation. It had been too good to be true.

Without awaiting an invitation, Caleb sat down in one of her visitor chairs. "I need you to help me locate someone," he told her briskly.

Daniela sat down slowly, disappointment making her throat ache. "Caleb, I really don't think I'm the best person to help you."

"Why not? You *are* licensed, aren't you?"

"Of course. But I can't…I mean, this is too awkward for me. Maybe one of my brothers can—"

"I don't want one of your brothers, Miss Roarke," he interrupted, his gaze intent on her face. "I want you."

Daniela's belly quivered at the husky timbre of his voice when he spoke those last three words. "All right," she said shakily. She searched for a pen and notepad beneath the clutter on her desk. As she did, she noticed Noah and Kenneth passing by her office and glancing inside with unabashed interest. When they doubled back and walked past again less than five seconds later, she smothered an exasperated sigh and got up to close the door.

"Sorry about that," she muttered to Caleb, returning to her chair. "I can't get any privacy around here."

She thought she saw a flicker of amusement in Caleb's dark eyes, but when he spoke, he was all business. "I'm on a tight schedule, Miss Roarke," he said, glancing pointedly at the watch peeking from beneath the snowy cuff of his shirt.

"Of course." Daniela found what she was looking for. With her pen poised above the notepad, she looked at Caleb, and promptly lost her train of thought. "I've never seen you in a suit before," she said, her voice soft with wonder. "You look incredible."

His mouth twitched. "Miss Roarke—"

"I know, I'm sorry. That was inappropriate of me. I'm supposed to be treating you like a real client." Clearing her throat, she continued in a brisk, professional tone, "This person you're looking for. How long have they been missing? And is the person male or female?"

"Female," Caleb answered. "And she's been missing for thirty-five years."

"What?" Startled, Daniela stared at him. "Thirty-five years? That's a long time!"

"I know," Caleb agreed softly.

Daniela's eyes narrowed on his face. "That's a bit unusual."

"Not really. It happens more often than you think."

"Well, yes, I have had clients whose loved ones have gone missing for many years. Thirty-five is a bit...extreme. Anyway, give me a physical description, and be as detailed as possible."

"Let's see... She's about five-seven, though she looks like she could be a bit taller, depending on the shoes she's wearing. I seem to remember her having something of a shoe fetish."

Daniela chuckled, taking notes. "Sounds like a woman after my own heart."

"Oh, I think you would have liked her. She had a great sense of humor, and the most incredible laugh you'd ever want to hear. And she had these quirks. Well, I guess you wouldn't really call them 'quirks.' I saw them as quirks because they're what made her really stand out to me, things that made her so damn sweet, and memorable." He paused. "Like eating ice cream with her coffee, instead of just ordering coffee ice cream."

Daniela kept taking notes, but the tears suddenly blurring her vision made it difficult to see what she was writing.

"She has this thing for fast cars and Harleys," Caleb continued. "And she loves watching romantic comedies, and golden sunsets. And she can slow dance even when there's no music playing. I loved that about her."

Tears spilled from Daniela's eyes and splashed onto

the notepad, smearing ink. She lifted her head and saw Caleb gazing at her with such tender adoration that her heart swelled painfully in her chest.

"You see, the woman I'm looking for had been missing all my life," he said huskily. "And once I finally found her, I lost her again. I need you to help me get her back, Daniela. Will you do that for me?"

Daniela nodded, tears of inexpressible joy flowing freely down her face. Caleb got up slowly, and before she knew it she was on her feet, rounding the desk and rushing into the open arms that awaited her. They closed around her with breathtaking force, holding her fiercely against him. Daniela clung to him just as tightly, fearing he would disappear if she let go.

"I missed you so much," she whispered fervently. "I'm so sorry for what I did, Caleb. So sorry I hurt—"

Cradling her tear-soaked face in his hands, Caleb bent his head and crushed his mouth to hers, swallowing the rest of her apology in a searing kiss that Daniela returned with equal desperation.

"I love you," Caleb uttered fiercely against her mouth. "I don't care about anything else. Just don't ever leave me again."

Her heart soared at his words. "I won't," she promised, so deliriously happy she didn't bother reminding him that *he* was the one who'd left her. "I love you, Caleb. Love you so much."

He drew back, still cupping her face in his hands. "Do you love me enough to make it legal?"

Daniela stared up at him, unable to believe what she was hearing. "Are you…are you proposing to me?"

His loving gaze swept her face. "That's exactly

what I'm doing," he said huskily. "Will you marry me, Daniela?"

Overcome with emotion, Daniela threw her arms around his neck, kissing him with all the love and ardor that had been bottled up inside her for too long. It wasn't until she felt Caleb smile against her mouth that she realized she hadn't given him an answer yet.

Keeping her arms looped around his neck, because she couldn't bear the thought of not touching him in some way, she pulled back slightly and looked at him. "I can't think of anything that would bring me more pleasure than becoming your wife," she told him in an achingly tender voice.

Grinning with elation, he lifted her into his arms and swung her around, making her squeal in delight. Instead of setting her back down on her feet, he planted her on the desk and stepped between her legs. Holding her gaze, he drew her hand to his lips and slowly, deliberately, kissed each fingertip. Her lashes fluttered as heat skirted along her nerve endings and pooled in her belly. She wanted him. She'd gone without him long enough.

He leaned forward, his eyes darkening, causing the blood to race through her veins. "Do you remember our first kiss?" he whispered against her mouth.

Daniela smiled at the delicious memory. "As I recall, it was in a closet not much bigger than this room."

He chuckled low in his throat, nibbling her bottom lip. "That was when I knew I was a goner. You're the only woman who's ever made me lose control like that."

Smiling with pleasure, Daniela slid her hands up his hard, muscled chest and reached to unbutton his shirt, desperate for the feel of his naked skin. "By the way, what's with the suit?"

"Faculty seminar downtown," he muttered distractedly as he tugged her blouse free of the waistband of her skirt. "Enforced dress code."

Daniela giggled. "And you actually *complied?*"

"I haven't been myself lately." He pulled pins from her upsweep until her hair tumbled down to her shoulders. With a masculine sound of approval, he sank his hands into the thick mass and slanted his mouth over hers in heated demand. They couldn't get enough of each other, couldn't get close enough.

A sudden thought penetrated the steamy fog of desire clouding Daniela's brain. Caleb groaned softly in protest as she drew back and gave him a worried look. "What about your father, Caleb? Doesn't he hate me?"

Caleb's mouth curved in a wry smile. "My father believes you're his only hope of ever getting any grandchildren. Believe me when I tell you he doesn't hate you."

Daniela grinned. "In that case, I'd better give him *plenty* of grandchildren. The more, the better."

Caleb chuckled, a wicked sound that curled her toes. "In *that* case," he drawled, making love to the pulse beating wildly at the base of her throat, "we'd better get started right away."

As their hungry mouths fused together, Daniela thought fleetingly of locking the door so that no one could walk in on them by acccident. But then she remembered the scene she'd stumbled upon between Kenneth and Janie, and she decided a little payback wasn't such a bad thing.

Caleb lifted his head and looked down at her, all the love in his heart evident in his smoldering gaze. "This is forever," he told her in a deep, intoxicating voice filled with lasting promise.

Daniela gazed up at him. "I'm looking forward to it," she whispered, then closed her eyes as his warm lips reclaimed hers in a kiss that showed her just how exquisite forever could be.